THE
ASTROLOGICAL
DIARY OF GOD

Bo Fowler was born in 1971. He studied Philosophy at Bristol University before attending the University of East Anglia where he studied Creative Writing under Malcolm Bradbury. His first novel, *Scepticism Inc.*, was published in 1998.

BY THE SAME AUTHOR

Scepticism Inc.

THE
ASTROLOGICAL
DIARY OF GOD

BO FOWLER

BLOOMSBURY

To Julie

Published by Bloomsbury Publishing, New York and London.
Distributed to the trade by St. Martin's Press

First published in Great Britain in 1999 by Jonathan Cape,
Random House UK

A CIP catalogue record for this book
is available from the Library of Congress

ISBN 1-58234-118-4

First U.S. Edition 2001
10 9 8 7 6 5 4 3 2 1

Printed in the United States of America
by R.R. Donnelley & Sons Company,
Harrisonburg, Virginia

How is it that hardly any major religion has looked at science and concluded, 'This is better than we thought! The Universe is much bigger than our prophets said, grander, more subtle, more elegant. God must be even greater than we dreamed'? Instead they say 'No, no, no! My god is a little god.'

CARL SAGAN

Only God knows how the world came into being – he only knows, or perhaps he knows not.

RIG VEDA

There is no such thing as obscenity. What is considered obscene in one country is holy in another.

MAN RAY

A man found masturbating in a public toilet in New York explained: it's all right I'm a Christian Scientist and I'm making love to my girlfriend in Florida.

G. LEYMAN
The Rationale of the Dirty Joke

THE ASTROLOGICAL DIARY OF GOD

(b. 1925)

A Diary of the day-to-day comings and goings during my time in captivity with a look back over my remarkable life intended to prove (were proving necessary) the divine nature of myself and my intimate and loving relationship with the cosmos.

HE-WHOSE-FIGURE-OF-BEAUTY-IS-TINGED-
WITH-THE-HUE-OF-CERULEAN-BLUE-CLOUDS-
AND-WHOSE-UNIQUE-LOVELINESS-CHARMS-
MILLIONS-OF-LITTLE-CUPIDS

AQUARIUS

Fort Knox, the 19th

Peace convention held in Washington	☽ v/c 8:11 am
Start of Russo-Japanese war	☽ △ ♂
Adolf Hitler becomes Minister	☉ ☍ ♅
USA launches probe to Venus	☽ ⊼ ♀
	☽ ☍ ♃
	☽ ⊼ ♄

Every year there is a reunion of retired kamikaze pilots in Hiroshima.

At these reunions everyone gets smashed on sake and eats truly prodigious quantities of dumplings. Most of the retired kamikaze pilots spend the rest of the time looking after the Shrines to the War Dead: they water the plants, sweep away empty Coke cans, pick up dogshit, tell screaming children to quieten down and chase away stray dogs. I, on the other hand, own nine highly profitable companies, am the rightful King of Adocentyn, the Holy Channel Island, and the Creator of the Universe.

This year's reunion is on the 13th of Leo.

It looks like I won't be going.

My name is Zizo Yasuzawa, or He-Whose-Figure-Of-Beauty-Is-Tinged-With-The-Hue-Of-Cerulean-Blue-Clouds-And-Whose-Unique-Loveliness-Charms-Millions-Of-Little-Cupids, although in the West I am better known as Japs Eye Fontanelle. I have rheumatoid arthritis, a weight problem, a heart condition, a hole in my head and no balls at all.

I'm accused by the UNCC (the United Nations Cosmology Commission) of killing Time.

It is something of a long story.

✳ ✳ ✳

After dinner God watched *Star Trek*.

THE 20TH

Publication of the *Communist Manifesto*	♆ ℞ 12:26 am
	☽ v/c 6:49 am
Ball of hair weighing 2.35 kg removed	☽ → ♍ 2:47 pm
from woman's stomach	♂ ☍ ♆
King of Hungary abdicates	☽ △ ♄
Walt Disney frozen	☽ ⊼ ♀
	☽ ⊼ ♆

I who have loved the world and all it contains, I the original seed of which the Old Testament speaks, the Monad, Pimander – the Divine Mind, the Awo-Bam-Do-Bop-Awo-Bambo!, the Light Unchangeable, Undivided Unity, I the sole possessor of what Dante called '*the love that moves the sun and the other stars*', await my trial for the killing of Time in a middle-of-the-range mobile home that contains towels with the letters UNCC sewn on them, a microwave, a radio, a small TV with terrible reception, a fridge, two beds, plastic crockery, a shower unit and a guide book to the Midwest which God probably won't be using.

The UNCC has also provided God with a nurse, whose name is Julie Hughes. She is a redhead and very pretty. Yesterday she told me that I was the fattest man she had ever seen. She did not say this with any malice, it was simply a statement of fact. Sometimes when she bends over God glimpses his nurse's underwear. God's nurse is a Capricorn with Mercury in a bad aspect to Mars, which means of course that she worries about things too much.

God tells her this often, full of compassion, but she does not believe me. In fact, she laughs at astrology. When she first arrived God asked her what she thought of the ancient science. She told God she thought astrology was a confused mess of half-baked anachronistic ideas and childish nonsense, mumbo-jumbo of the highest order, a demented and simplistic attempt to reduce the wonderful diversity and complexity of human personality into something that could be written on the back of a postcard. She added that it was a well-known fact that your midwife exerts more gravitational influence on you at your birth than all the stars and planets put together. God suspects my nurse has been given the job of looking after me by the UNCC precisely because she is so insensitive to the tenets of astrology.

Like all Capricorn women, my nurse's favourite colour is dark green, although for some reason she denies this.

God's mobile home is parked in the middle of the gold bullion depository vault in Fort Knox, Kentucky.

What they have done with the $100 billion worth of gold is anybody's business.

The vault is roughly the size of a baseball field, and has only one entrance.

Thirty-watt light bulbs illuminate the gold vault from 8 a.m.

to 10.30 p.m. There is one light switch by the entrance next to a coin-operated phone.

It is very cold here in the gold vault, even inside my mobile home. It is so cold, in fact, that the UNCC has issued God with a Norwegian combat overcoat. It has a fur hood, tissues in the pockets and the name Eric Woodall written in pen on the label. My nurse, has a similar coat, which fits her much better than God's fits him.

Normally God allows nothing to get between me and my creation, but it is just too damn cold in here to go around butt naked.

Even with the Norwegian combat overcoat the UNCC is worried God will catch pneumonia and be too ill to appear at my trial. This is a possibility as God is no spring chicken. I am very old. I am ancient. I will be eighty-five soon, and according to *The Guinness Book of Records*, the fattest man in the entire world.

God has never denied that I developed, towards the end of World War Two, something of a weight problem.

In fact I became the plumpest kamikaze pilot ever to take to the skies.

THE 21ST

Birthday of Ronald Reagan (actor)	☽ △ ♅
Birthday of Pedro Alvarez Cabral, Portuguese	☽ ∨ ♄
navigator (found Brazil)	☽ ⊼ ☉
	☽ ⊼ ♂
Frank Sinatra sings 'My Way' for the first time	☽ ⊼ ♃

God's jailers inside the gold vault are the whole company from the elite 82nd Airborne Division, known as the Screaming Eagles. Like God and my nurse they have been issued with Norwegian combat overcoats.

The commanding officer of the company of Screaming Eagles inside the gold vault, the head jailer, as it were, is Colonel Fleming. He is a Sagittarius, which means of course that he is in completely the wrong sort of career. He would be better off as a teacher, a librarian of some sort, a priest or in any sort of job to do with horses.

The day God was put inside the gold vault Colonel Fleming told me that he didn't want any funny business. God told him the Supreme Being didn't want any funny business either and suggested he seriously consider a career change.

Sagittarians prefer tea to coffee, dogs to cats, can't swim and are the least likely sign to be turned on by bondage. Their best days are Thursdays.

Colonel Fleming and his men were nervous and on edge when God's nurse helped the Creator of Everything piss in my mobile home for the first time under this posture of heaven:

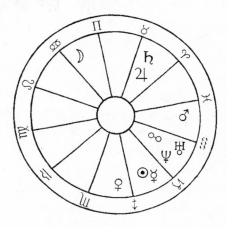

They heard us fumbling in the toilet and put two and two together. As my organ was held by nimble and cold fingers God could hear the soldiers outside whispering to each other. My nurse assists me in the bathroom because God is now so fat, such a mound of blubber, a living atoll, that I can no longer grasp my penis. To be perfectly honest God hasn't seen it in years – it has become something of a distant friend. They are estranged, God and his penis, despite all that they have been through together. If God walked past my own penis on the street I would hardly recognize it now. A penis that is worshipped across the globe. A penis that bends (God recalls) to the left. A penis that has definitely seen better days.

Colonel Fleming and his men are armed with Top Secret weapons that look like flashlights. A one-second burst from one of those things will kill you, God has been told. Just how it will kill you is Top Secret.

Every single Top Secret weapon in the gold vault has a giant label stuck on it. It is in bright green and says:

THIS IS NOT A FLASHLIGHT, THIS IS A TOP SECRET WEAPON!

THE 22ND

Birthday of Jean Fabre (naturalist (insects))	☽ → ♎ 3:19 am
Aircraft carrier first used in action	☽ △ ♆
Birthday of Sir Christopher Wren (architect)	☽ ☍ ♀
Deathday of the Earl of Mayo	☿ ⊻ ♃
Term 'swing' coined	☽ ✳ ♇

Every morning God's young nurse cooks God and herself break-fast, which we eat here in the mobile home. God's nurse is a good cook for a Capricorn. God tells her this often as she shovels spoonful after spoonful of scrambled egg and slivers of greasy bacon into God's mouth. Miss Hughes has to feed God because my arms are now so fat that they cannot get even close to my mouth. It is an anatomical impossibility. My arms are forced to rest in the air, suspended above mountains of wrinkled skin. It looks, God has been told on countless occasions, for all the world as if I am surrendering to some unseen assailant.

Colonel Fleming joined God and my nurse for breakfast today (he does this sometimes) and used his cutlery and the salt and pepper cellars to represent various critical moments in the Battle of the Pacific, explaining that his grandfather, Reginald Fleming, fought against the Japanese during the war. Colonel Fleming tells God that his grandfather, Reginald Fleming, crashed his plane on purpose on to the deck of a Mogami-class heavy cruiser during the battle of Midway, making him the only American kamikaze pilot God has ever heard of.

'What star sign was he?' God asked, still eating my breakfast.

Colonel Fleming's grandfather was a Libra and therefore preferred coffee to tea, enjoyed field sports and was twice unfaithful to his wife. He was a morning person and his best day of the week would have been Saturday.

Midway took place on a Thursday.

God missed Midway, I told Colonel Fleming, because of injuries sustained in what became known as the Battle of the Coral Sea.

Had God been present at Midway, God would probably have been killed.

Thus the Battle of the Coral Sea was a critical moment in the history of the Cosmos as is borne out by its chart:

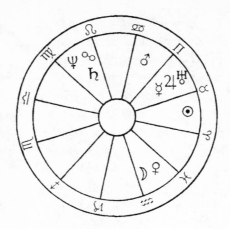

THE 23RD

Birthday of Charles Lindbergh (1st man

    to fly the Atlantic solo)

Invention of the telephone

Three-piece suit made from scratch in one

    hour thirty-four minutes

Deathday of Louis XIV (King of France)

$$\begin{array}{ccc} ☽ & □ & ♇ \\ ♀ & ✶ & ♆ \\ ☽ & ⊼ & ⛢ \\ ☽ & △ & ☉ \\ ☽ & ✶ & ⚷ \end{array}$$

Today, with the Moon in the cusp of Aries, God produced seven perfect little turds that lay at the bottom of the toilet bowl looking for all the world like the stars that make up the cluster known as the Pleiades, located in the constellation of Taurus. God pointed this remarkable similarity out to his nurse who laughed, dismissing it as mere coincidence, and flushed the toilet before God had taken a photograph.

    After ranting and raving about this missed opportunity, God had a meeting with a Mr Coleman, one of the best defence attorneys in the country. Miss Hughes made Mr Coleman a coffee and God told him that the Universe and God felt he was the best man for the job of defending the Supreme Being, He

That Was Before All Else. Mr Coleman said nothing so I showed him his horoscope which I had taken the liberty of drawing up after breakfast. God talked him through the various houses and explained how handling my case would be the pinnacle not just of his career but of his entire life. Mr Coleman thanked me for his birth chart, rolled it up into a tube, put it under his arm, put his hat on his head, thanked Miss Hughes for the coffee and informed the Creator of the Universe that he was at present too busy to handle my case.

God was speechless.

After leaving the gold vault, Mr Coleman spoke to reporters outside. He was on the lunchtime TV news. He was asked by a reporter how much God weighed. 'I guess at least a hundred stone,' he said, which is about right.

Mr Coleman was born under the sign of Cancer, which means he likes tea and coffee equally, collects china figurines, is bad at roller-skating, likes apples and is pedestrian in the bedroom department.

THE 24TH

Radar invented	☽ v/c 9:19 am
Man kills 201 mosquitoes in 5 minutes	☽ ♏ 4:10 pm
Largest shopping mall in the world opened	☽ ☍ ☿
	☽ ☍ ♄
	☽ □ ♆
	♀ △ ♇

God's nurse normally serves dinner here in the mobile home at seven.

Every night after dinner God's nurse clears away the dishes, removes God's bib and erects an old stepladder in the middle of the immobile mobile home. Then she deposits a black book and a pen on the top rung. God is positioned next to the ladder and in this manner I write my astrological diary, seeing what I write above my head with the help of carefully positioned mirrors around the mobile home.

God's nurse objects to erecting the stepladder and positioning the mirrors every night. She tells God it is bad luck to open stepladders indoors; God tells her she is thinking of umbrellas.

Normally at about ten o'clock Miss Hughes takes off God's Norwegian combat overcoat and tucks God into bed.

At 10.30 every night Colonel Fleming switches off the lights in the gold vault.

God misses the stars. The UNCC has provided God with a number of little stars that glow in the dark, and which Miss Hughes put on the ceiling of the mobile home, but they are just not the same.

They look like this:

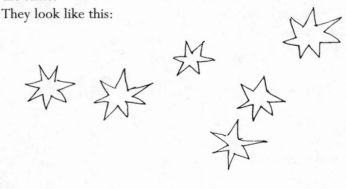

THE 25TH

✳

US buys Panama Canal	☽ → ♐ 3:48 am
Birthday of Pope John II	♂ ⚹ ♃
The song 'Honky Tonk Woman' is released	☽ ⚹ ♆
Napoleon marries Marie-Louise of Austria	☉ ⚹ ♃
	☉ ☌ ♂
	☿ ☌ ♄
	☽ ☌ ♇

Today God informed my nurse at breakfast that the Sun moves around the Earth but she did not believe me.

It is perfectly true though, I should know, I am God, after all.

Proof that the Sun goes around the Earth, were proof needed, can be seen clearly in the ancient science of astrology, for the horoscope, the very heart of astrology, is laid out with the Earth in the centre. God told my nurse that anyone who says astrology doesn't insist that the Sun orbits the Earth does not know what they are talking about. They are rascals. Nincompoops.

There's more: not only does the Sun revolve around the Earth but so do all the planets, all the stars and all the millions of galaxies.

We are, ladies and gentlemen, or more accurately I am, the very centre of the entire Universe. Yes indeedy.

Happy happy days.

THE 26TH

✳

The film *Easy Rider* is shown for the first time	☽ v/c 12:43 pm
	☽ → ♑ 1:40 pm
Rover robot lands on Mars	♉ → ♉ 9:10 pm
Manchu dynasty abdicates	☽ ⚼ ♂
Three-colour traffic lights installed in New York	☽ ⚼ ☉
	☽ △ ♄
	☽ △ ☿
	☽ ⊻ ♆
	♀ ⚹ ♅

The entire Universe was designed for mankind, God told my nurse this morning. The entire thing, the whole damn shooting match I, God, made with people in mind. Miss Hughes said nothing and started to do the washing up.

While she did so God recited a poem by John Donne. *'Man'* something something *'is all. He is not a piece of the world, but the world itself and next to the glory of God, the reason why there is a world.'*

And added that it was so true, so true.

✻ ✻ ✻ ✻

Later the two of us watched *Star Trek*.

THE 27TH

First Impressionist art exhibition, Paris	☽ ⌄ ♇
Birthday of Thomas Edison (inventor of the	☽ ⌄ ♅
light bulb, etc.)	☽ □ ♀
Man spits cherry stone 28.98 metres	☽ ✳ ⚷

The hundred and twenty soldiers that guard God here inside the gold vault all wear blue helmets under the fur hoods of their Norwegian combat overcoats. So do the six doctors who, on Mondays after breakfast, enter the gold vault in single file and pile into God's mobile home. They are polite but refuse to tell God their star signs. They act as if they are visiting someone who has just suffered a bereavement.

'Good morning, Mr Fontanelle, how are you today?' the head doctor says.

'I am good and the Universe is good,' God normally says.

The six doctors then examine God. They climb all over God, prodding, pinching, slapping. God is weighed, measured, photographed and weighed again. Special attention is paid to the hole in the top of God's head. God's astrolabe, a perfect brass model of the zodiac, is removed and placed carefully on my bed. God's *hachimaki*, the white cloth worn around the heads of all kamikaze pilots, is untied. Then the half-dozen doctors look into the hole in the top of God's head like children peering into a well.

While all this is going on a psychiatrist with odd socks shows God various ink blots on bits of card.

'What does this look like?' he asks.

'Stars.'

'What about this one, what does it look like?'

'More stars,' says God.

After they have checked out God's head and its crater the doctors focus their attention on my crutch. One of them squeezes between God's legs armed with a flashlight. It is not, God is assured, a Top Secret weapon.

This is done to make sure that God's balls haven't grown back.

God was castrated around about a year ago. It was in all the papers. The facts were, of course, heavily distorted and for a while God considered legal action.

My balls, God has to say, are in better shape than I am. They are sitting comfortably on cushions in the inner air-conditioned chambers of two very ostentatious temples called the House of the Right Ball and the House of the Left Ball.

The House of the Right Ball is in Hiroshima, the House of the Left Ball is in Jersey.

I get around.

I would like to think that God's right ball is in the House of the Right Ball and that God's left ball is in the House of the Left Ball, but this is by no means certain. After the castration things were pretty hectic, as you can imagine.

The precise locations of the House of the Right Ball and the House of the Left Ball are known only to my most devout followers, including God's second wife. This is so God's balls do not fall into my enemies' hands.

Both of God's balls are attached to life-support machines.

God has been told by the world's most eminent specialists that my balls will last a thousand years.

Happy happy days.

THE 28TH

Birthday of Galileo (astronomer)	☽ v/c 4:54 pm
Birthday of John Wayne (actor)	☽ → ♒ 9:31 pm
Deathday of Queen Victoria	☽ ✳ ♃
Oregon and Arizona become US states	☿ □ ♆
China boycotts all US goods	☽ △ ♂
	☽ △ ☉
	♀ ⊼ ⚷
	☽ □ ♄

I am the benign creator of Everything. I am The One Who Hath Made All Things, The Spirit of Spirits, The Old One of which the Egyptians spoke. I started the Ball Rolling. I have existed from of old and was when nothing else had being, and what existeth I created after I came into being. I am the Eternal One, infinite. I am Cosmic Being, Perfectus, I am The Light, I am Elvis, I am Undivided Unity, I am . . .

God's nurse is really very pretty. She reminds God of the film star Kim Basinger. Actually God's nurse reminds God of lots of things.

At breakfast today, God told Colonel Fleming that he is in the wrong profession. It is written up above, God told him. 'Sagittarians don't make good soldiers, they make good teachers,' God explained. Colonel Fleming said that he didn't want to be a teacher. So God suggested he think about something to do with horses.

Colonel Fleming then tried to change the subject. He asked about World War Two, turning his fork into a US aircraft carrier steaming through the Pacific Ocean towards the edge of the table/world.

God did not feel like talking about WWII.

God told the Colonel that World War Two had taken place a thousand years ago and I was no longer Japanese but Egyptian.

'Besides,' God said, 'God was catatonic for most of it anyway.'

After that God told Colonel Fleming that God is a fat old man, that the past is the past and even I, God, cannot change that.

Lieutenant Lang, Colonel Fleming's executive officer, has never once sat down to eat with Colonel Fleming, Miss Hughes and God in the mobile home although God has made a point of inviting him on several occasions. This puzzles God. God asked the Colonel if Lieutenant Lang has something against fat people.

'Oh, it's nothing like that,' said Colonel Fleming.

'Is he racist?' God asked.

'No.'

'An atheist?'
'Nope.'
'What is it then?'
'He thinks you've slept with his ex-wife.'

'It is perfectly possible, I suppose,' God said after a little think.

God then told Captain Fleming, as God has done on other occasions, that in a former life he and God were complete strangers.

No one said anything after that and then God asked the Colonel how long God is going to be locked up like this in the gold bullion depository vault in Fort Knox.

'For as long as it takes, I guess,' he said after a little think.

Some nights I think I am back in Kyoto, the city of eight thousand shrines. Some nights I think I am back in Egypt and some nights I think my penis and my balls absolutely despise me.

THE 29TH

Largest gathering of clowns in the world (820)	☽ → ♓ 3:04 am
Franco-German agreement on Baghdad Railway	☽ ⊻ ♆
Boy Scout Movement founded	☿ ⊼ ♇
Nimbus 2 satellite put into orbit	☽ □ ♇
	☽ ✳ ☿

God was born on the 20th of Scorpio 1925 at 3.30 in the afternoon in the Holy City of Kyoto. At the time no one thought to prepare a birth chart, but when this error was corrected years later, in the aftermath of WWII, by yours truly, what a birth chart it was. It is just about as fine and dandy a birth chart as you are ever likely to come across, a chart filled with profundity, if ever there was one.

A few weeks after I was born doctors noticed that (due to incomplete ossification of my cranial bones) God had a hole in the top of his head. A sort of fissure, a tiny Grand Canyon. My wet brain was revealed to the sky: my mind perpetually flashed the heavens, as it were.

When several weeks had gone by and still the hole refused to close up, doctors decided to screw a sheet of steel to the top of God's head. The sheet of steel measured four inches by four inches and had the name of the doctor who performed the operation engraved on it, as well as an old Japanese proverb which went:

WE ARE LIKE BLIND MEN
PEEPING THROUGH A FENCE

Four little holes were made in God's skull with a hand drill, while God was wide awake, and then the sheet of steel was screwed in place.

From the age of four God wore a toupee.

Millions have had the chance to see God's glorious birth chart, to gaze at its perfection. It has been printed in hundreds of newspapers all over the globe. God's nine companies manufactured table mats, shower curtains, jewellery, posters, blankets, jumpers, carpets and bumper stickers with my birth chart on, or rather they did before being shut down by the UNCC.

Here, in all its majesty, in all its sublime splendour, is God's holy birth chart:

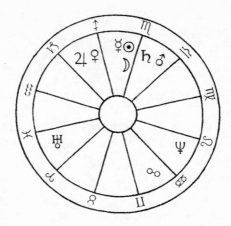

The Les Mielles golf course on the western tip of Jersey had a giant copy of my awesome birth chart painted on it by three hundred Pisceans. God has to say that when it was finished it was quite the most beautiful thing I have ever seen. When God drove around it in a little white electric car it brought tears to God's all-seeing eyes.

This fine work of art, this giant rendition of God's birth chart was not God's idea. It had been the brainchild of the Lieutenant-Governor of the island.

It took nearly six months to complete and nearly half the artisans who worked on it died from scorpion bites. Tragically, the whole thing was destroyed by cruise missiles during the early stages of the UN invasion of Jersey.

God's followers still have framed copies of my birth chart over their mantelpieces and it remains the most analysed chart ever drawn up, with the possible exception of Hitler's.

THE 30TH

Birthday of Henry Stanley (found Dr Livingstone)	3rd – 9:30 am
	☽ v/c 11:06 am
Last heretic burnt by the Inquisition in Mexico	
Spain proclaimed a republic	☽ ☍ ☉
Singing mice perform on US radio	☽ ☍ ♂
	☽ △ ♃
	☽ ⊼ ☿
	☽ ⊼ ♄

God's followers, those that are left, appeared on TV news programmes regularly. God's followers are denouncing my trial as a sham, they say the whole thing is a set-up, that God has been framed. God's followers are picketing the UN building in New York every day, holding giant papier mâché models of the planets and shouting, 'It is true, without falsehood certain and very real that that which is on high is as that which is below and that which is below is as that which is on high!'

After my followers were shown on the TV, the spokesman for the Committee for the Scientific Investigation into Claims of the Paranormal was interviewed.

'Your organization believes all legal proceedings against Mr Fontanelle ought to be dropped immediately?' the reporter asked.

'That's right,' said the spokesman.

'And why is that?'

'Mr Fontanelle is guilty of many things but killing Time is not one of them.'

'So you would like to see him released.'

'Yes, immediately, and then re-arrested.'

'Re-arrested for what?'

'For breaking the Trade Description Act, for pretending to be the Creator of the Universe when he isn't, for peddling astrology, for being as insane as it is possible to be.'

'If you could speak to the accused tonight, what would you say to him?'

'I'd say, "Come in, number 9, your time is up."'

I am stoical. I'm God and so have to be.

You can spot a member of the Committee for the Scientific Investigation into Claims of the Paranormal easily: they all wear orange life jackets.

Miss Hughes asked God during a commercial break why all the members of the Committee for the Scientific Investigation into Claims of the Paranormal wear orange life jackets.

God told her God has often wondered about that myself.

God is having something of a problem getting an attorney. Those that God phones are always in a meeting or out to lunch and never return God's call. No doubt they do not feel worthy enough to represent God. God can understand this but all the calls I am making are costing money. God owes my nurse five dollars and sixty cents and Colonel Fleming three dollars. God tells them as the Creator of Everything God is good for it. However, since the UN has frozen all of God's assets and bank accounts, God is effectively penniless in my own Universe.

You can have no idea just how embarrassing this is.

How God will pay my attorney when I find one willing to take my case, God hasn't a clue.

Here is God's father's birth chart. He was not my real father; technically, of course, I am my own father just as I am also my own mother, brother, cousin, niece and any other relative you care to mention:

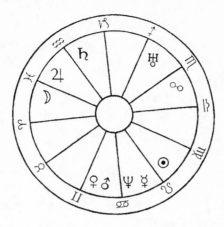

God's father was a quiet man who made mats for monks in Kyoto to sit on in their 8,000 honey-coloured temples as they contemplated the infinite.

God's father used to tell God that there was money to be made from the infinite, lots and lots and lots of money.

As if to prove his point God's father made a fortune, enough even to send me to the very best schools and later see that God was accepted, no questions asked, into the Naval Academy.

God's 'mother' died in a freak accident when God was nearly eight involving a crab trap and the deep blue sea. As her chart clearly indicates she would, she drowned.

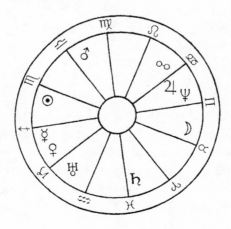

THE 31ST

Birthday of Henry Moore (sculptor)	4th – 11:36 pm
2.5-tonne hamburger made	☽ □ ⚷
Destruction of USS Main in Havana	☽ ✳ ♀
	☽ ⅄ ♃
	☉ ⅄ ♄
	☽ □ ♂
	☽ ✳ ♄
	☽ □ △

After breakfast, while she was clearing up, my nurse told God that I was a complete and utter slob. God told her to try and look at the Big Picture.

World War Two broke out under this face of heaven:

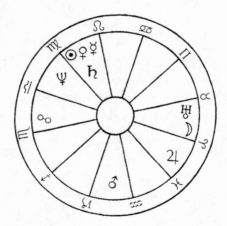

My arms, God explained to Miss Hughes, did not point heaven-ward as a consequence of any weight problem back in 1941. God was, when war broke out, what most people would consider average in build. God also had no idea just how special or important I was. I had absolutely no idea that I made the Universe or even that I was the saviour of all mankind.

24

God had graduated from the Naval Academy and married a young Leo girl from another mat-making family. We had first been introduced at an anti-western rally. We became two politically active lovebirds. We discussed Japan's natural superiority and divine origin staring into each other's eyes. We loved each other nearly as much as we loved our glorious sugar daddy, our hero, our pop star, our idol, our Cliff Richard: the bespectacled Emperor Hirohito.

Leo women like having their breasts caressed, going on picnics, and watching movies in the daytime. Leo women have sex on trains and eat quite a lot of pizza.

My wife and I built a shrine to the Emperor in my backyard together in secret one summer day out of used shoeboxes.

Six weeks before the start of the war my little wife, whose name was Misao, was carried in a litter to my father's house. We drank sake together and were married. On our wedding night we discussed politics furiously and made love for the very first time under white sheets and the bemused gaze of heaven.

On our first night of lovemaking my new little wife kissed the metal plate screwed to the top of my head. No one had ever done that before. It sent a shiver of electricity down God's skull, along my spine and out through the hairs in my armpits. It sent invisible blue sparks shooting everywhere.

I am convinced that that first fuck was carcinogenic, to my mortal wife at least. It was akin to the mythical lovemaking of the God Shiva (an aspect of myself) and the Goddess Parvati (another aspect of myself) that created so much friction that the other gods (also aspects of myself) became terrified and sent the God of Fire (yours truly) to tell them (me) to cut it out.

* * * *

When we had finished my wife said 'O-mito-fo' and went fast asleep in my then normal-sized arms.

O-mito-fo is the name of the Buddha of Boundless Light. His eternal paradise can, it is believed, be reached by anyone who utters his name in sincere devotion.

Pretty much the same thing can be achieved by uttering my Western name, Japs Eye Fontanelle, in a similar state of devotion.

Try it. It will change your life.

* * * *

My first wife and God made love approximately 1,238 times. God says approximately for God was not keeping records of such things then, unfortunately.

The position of the Zodiac that first night God has calculated was thus:

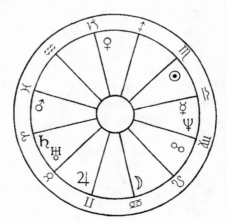

On the very last night we were together, while God was on leave from the Front, the stars were so:

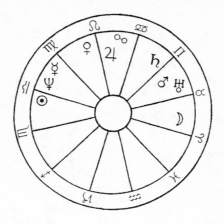

Need God say any more?

THE 32ND

Start of Picasso's Blue Period	☽ △ ♀
Birthday of Charles Darwin	☽ ✳ ♅
Deathday of Richard Wagner (composer)	☽ ∨ ⚷
John Harwood invents self-winding wristwatch	☽ ☐ ♃

This morning, Colonel Fleming brought God nine death threats and thirty-four letters of support.

God's nurse gave the death threats to Private Jones, who burned them in an old oil drum just outside the mobile home in an attempt to keep warm. Jones is a Leo and one of the few people in the gold vault with any kind of understanding and respect for astrology.

Leo men make a lot of noise at climax, write with biros and holiday in Italy and Madagascar.

27

The thirty-four letters of support all come from people living in Jersey. The thirty-four letters of support say it is a terribly sad thing that I am being tried for the killing of Time. They say this is no way to treat God. God agrees.

All of the letters from Jersey ask for astrological guidance.

After dinner, God writes back to the thirty-four people living in Jersey, leaning against my stepladder, informing them of the position of the stars and planets and the effects these will have on their lives, then God expresses my thanks for their support and states the conviction that everything will turn out well for them. Towards the end of each letter I write 'things will be good for you'.

Each letter is signed: Zodiac Man.

The oldest horoscope in the world comes from Mesopotamia and concerns the birth of a nobleman on the 8th of Taurus 410 BC. The prediction is short and sweet and goes: '*Things will be good for you.*'

Taurus men enjoy spanking, telephone sex, wife-swapping and Chinese food.

PISCES

FORT KNOX, THE 1ST

Discovery of Admiral Islands	☉ → ♊ 1.05 am
	☽ v/c 2:45 am
Manhattan Bridge opened	☽ → ♈ 6.06 am
Germans launch V-2 rocket	♂ ⊻ ♄
	☽ ⊻ ♄
	☽ ✳ ♂
	☽ ✳ ☉
	☽ ✳ ♆
	☽ △ ♇

After lunch today Colonel Fleming asked God about the raid on Pearl Harbor. God told him that the idea of staging a raid on Pearl Harbor was dreamed up one sunny day in 1939 on the boating lake of Regent's Park in London by Minoru Genda (a Virgo), then an assistant naval attaché at the Japanese Embassy, and that God had taken part in the raid.

Virgo males hate blow jobs. Their favourite colour is navy blue. They hardly ever use knives and always make their own furniture.

Colonel Fleming insisted God recount the part I played in the raid. The Colonel constructed a scale model of the island of

Oahu, where Pearl Harbor was situated, out of the food on his plate. God suggested minor improvements to the coastline and airstrips and told the Colonel how on the morning of the 3rd of Sagittarius God and the rest of the carrier group left Hitokappu Bay and headed eastward towards Pearl Harbor.

* * *

God's first wife's last words to him had been:
'Always wear clean underwear in case you crash, Zizo.'

* * *

God told Colonel Fleming that at around 09.40 on the day we sailed out of the bay, God went to the lavatory on my carrier the *Zuikaku*. God was just sitting there smoking and thinking things over when I discovered a small growth on my left testicle.

'There you were in the midst of history and all you can tell us is how you kept scratching your balls,' Captain Fleming said, putting the finishing touches to his model of the island of Oahu on his plate.

'Captain Fleming,' God retorted, 'my balls *are* history.'

* * *

Which they are.

THE 2ND

Premier of Egypt assassinated by nationalist fanatic	☽ v/c 4:13 am ☽ → ♉ 7:06 am ♂ → ♊ 10:42 am
Birthday of Burt Lancaster (actor)	☽ ☌ ♄
Ireland legalizes sale of contraceptives	☉ △ ♆
Plane crosses the Atlantic in 16 hours and 27 minutes	☽ ⊼ ♂
	☽ □ ♆
	☽ ⊼ ☉
	☽ ⊼ ♇
	☿ ☍ ⚷

God now owes my nurse and Captain Fleming a total of thirteen dollars and still God, The Archetypal Form, The Emanator of the Created, The Fountain of All Things, The Principal Essence, has yet to find myself a lawyer.

According to today's TV reports my followers are still protesting outside the UN and the orange-life-jacket-wearing Committee for the Scientific Investigation into Claims of the Paranormal are still insisting I am nothing but a fake.

God tells my nurse that ever since the late seventies the Committee for the Scientific Investigation into Claims of the Paranormal has campaigned against God and against the ancient science of astrology. For years they have wanted a warning label to accompany my horoscopes printed in newspapers across the globe.

They first suggested the warning should go something like this:

> *The following astrological forecasts should be read for entertainment value only. Such predictions have no reliable basis in scientific fact.*

Later they changed it to:

> *For Christ's sake, your midwife exerts more of a gravitational influence on you at your birth than all the stars and planets put together. Why on earth do you read this crap?*

Miss Hughes asked God why all the members of the Committee for the Scientific Investigation into Claims of the Paranormal wore orange life jackets.

'I don't know,' God said.

Then God told his nurse that he did not make the world in six days.

God finished it, or rather was unable to work on it any more, about a year ago. The Earth was the very first thing God made after empty space, which was easy. The Earth is thus the oldest thing in the Universe, aside from God himself, of course. This fact is something most scientists can't bring themselves to accept but it is perfectly true. The Sun and the Moon appeared some eight seconds later, then came Mars, Venus, Mercury, Jupiter, Neptune and Saturn. God didn't make Pluto until God was five years old. It was a birthday present to myself. A birthday present covered in frozen methane and only slightly smaller than the Moon.

THE 3RD

Elvis records 'Heartbreak Hotel'	☽ ⊻ ♅
Gödel questions the possibility of establishing	☽ △ ⚷
	☽ ⊻ ♀
dependable axioms in mathematics	☽ ☌ ♃

'As the carrier force and its escorts sailed on towards its date with infamy,' God told Colonel Fleming today at breakfast, 'the growth on my left testicle got bigger.'

God then told Colonel Fleming how God inspected my balls hourly in the lavatory at the rear of the carrier with growing concern, scratching the metal plate on the top of my head and wondering what to do.

On the 10th of Sagittarius, coming back from one of these inspections, God was sent down to the armoury to get a revolver for everyone in my squadron.

The revolvers God collected from the armoury were

unusual; they did not have any sights. They didn't have any sights because if we used them we weren't going to have to aim very hard. The guns, God told Colonel Fleming, were for us to shoot ourselves should we get captured.

Getting captured was a big no-no.

After lunch the entire squadron lined up on the hangar deck and practised killing themselves.

God was very nearly killed in the chaos and confusion following the cosmically unharmonious invasion of Jersey. God is convinced that God would have been shot if God hadn't been as fat as I was. By the time of the invasion my arms had been forced into their position of capitulation.

THE 4TH

	2nd – 3:19 pm
Hundreds of Kuwait oil wells are set alight by Iraqi forces	☽ ⚹ ♇
	☽ ⚹ ♅
Joan of Arc canonized	☉ ⚺ ♃
Ketchup sold for the first time	☽ △ ♃
Start of the California Gold Rush	☽ ▢ ☉
	☽ △ ♀
Deathday of Harry Houdini (escapologist)	☽ ▢ ☿

God stayed up last night until around 3 a.m. with my nurse watching wildlife programmes on TV.

God still does not have an attorney.

* ** *

After breakfast Colonel Fleming asked God to continue my account of the attack on Pearl Harbor.

God explained how one Captain Fuchida, a Capricorn and the man who would shortly lead us into battle and become known in the process as the Hero of Pearl Harbor, found God on the eve of the raid fiddling with myself in the toilet. Captain Fuchida was furious. He was going to have God court-martialled. God offered him a cigarette. He calmed down a bit after that, though he was still hopping mad.

Captain Fuchida's last words to God in the men's room before Pearl Harbor were:

'Think of our glorious Emperor and stop playing with yourself.'

* ** *

Capricorn men like status symbols, slippers, nightclubs, potatoes and an average of 4.5 minutes' foreplay.

* ** *

At five o'clock the next morning we were given our orders to attack.

God took a shower. I examined my left testicle once more. The growth had without a doubt got bigger. In mad desperation God squeezed it. It exploded.

It had been nothing more than a zit.

God donned my flying gear and clambered into my plane completely overcome with relief.

* ** *

Colonel Fleming wanted God to go on but God said he was feeling tired and would tell him the rest some other time.

* ** *

Tomorrow, apparently, God is being taken to New York.

✳ ✳ ✳

God loves New York.

THE 5TH

Mussolini founds Fascist party	1st – 2:32 pm
Disneyland opens	☽ → ♊ 7:25 am
Thompson invents sub-machine gun	☽ ⚹ ♄
	☽ ☌ ♂
	☽ △ ♆
	☽ ☌ ☉
	☽ ☍ ♇

God, my nurse, Colonel Fleming and his one hundred and twenty soldiers left the gold vault this morning and were put on board the same supersonic train that had originally brought God to Fort Knox.

As soon as we were outside the gold vault we all took off our Norwegian combat overcoats. The trip to New York was uneventful; at one o'clock God's nurse fed me some sandwiches and a Coke. At two she escorted me to the toilet. At three God said I felt seasick. At four God said I was bored. At six we pulled into Grand Central Station.

Waiting for us were hundreds of police, agents from the FBI's New York office, members of New York Police Department's Anti-Terrorism Task Force and UN officials. They were all wearing dark sunglasses, would not tell God their star signs and were generally pretty unfriendly.

God, my nurse, Colonel Fleming and about thirty Screaming Eagles were put on board a yellow school bus and, amid a sea of police cars, driven east to the United Nations Headquarters.

The rest of the Screaming Eagles followed in three more buses.

Outside the United Nations Headquarters was a M-1B Ragan tank painted completely blue with the initials UNCC stencilled on its turret. Colonel Fleming informed God that the tank had a 120mm calibre Top Secret main gun and 380mm of Top Secret armour, as if God did not already know this.

The school buses and police cars sped past the tank and came to an abrupt halt outside the main entrance of the UN Headquarters. The cops and the FBI men got out of their cars, their guns drawn, then the UN officials got out and one of them shouted, 'OK, God, come on out, but do it real slow.'

Colonel Fleming and some of his men eased God from the bus while others pointed their Top Secret Weapons in every direction. Once we were out of the bus God was led quickly inside to the General Assembly Hall, which was completely empty except for some cleaners and the fifteen members of the International Court of Justice.

The chairman of the International Court of Justice tapped a microphone in front of him. 'Are you Zizo Yasuzawa?' he asked. 'Also known as Japs Eye Fontanelle, the Zodiac Man, He-Whose-Figure-Of-Beauty-Is-Tinged-With-The-Hue-Of-Cerulean-Blue-Clouds-And-Whose-Unique-Loveliness-Charms-Millions-Of-Little-Cupids, the Creator of the Universe, King of the Holy Channel Island of Adocentyn, God, the reincarnation of Maitreya Buddha, Avatara of the Hindu deity Vishnu, Iman Mahdi, the Saviour of Humanity, Maker of the Cosmos, Holy Emperor and the reincarnation of the Thrice Great One, author of The Emerald Tablet, Hermes Trismegistus, maker of the holy pyramids of Egypt. Awo-Bam-Do-Bop-Awo-Bambo?'

'Yes indeedy,' God said.

'You are hereby charged with the killing of Time.'

'God had nothing to do with it,' God said.

'You will be brought before this court in two weeks' time to stand trial,' the chairman said.

'Two weeks!' shouted God in disbelief.

'Take the prisoner away,' the chairman said.

'But I don't even have an attorney yet.'

We left the General Assembly Hall and got back into our yellow school buses. At this point one of Colonel Fleming's men reported that Miss Hughes was missing. The entire UN Headquarters was searched and she was found in the gift shop in the basement buying souvenir mugs which had the letters UN printed in blue on them. After Miss Hughes was put on board the bus we went back down East 42nd Street and boarded the train which took us back to Fort Knox.

On the trip back Miss Hughes told God that she had never been to New York before and God told her that this whole thing, God's incarceration, his trial, this travelling up and down America, is the fault of just one silly little man.

If it wasn't for Commissioner Pizarro, the rascal, God told his nurse, God would still be on Jersey, left to my own devices, doing the vital work of harmonizing the Microcosm with the Macrocosm and free to attend, as God has always done, the annual reunion of retired kamikaze pilots in Hiroshima. Commissioner Pizarro is insane, obsessed about me and born under the star sign of Libra which means, of course, that he likes his women on top, votes Republican, has a small penis and should avoid finalizing anything on a Wednesday.

THE 6TH

✳

Launch of largest liner ever built	☽ v/c 6:43 am
Birthday of Greta Garbo (actress)	☽ → ♋ 8:58 am
Uruguay declares war on Argentina	☽ ✳ ♀
W.H. Carothers makes nylon stockings	☽ ✳ ♄
	☽ ⊼ ♆
	☽ ⊻ ♂
	☽ ⊻ △
	☽ ⊼ ♇

Colonel Fleming gave God another batch of mail today. One of the letters is from God's second wife, Dr Hultcravitz, who has been in hiding in Japan ever since the invasion of Jersey. Dr Hultcravitz said in her letter that she hopes God is being treated well. She tells God my ball is doing fine. In fact, she says it is just dandy.

God's second wife's letter ends by telling God to be strong.

Enclosed with the letter is a picture of God's right, possibly left, ball, drawn by Dr Hultcravitz herself.

God got my nurse to hang the picture of my ball above the table in the mobile home. God's nurse thinks that the picture of God's right, possibly left, ball is of a sunset or a sunrise. God told her she was close.

When God and my balls were together I had made love 15,003 times to my second wife.

God and my nurse watched *Star Trek* later. Tonight's episode was about a planet on which embarrassing silences were not embarrassing.

THE 7TH

Germany annexes Tanganyika and Zanzibar	☽ ⊻ ☿
Federal income tax introduced in the US	☽ ✳ ♅
Bob Dylan (singer) falls off motorbike	☽ ⊼ ♇
	☽ ♂ ♀
	☽ ⊻ ♃
	☿ □ ♅

After a distinguished career as Foreign Minister of Nicaragua Pedro Pizarro was appointed Commissioner for the Prevention of Natural Disasters in 1945. He was given a little room in the corner of the brand new UN building and an equally brand-new bright-eyed Virgo secretary who could type seventy-five words a minute.

On the door to his office he put up a sign which said:

There is no such thing as an accident.

Pizarro was the natural choice for the post of Commissioner for the Prevention of Natural Disasters, seeing that Nicaragua's capital Managua had twice been completely destroyed by earthquakes and, back in 1835, the country had experienced the most violent volcanic eruption ever to hit the western hemisphere.

Virgo women are vegetarians, and are turned on by hotel rooms and boxer shorts. Their lucky soup is tomato.

Pedro Pizarro loved his work. He engrossed himself in his subject, becoming an expert on the destruction of Pompeii in AD 79 and proposing a theory that explained the disappearance of Atlantis, the plague of darkness and the parting of the Red Sea, both reported in the Bible, and as if that were not enough, the curious disappearance of the Minoan Civilization, on the eruption of the volcano Santorini in the Aegean Sea.

Commissioner Pizarro's basic theory was elaborated later by Professor George A. Galanopoulos, an Aquarius and director of the Seismological Laboratory of the University of Athens.

Aquarius men do not enjoy pissing on their partners or being pissed on; their best time of day is 4.32 p.m., their lucky numbers are 1, 2, 3, 4, 5, 6, 7, 8, 9 and 10.

Pedro Pizarro criss-crossed the Earth, witnessing the aftermath of every kind of natural disaster – floods, earthquakes, tornados, storms – the whole shooting match. Everywhere he went he would take photographs, make measurements and collect eye-witness accounts.

Whenever there was a natural calamity Commissioner Pizarro would be there. He became something of a celebrity. When a country was blighted by an avalanche or a flood, the people would say 'Commissioner Pizarro will be here soon', and he invariably was.

God asked my nurse, while God was standing partially under the shower, as she scrubbed some part of my tremendous body (safely under the influence of Neptune), to describe my penis to me. She thought for some time and then reported that she supposed it looked like a miniature one of those Dead Sea Scrolls.

God thanked her profusely.

God has decided to write a book while in captivity. It will be called *How to Fix your Car with the Help of Astrology* and will be a runaway success.

THE 8TH

First UFO sighted by Kenneth Arnold	☽ v/c 1:09 pm
	☽ → ♌ 1:38 pm
London University moves from Kensington	♀ → ♉ 6:32 pm
to Bloomsbury	☽ ✱ ☿
Louis Pasteur cures hydrophobia	☽ △ ♃
	☿ ✱ ♃
Thermos bottle invented	☽ □ ♄
	☽ □ ♀
	☽ ☍ ♆
	☽ ✱ ♂

God's nurse said this morning that God snores in his sleep. God categorically denies this.

Colonel Fleming came by for breakfast as usual and wanted to hear more of the raid on Pearl Harbor.

So God told him the growth on his ball had turned out to be just a spot and that God had taken off along with everyone else on the raid.

'I know that,' said Colonel Fleming, 'you told me all that last time, what happened next?'

God told him that we reached an altitude of 9,000 feet and an hour later, through thick cloud cover, an island appeared ahead of us. It looked a lot like Jersey. So much so in fact that when God flew over that particular Channel Island many years later I would be struck with a powerful sense of déjà vu. Our original orders had been to protect the dive-bombers and torpedo planes from enemy fighter aircraft, but no American planes got into the air, so after a while, for something to do, my squadron of Zeros began strafing the airfields on the island while the bombers destroyed the United States Pacific Fleet in Pearl Harbor.

One after the other we machine-gunned American aircraft

that were parked along the runway, wing tip to wing tip, like some giant zip sown into the ground.

Colonel Fleming, listening intently, simulated our attacks by poking his food with his fork and making what he considered to be machine-gun noises with his chapped lips.

It was on God's second strafing attack, God told the Colonel, as God started to pull up out of my dive, that the control stick came away in God's hands.

God then told the Colonel that human beings have not one drop of free will. Free will is an idea directly in contradiction to the glorious tenets of astrology, God said, adding that this was obvious, and that a child could see it. How can mortals have free will if fashion, business, interior decorating, sports, television, childcare, careers, cosmetics, health, interpersonal relationships, sex and art are all determined by the motions of the stars?

Free will is a silly idea if you ask God. Humans have about as much free will as Lake Michigan or an eggplant, which is zip. Zero. Nil.

What critics of astrology always fail to see, God told Colonel Fleming, is that people simply do not want to have free will, they can't stand it, they just hate it. When you get rid of free will, you get rid of the terrifying burden of daily responsibility, of having to think for yourself. Man was never meant to think for himself.

'Why else do you think I invented astrology?' God asked, then told the Colonel the very first astrological prediction God ever made. It was for Leos and appeared in the newspaper *Yomiuri* in 1946 and went like this:

> *You will meet a tall dark stranger or a short dark stranger. He or she will definitely not be medium in height. That much is clear. You will get some money soon which you should spend wisely. You will buy a new pair of shoes and eat something quite spicy.*

Leos have two orgasms a night and have a special cosmic relationship with all citrus fruits.

THE 9TH

✳

Deathday of Monet (artist)	☽ ✳ ☉
Alabama explored for the first time	☽ △ ♅
Food blender invented	☽ □ ♃
Earthquake in Peru	☉ ✳ ♅ ☽ ⊼ ♄
	☽ ✳ ☿ ☽ ✳ ♂
	☽ ✳ ♄

In 1947, while God was just starting out on my mission to save mankind, Commissioner Pizarro was picked up by a tornado he was following in Oklahoma and transported two miles. Throughout the ordeal the Commissioner continued to make notes.

God told Miss Hughes this while she was making lunch. She was not very interested but God was bored and just kept going, explaining how, a few months later, Commissioner Pizarro was in India following a massive landslide that had killed thousands. He returned to New York only to witness at first hand the terrible snowstorm of the 4th of Capricorn 1947. Ninety-nine million tons of snow covered the city of New York. The United Nations building's heating broke down and New York cab drivers charged kings' ransoms for rides.

When New York thawed, Pizarro went back to criss-crossing the world following one natural disaster after another. It was all he did.

Then came the high point of Pizarro's career – the earthquake at Assam, a real show-stopper, the biggest earthquake ever seen. It set needles skidding off seismographs. It was so monstrous that American scientists assumed the quake was occurring in Japan while Japanese scientists stated that the quake had to be taking place in downtown Kansas City.

When Commissioner Pizarro arrived the quake was still going on. The ground rose up and greeted his white UN jet. For five full days the world quivered, shuddered as if in the grip of some monstrous orgasm, an orgasm to end all orgasms.

O-mito-fo.

Whole towns disappeared and, of course, thousands of people perished. Survivors clung to the uppermost branches of trees and ate leaves. In the tree in which Commissioner Pizarro found himself hanging for his life, a woman gave birth to a Virgo, an Earth sign.

When the ground finally stopped moving nearly a week later, Commissioner Pizarro's tree fell over. All the Commissioner could hear, he told reporters later, still in the tree's branches, was the smacking sound of the newborn Virgo sucking its terrified mother's nipple.

Commissioner Pizarro interviewed the few survivors. He asked them, 'So the ground just started to move, to shake violently, is that right? And you never saw anyone provoke it in any way, you never saw anyone kick it or call it names?'

After the earthquake in Assam, India, in Leo, 1950, Commissioner Pizarro did two extraordinary things. First he swore never to touch the ground again for as long as he lived, getting about on a pogo stick which he quickly mastered, and second when he returned to America he called a press conference, declared the world a crime scene and formally indicted Nature for crimes against humanity.

THE 10TH

<hr>

First footprint of Yeti found by Col. Howard-Bury

F. Galton proves permanence and individuality

  of fingerprints

China declares Korea to be an independent state

Charles Emmanuel IV of Sardinia enthroned

Great Fire of London

☽ v/c 7:23 am
☽ → ♋ 2:10 pm

♂ ♂ ♄
☽ △ ♀
☽ ⊼ ♆

<hr>

At lunchtime today the phone in the gold vault rang.

It had never done this before.

It sounded like this: Berrr Berrr Berrr Berrr.

Colonel Fleming answered it. 'It's for God,' he said.

A dozen soldiers, complaining that this was not the sort of thing they had in mind when they had joined the army, squeezed God out of the mobile home and escorted him to the phone.

'Hello,' God said into the receiver the Colonel held to my mouth. 'Hello?'

'Thrice Great One, is it really you?'

'Yep.'

'I can't believe I am actually speaking down the phone to God himself.'

'Who is this and how did you get my number?'

'My name is Ilgi Spillsbury, I lived on Jersey during your glorious reign. I was a corporal in the Leo Legion.'

'And?'

'And I was an attorney here in America before I gave all that up to devote myself to the Zodiac and You.'

'Mr Spillsbury,' God said, 'you're hired.'

* * *

Leo men's best days are Sundays, they enjoy crime novels, hate taking cabs and have had at least twenty sexual partners by the age of forty. They have a feeling that their sex life would improve if they had bigger penises. They are right.

Mr Spillsbury was phoning from a motel just outside Fort Knox. An hour later he was kneeling before God in the mobile home, telling God the story of his little finite life.

He would have come to my assistance earlier only he was fighting the US Marines who stormed the island of Jersey. God had been under the impression that organized resistance ceased within twelve hours of the assault. God asked Mr Spillsbury how many others there were still holding out on the island. There were about one hundred. God asked how the Resistance fighters were doing. Not so well, Mr Spillsbury said. All attempts to blend in with the civilian population fail because the Resistance fighters insist on wearing their brightly coloured uniforms, the colour of which corresponds to their individual star sign. Worse, the Marines know that the Resistance only attacks when Mars is favourably aligned with Saturn and have so far always been waiting for the attack when it happens. Apparently being armed only with bamboo spears doesn't help much either.

Mr Spillsbury, when he heard that I was unable to find myself an attorney (God's predicament having been reported and commented on by all the major TV networks), left the Resistance hideout and gave himself up – handing over his bamboo spear to a Marine sergeant who had said, 'Thank you very much.'

Mr Spillsbury told God how after that he was given non-astrological clothes to wear and spent a week in what had formerly been the Temple of God's Illustrious Gonads, and before that, Fort Regent's Leisure Centre, where he underwent brainwashing. Mr Spillsbury had to renounce all his most cherished beliefs, he had to utter blatant untruths, he had to say that astrology was a confused mess of half-baked anachronistic ideas and childish nonsense. He had to say it was mumbo-jumbo of the highest order, a demented and simplistic attempt to reduce the wonderful diversity and complexity of human personality into something that could be written on the back of a postcard. It was accordingly an affront to the human spirit and an insult to tell someone that they were basically a Capricorn or an Aries or what have you.

Poor Mr Spillsbury had to shout out that in his opinion the stars were just tremendous spheres of very hot gas getting their energy from hydrogen. 'Other than sending out light and other forms of radiation, the stars affect my life not one zip!' is what Ilgi Spillsbury had to shout.

He also had to sign a piece of paper that stated that the Zodiac had been made up a long time ago by people with bad eyesight or too much to drink or not enough to eat who saw things that were not there.

Then the US Marine Corps made Mr Spillsbury invent his own Zodiac, made him draw it on a map of the stars. Mr Spillsbury's Zodiac was made up of anything he could think of, table lamps, chairs, fruit, a chicken crossing the road and a 747 with its landing gear down.

The night before Mr Spillsbury was made a free man he and some other former astrologers were marched outside and asked by a Marine counter-intelligence officer if they could see something like a crab, or two guys standing together or a bull or anything like that in the sky above them.

'We looked real hard for a while and then said nope.'

The Marine counter-intelligence officer kept Mr Spillsbury and the others looking for fish, rams, women carrying pitchers of water, and centaurs all night. When the stars faded from view and the sun rose Mr Spillsbury was released and caught a plane for New York.

'The Universe forgives you, Mr Spillsbury,' God told him after I had heard his harrowing story.

'Thank you very much,' he said, adding that not for one second did he actually believe what they were telling him about astrology. He said he couldn't because to entertain what the Marine counter-intelligence officer was saying would expose his life as a complete and utter sham.

Leo men prefer tea to coffee, they are not good with children, their lucky piece of cutlery is the teaspoon.

The Universe needs more men like Ilgi Spillsbury.

THE 11TH

Bob Dylan gets religion	☽ v/c 9:35 am
	☽ → ♌ 9:36 pm
Peace between Turkey and Serbia	
	☽ □ ♄
29.43-metre tall snowman made	☽ □ ♂
	☽ ⊼ ♀

Mr Spillsbury, my attorney, insists on kneeling in God's presence, even when we eat. God is touched.

When Commissioner Pizarro charged Nature with crimes against humanity the judicial system laughed, the press had a field day, religious leaders complained and the UN Secretary-General, a Gemini, ordered Commissioner Pizarro into his office. 'What's the big idea?' the UN Secretary-General asked.

Gemini men dislike all shades of yellow, cannot stand classical music or mice and are the hardest to arouse of all the signs.

Commissioner Pizarro replied, bouncing up and down: 'I just thought something ought to be done, sir.'

'Oh, you did.'

'Yes, I did. Things have been going on like this for too long.'

'Like what?'

'The indiscriminate murdering of people by Nature,' explained Commissioner Pizarro.

'Jesus,' said the Secretary-General.

Here is what Commissioner Pizarro had said at his famous press conference:

'People say Nature is beautiful, and all right, things like the Niagara Falls and sunsets are nice and everything, but, well, what's beautiful about cancer? What's beautiful about a gazelle being ripped to pieces by a lion? What's so wonderfully touching exactly about death? Why do we have to die? Why do stars have to go out? Why does there have to be so much pain everywhere? And why does shit have to smell so bad? Why is the weather not better? Why do we have to spend half our life doing nothing but sleep? Have you ever stopped to think how completely stupid and pointless sleeping is? Why can't we travel faster than light? Why is there no air in space? And why why why are there things like earthquakes and landslides, and floods and hurricanes? Why do things have to darn well hurt so much so much of the time? Why?'.

People watching Commissioner Pizarro's press conference on their TV sets stood up, looked around them, thought for a while and then said, 'Yeah, why do things have to darn well hurt so much so much of the time?' Some of them even shouted the question out of their windows into the night.

Commissioner Pizarro went on and on. He said that if he were Mother Nature, if he were God, he would have designed things a hundred times better. He said he would have done a better job with both his hands tied behind his back. Then Commissioner Pizarro read aloud something a philosopher had written more than two hundred years before. The philosopher's name was John Stuart Mill. He was a Gemini, which meant he liked light meats such as chicken, had dangly testicles and his lucky mathematical sign was 'divide'.

Here are the words of John Stuart Mill, that Commissioner Pizarro read out at his press conference:

> *Everything, in short, which the worst men commit either against life or property is perpetrated on a larger scale by natural agents . . . Not even with the most distorted and contracted theory of good which ever was framed by religious or philosophical fanaticism can the government of Nature be made to resemble the work of a being at once good and omnipotent.*

To which I, God, retort: Blow it out your ass.

THE 12TH

Formation of the Black Panthers

Man tap-dances 37.36 kilometres

Ohio and Nebraska become states of America

50lbs of rock brought back from the Moon

President Theodore Roosevelt shakes 8,513
  people's hands at an office function

$\math{D} \to \math{m}$ 8:26 pm

$\odot \; \pi \; \hbar$

$\math{D} \; \delta \; \varphi$

$\math{D} \; \pi \; \Psi$

$\varphi \; \vee \; \Psi$

Commissioner Pizarro went on to say in his press conference that he considered the Third Law of Thermodynamics a complete disgrace. According to him, evolution was immoral, little better than Fascism, and Gravity absolutely sucked. He said he had spoken to all the world's religious leaders asking for an explanation of why parts of Nature had to be such shit. The world's religious leaders had said that without bad things happening there would be no way to recognize good things.

Commissioner Pizarro had thought this argument was a pile of bullshit. Why, he wanted to know, couldn't the world be full of dull things and good things, or only very slightly scary bad things and good things? Instead of what we had which was a world with a hell of a lot of dangerous bad stuff and hardly any good. Why hadn't God made a world full of good things and very good things, the Commissioner wanted to know.

People all over the planet agreed with the Commissioner and kept asking themselves, 'Why do things have to darn well hurt so much so much of the time?', shouting the question out their windows into the night.

And then the North Koreans invaded South Korea and everyone forgot about the UN official who was trying to take Nature to court. Commissioner Pizarro, however, went on compiling his case, went on gathering his evidence, out of the limelight, madder than ever. When the Hwai and Yangtze rivers flooded in eastern China, Commissioner Pizarro was given permission to visit the area. Hundreds of towns and cities had been wiped out and Commissioner Pizarro, viewing the scene from a Chinese navy patrol boat, could hear cries for help coming from every direction, above the noise his pogo stick made on the wooden deck.

For the next ten years he went on compiling his case, went on bitterly criticizing the Natural Order of Things.

After dinner Colonel Fleming asked if God wanted to join him and Miss Hughes in a game of poker.

God lost. He now owes the Colonel and Miss Hughes a total of $52. That God lost is not surprising really when you consider that I was unable to see my hand thanks to the ridiculous positions of my arms.

THE 13TH

Hirohito ascends to the throne on the death	☽ △ ♇
of his father, Emperor Yoshihito	☽ ✳ ☉
Shelley von Strunckel takes over from the	☽ ☍ ♅
late Patric Walker as the London	☽ □ ♄
Evening Standard's astrologer	
End of Taiping Rebellion in China	
Texas declares itself independent of Mexico	

Colonel Fleming, during breakfast, asked God what had happened when the control stick of my plane had come away in my hands over Pearl Harbor.

'Well,' God said, 'first God just looked at the control stick for five or six seconds. Then God started to shout like mad. God swore, then God spent perhaps another four seconds insulting my plane and my fellow countrymen who had built it, spinning towards the ground.' God told Colonel Fleming that God then scratched the metal plate on the top of my head. God then tried to bail out but my canopy refused to open. After that God swore a bit more. Then God took a good look around. Then God groped frantically at what was left of the control stick and managed to level out.

God was maybe ten feet above the ground, flying over the heads of terrified Americans. Already the sky was black with burning oil, billowing from crippled warships in the harbour.

I made it back to the carrier group, the last plane to do so. God was hoisted on to the shoulders of two ground crew amid cheers and applause. God was light enough back then to be picked up by just two men.

When God had finished Colonel Fleming dropped his fork and listed out loud the names of the eleven US battleships heavily damaged or destroyed in the raid, pushing his plate away from him as he did so.

'The USS *Virginia*, the USS *Tennessee*, the USS . . .'

'It was a neon ago,' God interrupted.

'An aeon,' corrected Miss Hughes.

'Yes,' said God, 'an aeon ago and lots of shit has passed under the bridge since then.'

THE 14TH

The rubber hose is invented	☽ ⊼ ♆
Florida becomes US state	☽ ⊼ ♇
Albania declared first atheist country in the world	☽ ✳ ☉
Authorized Version of the Bible rendered into	☽ ⊼ ♅
English by 47 translators	☽ ✳ ♂
Man tells 345 jokes in a hour	

God sat on my holy arse and did nothing at all today. Mr Spillsbury wanted to start work on God's defence but God told him God didn't feel like it and suggested he go kneel somewhere else.

WWII started well for Japan. We liberated Malaya, Thailand, the Gilberts, Guam, Northern Luzon, North Borneo. On and on we went all the way to the Philippines.

We were invincible, at least to start with.

Three months after Pearl Harbor God took part in the Battle of the Coral Sea. The Americans lost a carrier, a destroyer and a tanker, while we lost only a light carrier, the *Shoho*. So long, *Shoho*.

The Americans considered it a win for them all the same, as it forced us to call off our invasion of Port Moresby and, more importantly, forced God's carrier, the *Zuikaku*, and another, the *Shokaku*, to return to port for repair work, thereby missing the Battle of Midway.

God's Zero fighter was badly shot up during the Battle of the Coral Sea. Ground crew counted thirty-eight bullet holes in the plane altogether.

In many ways Midway was a repeat of Pearl Harbor. Admiral Yamamoto's task force sailed eastward from Hitokappu Bay towards the island of Oahu and Pearl Harbor just as we had done in '41. Only this time the element of surprise was on the American side.

Admiral Yamamoto, being a Libra, loved all shades of red, never used a public toilet, had a weakness for gambling and had never had sex on a Monday.

American planes (one flown by Colonel Fleming's grandfather) destroyed a number of ships including four aircraft carriers.

As anyone will tell you it was the turning point of the war in the Pacific. With those four carriers we lost the ability to wage offensive warfare. After Midway we could only defend what we had already taken.

Years after the war, Captain Fuchida, the hero of Pearl Harbor and the man who had found God on the eve of the raid fiddling with himself, would say that before Midway we could 'zap zap', after it we could only 'poo poo'.

Towards the end of his life, Captain Fuchida came to believe among other things that Midway was caused by the divine intervention of the Archangel Gabriel.

THE 15TH

Deathday of Dizzy Gillespie (jazz musician) ☽ v/c 2:30 pm
Galileo discovers Jupiter's moons ☽ □ ♇
James Monroe elected President of the USA ☽ ⊼ ♅
  ☽ ☊ ♃
Shampoo used for the first time ☽ ⊼ ☿
End of Anglo-Persian War ☿ ⋎ ♃
  ☽ ✳ ♄
  ☽ ⊼ ☉

On the six o'clock news tonight a four-star Marine general announced that all armed resistance on the island of Jersey had ceased and the island was an 'astrology-free zone' following a raid on the Resistance movement headquarters, the House of the Left Ball, formerly God's command bunker and before that an art gallery and before that a WWII German medical bunker. The TV showed a pile of bamboo spears captured in the operation and a number of bath mats and key chains with God's birth chart printed on them. Most shocking of all was the news that the US Marines have confiscated God's left (possibly right) testicle. There were pictures of it being carried out of the temple by soldiers wearing gas masks. It looked so defenceless.

On seeing these shocking pictures God Almighty burst into tears. Miss Hughes tried to comfort me saying, 'There, there, Mr Fontanelle, it will be all right.'

'Please,' God said, 'call me God.'

In 1960 Commissioner Pizarro, still ranting against Providence, had what many saw as a breakdown when one of his filing cabinets collapsed on top of him as he worked late. The 'accident' happened on Friday night and he was not found by his secretary until Monday morning.

He insisted that Nature had been to blame. By this stage his office was a tip, files were everywhere. He had let himself go – he had also beaten the world record for continuous pogo-hopping, which had been set by Terry Cole.

The UN Secretary-General told him to take a vacation. It was an order and it was Pizarro's first real vacation since becoming Commissioner for the Prevention of Natural Disasters fifteen years before.

He went to the island of Fiji, drank out of coconuts, mastered the art of bouncing on sand (not an easy thing) and watched girls in straw dresses laugh at him. On his second day there heavy rain and storms engulfed the island. Fourteen people died, hundreds of homes were destroyed and Commissioner Pizarro's pogo stick was washed out to sea. He got another one.

THE 16TH

Deathday of Walter Chrysler (industrialist)	☉ ♂ ♇
Jodrell Bank Radio Telescope completed	☽ ⊼ ♅
E. Fermi suggests that neutrons and protons	☽ △ ♨
are the same fundamental particles in two	♀ ♂ ♄
different quantum states	
Man shot attempting to leave East Germany	

During the Battle of the Coral Sea, one of those thirty-two bullets that ripped through God's plane happened to hit the metal plate that had been screwed to my head when God was six months old. The plate was dented bang in the centre and the proverb engraved on it was ruined.

God made it back to the *Zuikaku*, the bullet still smouldering on the top of his head. My ground crew started to count the number of bullet holes in my plane. They did this by pushing their podgy fingers through the still warm holes. Before they had finished God was in a coma.

It was a coma from which God would not recover until October 1944. Some two and a half years later.

God was taken to the head injury ward of Miyazaki Hospital on the home island of Kyushu, where God lingered, all attempts to bring me back to this world failing.

My first wife visited me regularly and left neatly folded pairs of brilliant-white underwear on the chair next to God's bed, most of which were stolen and later sold on the black market, ending up in the far corners of the South Pacific Theatre of Operations.

While God lay in Miyazaki impersonating an inanimate object, the war continued to worsen for Japan. The Solomon Islands were successfully attacked by the US Marine Corps and British forces began clawing back parts of Burma.

Things, in short, did not look good:

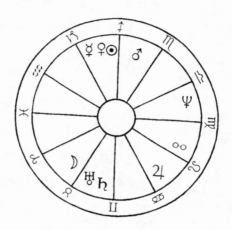

THE 17TH

Deathday of Mao Tse-tung	☽ v/c 12:09 am
	☽ → ♋ 7:27 am
Birthday of first test-tube baby	☽ □ ☿
Start of regular airmail service between	♂ ✳ ♆
	♀ ☌ ♆
London and Australia	☽ ⊼ ♆
	☽ ⊼ ♀ ☽ □ ♂
	♄ ⊼ ♎ ☽ △ ♃
	☽ ⊼ ♇

Spent most of today in bed with a cold. Sent Mr Spillsbury back to his motel room, telling him we will work on God's defence later.

Miss Hughes has been feeding me chicken soup all day. Something really has to be done about the heating in here.

THE 18TH

Pavlov begins working with dogs on

  conditioned reflexes

Largest ice-cream sundae made of 20.27

  tons of ice cream

The number of domestic refrigerators in

  the US tops 2 million

India declares war on Pakistan

☽ v/c 9:47am
☽ → ♊ 8:56 pm

☽ ⚹ ♃
☽ ⚹ ♀
☽ ⊻ ♄
☉ ⊼ ♇

Commissioner Pizarro issued one hundred court summonses on Nature and posted them to the four corners of the Earth. Nature naturally never showed. In utter frustration the Commissioner took to bouncing around shouting, 'Kiss my ass, Mother Earth, kiss my ass!' saying it made him feel a little better.

And then on the 30th of Sagittarius 1972, Managua, the capital of Nicaragua, was destroyed for the third time by an earthquake. God had, of course, seen it coming astrologically way off.

Seven thousand people died and over 20,000 were made homeless. Everything Pizarro remembered from his childhood, his parents' house, his old school, the church, were miraculously turned into wonderfully neat piles of rubble.

People fled the city in the morning light moments after the quake struck. Mutilated bodies were everywhere. The people of the former city of Managua were cut off from the rest of the world except for a ham radio operator whose name was Enrique and whose star sign was Pisces.

Pizarro, like millions of others, listened to Enrique's broadcasts. They were all pretty much alike. They went like this:

People run through the streets like zombies, with terror.
Big buildings are cracked. There is blood on people's faces,
legs, arms as they leave their homes. We have never seen
a catastrophe like this.

They had, of course. Twice.

That night, Managua burned and it looked for all the world like Tokyo the night the Americans set it alight with thousands of incendiary bombs, the size of penises, turning the city into a beautiful ice storm of little fires, reminiscent of the Milky Way, towards the tail-end of World War II.

Pisces men never fail to climax. Their lucky number is 1,324. They like purple and greeny-blues and hardly ever brush their teeth.

After dinner God watched *Star Trek*.

In tonight's episode the crew of the Enterprise made contact with a self-conscious Nebula of compressed hydrogen and helium.

The crew of the Starship Enterprise asked the Nebula what it was doing. The Nebula told them that it was just hanging around.

THE 19TH

Birthday of Billy Graham (businessman)	☽ v/c 10:32 am
Start of cholera epidemic	☽ → ♓ 8:07 pm
Invention of the paper clip	☽ ⚹ ♄
	♀ △ ⚨
	☽ ⚹ ☉
	☽ ⚺ ♆

God told Colonel Fleming, Mr Spillsbury and my nurse this morning that all things manifest are in degrees of representation of the Divine Pattern Above. In humanity there is the greatest number of degrees, for mind is present in man. The human soul is the Microcosmic unit of the Macrocosm and possesses the Divine Spark.

Mr Spillsbury broke into applause while my nurse told me to shut up as I was spitting bits of porridge all over the place.

✳ ✳ ✳

The Solomon Islands were abandoned, Guam bombed by US planes, the Marshalls taken, Les Negros invaded, effectively cutting off our forces in the Bismarck Archipelago, and all that time God remained in my coma, in my own tiny weeny cosmos, the size of my head.

THE 20TH

Discovery of Peking man in China	☽ v/c 3:21 pm
Turkish troops massacre Bulgarians	☽ → ♋ 10:57 pm
Formation of the anti-saloon league in US	☽ □ ♃
Spring mattress invented	♀ ⚺ ♄
	☽ ⚹ ♄
	☽ □ ♀
	♂ □ ♅

Mr Spillsbury and God Almighty spent today preparing for God's impending trial. We spent most of the day trying to lower my arms. Mr Spillsbury feels that, raised as they are, they will give the wrong impression in court. God is inclined to agree with him. We have tried everything we can think of but so far nothing seems to work. As if this wasn't bad enough Mr Spillsbury now seems to be getting the flu. It is still terribly cold in here and for some reason Mr Spillsbury has not been issued with a Norwegian combat overcoat.

THE 21ST

Van Allen discovers radiation belts round	☽ v/c 6:33 pm
the Earth	☽ ⊼ ♅
Deathday of John VI of Portugal	☽ △ ⊙
Birthday of Shoko Asahara (poisoned Tokyo	☽ △ ⚷
underground)	☽ □ ♄
Invention of underarm deodorants	
Britain and France recognize independence of Zanzibar	

Discussed astrology for most of the day with my attorney, who, every time I stopped for breath, clapped wildly.

After Managua had been destroyed for the third time Commissioner Pizarro was put on a course of Prozac, took early retirement and spent his days in a convalescent home in Brooklyn that had sufficiently lax house rules to allow for his pogo stick. The post of Commissioner for the Prevention of Natural Disasters became vacant and remained so.

Pizarro's colleagues at the UN, who visited him from time to time, reported that he still ranted about how shit Nature was, how he could have done a better job with his eyes closed, how he still kept saying 'Kiss my ass, Mother Earth!' as he bounced around, but a lot of the fight had gone out of him. He took up chess and became, everyone seemed to agree, a rather mediocre player.

No doubt Pizarro would have eventually died on the toilet in that convalescent home as people, especially Virgos, Leos and Scorpios, are prone to do.

He didn't die. Instead, God, holding a sparkler and talking about astrology, showed up.

God had just finished months of intense testing at the Stanford Research Institute, the results of which had been published in the magazine *Nature*. My name was on everyone's lips. God was giving two performances a day, and picking up followers willy-nilly.

God performed everywhere to packed crowds, in baseball parks, ice rinks, at swanky hotels, private parties of the rich and famous, concert halls, nightclubs, and yes, even convalescent homes.

That was how Pedro Pizarro saw God in action for the first time. It took place in the main lounge with one hundred and twenty-five armchairs filled with the ageing placed in a semi-circle around me.

Pedro Pizarro looked on with a mixture of dread and fascination, bouncing up and down behind the armchairs.

God left and within three hours was at it again in a Lebanese restaurant on Third Avenue.

When God had gone, Pedro Pizarro, the former UN Commissioner for the Prevention of Natural Disasters, was on the phone whipping up a storm all of his own.

THE 22ND

✳

CS gas first used in riot control   ☽ ☐ ☿

D. Griffiths sets sneezing world record   ☽ ⋎ ♅

Marlene Dietrich appears in her first film   ☽ ✳ ♀

Dirac, Milne and Dingle engage in controversy   ☽ ✳ ♆

    about the age of the world   ☽ ✳ ♃

On the 1st of Virgo 1944, God regained consciousness. My world
in one head-jerking nanosecond expanded from something like
three inches in diameter to the current size of the Universe.

My sweet little first wife had awoken me from a two-and-a-
half-year slumber by nibbling my cock, the heavens at the time
being disposed thus:

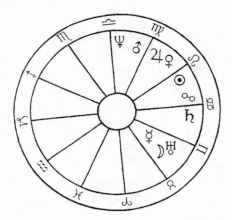

God has no illusions about her motives, she did it primarily for
the Emperor. There was, after all, a war going on.

God got spunk all over his Pearl Harbor medal which was
attached to the breast of my, what Americans call, PJs.

God had thirty-eight spare pairs of PJs.

More spare pairs of PJs, in fact, than God knew what to do with.

THE 23RD

Birthday of Mahatma Gandhi (politician)	☽ v/c 6:10 pm
First episode of *Monty Python* broadcast	☽ △ ♀
Independence of China declared	☽ ⊻ ♇
	☉ ♂ ♄
Atom split for the first time	♀ □ ♇
Term surrealism coined	☽ ⊼ ☿
	☽ □ ♅
	☽ △ ♃ ☽ ♂ ⚷

Mr Spillsbury came into the gold vault to continue working on my defence today. He was sneezing a lot and Miss Hughes made him some chicken soup. Rather than work on our defence God told his attorney how, just after WWII, God had eaten something that must have been off and spent days shitting and puking everywhere. In such a state it was impossible for God to make predictions and for nearly a week the astrological pages of several papers had the following message:

Unfortunately Zizo Yasuzawa, He-Whose-Figure-Of-Beauty-Is-Tinged-With-The-Hue-Of-Cerulean-Blue-Clouds-And-Whose-Unique-Loveliness-Charms-Millions-Of-Little-Cupids, is unwell and cannot do any detailed forecasts, he has however been able to compile a general prediction for all star signs which is as follows:

THINGS WILL HAPPEN

After telling him this God sent Mr Spillsbury home.

THE 24TH

O.P. Karrer claims to have isolated vitamin A	☽ △ ♆
Heisenberg propounds 'The Uncertainty Principle'	☽ ☍ ♇
O.P. Karrer withdraws claim to have isolated vitamin A	☽ ⊼ ☉
Birthday of Kurt Vonnegut (novelist)	☿ ⁎ ♅
	☽ ⊼ ♂
	☽ △ ♅
	☽ ⁎ ☿ ☽ ⊼ ♄

The UN felt sorry for Pedro Pizarro for the toll his job had taken on him, not least his psychotic jumping. They wanted to help him, they felt they owed him and they probably did. And so when he presented his madcap proposal they smiled, they touched him on his shoulder and gave him their blessing.

That was how the UN Cosmological Commission was formed.

Pizarro had finally found something tangible to fight, something to hold accountable for Nature, something that he could actually bring to book – me.

That was how it began and God was oblivious to it all.

Working almost completely alone and living entirely in the field, Pizarro followed me and my performances all over the place.

It went on like this for years, God told his nurse, I never once noticed the little man on the pogo stick taking pictures. I know that must be hard to believe but it's true. I suppose I was preoccupied with making the Universe what it is today.

Pizarro photographed God everywhere, putting the film in giant brown envelopes marked TOP SECRET, which he sent to his old secretary who opened the envelopes with great care and put their contents into thirty-eight silver filing cabinets in the basement of United Nations Headquarters.

Pizarro lived in motel rooms and had no social life at all. I was his world. I was his reason for being. He was almost happy.

It is said that everywhere he went Commissioner Pizarro bought a copy of my birth chart which he used, late into the night – it pains me terribly to write this – as a dart board.

Commissioner Pizarro was even worse at darts then he had been at chess, on account of his pogo stick.

Later God and my nurse watched *Star Trek* together.

THE 25TH

First use of a parachute

Deathday of Salvador Dali (artist)

C. Birdseye extends deep-freezing process
   to pre-cooked foods

☽ ☐ ♃
☽ ∨ ♂
☽ △ ♄

God spent two short weeks with my first little wife back in Kyoto before being ordered to join the 201st Air Group operating out of the Philippines. On the 25th of Libra 1944, God landed at Mabalacat airfield on the island of Luzon just as dusk was setting in.

Climbing down from my plane with my belongings – a towel, some maps and charts, three pencils, a pencil sharpener, and thirty-six pairs of underwear – God made my way over to the airfield command post trying to look as much the flying ace as possible. Crammed into the room was every single pilot of the 201st Air Group, standing to attention in front of a man God would later learn was Commander Tamai.

Suddenly every hand in the command post shot upward. Everyone was on tiptoes. God deduced, incorrectly as it turned out, that Commander Tamai had ordered everyone to touch the ceiling.

With every single pilot reaching upward, stupid grins on their faces, God did likewise (what patriot would not have?) blissfully unaware that when God reached old age he would find himself unable to strike any other pose.

Commander Tamai beamed with satisfaction and clapped.

We all clapped, although we were nowhere near the ceiling.

Then Commander Tamai said that obviously secrecy was critical and wished us all a good night's sleep.

Commander Tamai was born under the sign of Aries and consequently had a passion for sports cars and radishes and would have liked his partner to make wombat noises during sex.

It was only later, as God spoke to the other pilots in the back of one of the jeeps returning to our billet, a Western-style building of huge proportions in town, a giant doll's house minus the giant hinges on the corners, that it dawned on me that I had been that night, just outside Mabalacat on the island of Luzon in the Philippines, a founding member of the volunteer Kamikaze Special Attack Corps.

Commander Tamai's lucky number was 0.003. He would never, alas, know this.

THE 26TH

✳

Mt St Helens explodes	☽ v/c 2:35 am
Revival of the Olympic Games	☽ → ♈ 9:31 pm
Birthday of Albert Einstein	♂ ⊼ ♇
Start of European Monetary Union	☽ ☌ ♃
Deathday of Karl Marx	☽ ☌ ♀
	☽ ⊻ ♄

My attorney and God spent four hours trying to lower God's arms before giving up today. We spent the rest of the day discussing the case itself.

Apparently it all comes down to how much gravity there is. If there is too much then the Universe will collapse back into itself, implode, experience a sort of Big Bang in reverse. The UNCC thinks by making all the galaxies God has, I have made too much mass and thus too much gravity.

If there is a Big Bang in reverse – a Big Crunch – then Time will go down the plughole along with everything else.

Mr Spillsbury showed God a book on cosmology that showed the two possible fates of the Universe and everything in it.

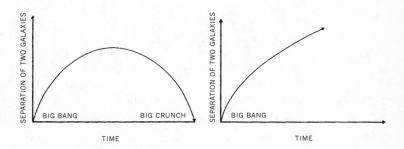

The first chart, Mr Spillsbury says, showed what the UNCC thinks will happen to the Universe thanks to God: at some point the distance between all the galaxies will decrease to zero.

The second chart showed the Universe constantly expanding at a uniform rate, because the gravitational attraction between galaxies is not strong enough to stop them speeding apart.

To be found innocent at the trial, Mr Spillsbury and God will have to show that the fate of the Universe resembles the second chart, not the first. How we are going to do this God has absolutely no idea.

THE 27TH

British conquest of northern Nigeria completed	☽ ✳ ♆
	☽ ⊻ ☉
	☽ △ ♇
Military rule ends in Brazil	☽ ⊻ ♂
	☽ ☌ ☿
	☽ ✳ ♅
	☽ ⊼ ♄

God's trial for the killing of Time is to start tomorrow. It will be shown live on every TV network in America and in all 201 nations that make up the UN. An estimated six billion people will be watching.

✳ ✳ ✳

My supporters are shown on TV tonight protesting outside the UN building, chanting about the Oneness of the Universe and demanding my immediate release. The spokesman for the Committee for the Scientific Investigation into Claims of the Paranormal, still wearing an orange life jacket, made an impassioned plea for me, God, to confess tomorrow in court that I have nothing to do with galactic formation, that I do not have the power I claim, in short to come out and say that I am not in fact God. If I were to do this the spokesman for the Committee for the Scientific Investigation into Claims of the

Paranormal said the UNCC would be forced to drop all charges and I would be able to leave the gold vault a free fat old man. The spokesman for the Committee for the Scientific Investigation into Claims of the Paranormal ended his plea by shouting, 'Come in, number 9, your time is up!'

* * *

The idea that I deny my own divinity made God laugh hysterically.

THE 28TH

Creation of the first national anthem	☽ △ ♅
Cocaine used as an anaesthetic	☽ ⊼ ♎
Nationalization of Japanese railways	☽ ⊻ ☿
	♂ △ ♆
	☽ □ ♃

The opening of God's trial was delayed by two hours. It was not God's fault. It was completely out of my control. A number of my followers decided to throw themselves on to the tracks in front of our train and had to be pulled off, one by one, by my guards. When we finally arrived at Grand Central Station we were met by hundreds of police, reporters, photographers, FBI agents and UN officials and put into our yellow school buses again. Pulling out on to East 42nd Street, we didn't go east as we had before, but headed west, passing the New York Public Library and ending up in Times Square.

There, forty-two giant stands had been erected, on which sat 100,000 people. The 100,000 people ate hotdogs, did the wave, and asked each other the time.

In addition to the 100,000 members of the public, the entire General Assembly of the United Nations was there, as was

Congress and the House of Representatives. The President of the United States of America was there with his family as was the UN Secretary-General and about a hundred foreign heads of state.

As God took his place in front of the International Court of Justice, scuffles broke out in the stands between those that thought God was innocent and those that thought I was not. In the commotion one of the giant stands collapsed. Two hundred people were killed and nearly a thousand were taken to hospital. Hardly anyone noticed. Everyone was watching Commissioner Pizarro negotiate his way through the crowds of people, police, Screaming Eagles, camera crews, on his stupid stupid pogo stick. When he finally made it the whole of Times Square erupted in applause.

Then the Secretary-General of the United Nations stood up, coughed, wondered out loud if the UN's founding fathers had had this sort of thing in mind when they had set it up, then said, 'Let's get this show on the road.'

Again Times Square erupted in applause. Everyone clapped and clapped and clapped, everyone, that is, apart from God. God didn't clap because I am so fat, am such a complete mound of blubber that I can't. Clapping, like so many things, is for God, an anatomical impossibility.

When everyone apart from God had stopped clapping, the chairman of the International Court of Justice declared the court in session.

'The defendant will stand,' the chairman said.

Colonel Fleming, Miss Hughes and my attorney helped God up.

When God was standing the chairman said, 'The defendant can lower his arms. We are all aware of his status as prisoner of the UN.'

God's attorney stood up. 'I am Mr Spillsbury, God's legal representative. My client, your honours, cannot lower his arms.'

'We've tried everything you can think of,' God said, smiling.

'It's because of my client's weight problem, caused by the horrors of World War Two,' explained my attorney.

'And a major Venus affliction,' God added.

The fifteen judges conferred briefly.

'Very well, the defendant may keep his hands in the air if he must,' said the chairman. Then he read out the charges.

'Mr Fontanelle, you are charged with 1,034,480 counts of the wilful creation of matter and the killing of Time. You are also charged with 102,000 counts of wanton volcanic eruption, 203,330 counts of premeditated avalanches and landslides, 100,000 counts of wilful droughting, 230,000 counts of creating cyclones without due regard to human life or property, 550,000 counts of other meteorological incompetence including hurricanes, snowstorms, tornados and typhoons. You are also charged with the creation of all known diseases, viruses, plagues and pestilences, with making the laws of physics downright unfriendly, for making gravity a pain in the ass and for inventing evolution with its amoral notion of the survival of the fittest. You are also charged with . . .'

At this point God's attorney started shouting objection, insisting that his client was here to face the charge of killing Time, all the other charges being irrelevant. The precise wording of UN resolution 231337, argued Mr Spillsbury, called for the arrest and trial of God for the killing of Time. It made no mention of earthquakes or anything else like that.

The International Court of Justice conferred. After five minutes Mr Spillsbury's objection was sustained. God would stand trial solely for the killing of Time. Commissioner Pizarro was clearly hopping mad but there was nothing he could do about it.

'How do you wish to plead?' asked the chairman of the International Court of Justice.

'The primal truth is not a body, but is one, one truth, one unity,' God explained. 'All things come from it and through it receive truth and unity in the perpetual movement of the stars.

There is a hierarchy of things, and higher things descend to lower things. Man is a little world reflecting the great world of the cosmos.'

'How do you plead?' inquired the chairman again, who seemed to have completely failed to take in anything God had just said.

'I, Japs Eye Fontanelle, the Zodiac Man, God, am well. God has been living for the last two months in a mobile home in the gold vault in Fort Knox. God has no idea where they have put all the gold. It is very cold inside the gold vault.'

'Kindly get to the point, Mr Fontanelle. How do you wish to plead?' said the chairman.

'We are the centre of the Universe, or at least I am. The Universe revolves around me, or more specifically my splendid balls. The Universe loves you, it really does, believe me. Fontanelle will now make predictions for his faithful followers. During the rest of Pisces the blind will see little and the deaf will hear poorly, Virgos will get mild diarrhoea today, getting progressively worse as evening approaches. Sagittarians will have OK sex tonight, but with the Moon in —'

'Your plea?'

God admitted to the creation of matter but pleaded not guilty to the killing of Time.

After God had pleaded not guilty the Committee for the Scientific Investigation into Claims of the Paranormal began to make an unholy racket with six brass drums, twenty-two cymbals, eight trumpets, three French horns and a bassoon they had smuggled into Times Square.

Due to the unholy racket the chairman of the International Court of Justice decided that the court would reconvene in the morning.

God, my attorney, my nurse and my guards were put back on board their yellow school buses and driven down Broadway to the Manhattan Correction Center where we spent the night.

THE 29TH

Airplane flies over the North Pole	♀ → ♓ 12:38 am
	☽ v/c 11:41 pm
Airplane flies over the South Pole	☽ ⊼ ♃
Flashbulb invented	☽ △ ☉
	☽ △ ☿
	☽ □ ♇
	☿ ☌ ☉
	☽ △ ♄
	☽ △ ♂

At nine today Commissioner Pizarro gave his opening speech. It was, despite his age (the Commissioner like God is no spring chicken), a magnificent performance. He spoke as if shouting a long way away over some unseen, unheard waterfall.

This is pretty much what he said:

'Unfortunately, God is not here to explain to us all the natural disasters he has seen fit to visit on mankind, God is not in court today to answer to any of that. He is here on a charge of premeditated murder. The killing of Time by the wanton creation of matter. As you heard yesterday, the accused denies the whole thing, but the evidence I have amassed establishes without doubt the Supreme Being's complete guilt.'

Commissioner Pizarro said nothing for a few bounces, entirely for effect, then went on:

'What is almost more shocking to civil people than the act of murder itself is the total indifference shown by the accused. Not once has he exhibited any sign of guilt, repentance or grief. Look at him, members of the court, ladies and gentlemen, does he look as if he feels any remorse?'

God wriggled my fingers. God's attorney advised me to stop.

Commissioner Pizarro went on to speak of God in the most disrespectful manner you can imagine, to say he blasphemed would be to understate things.

He called God a buffoon, a dickhead and an asshole. On several occasions he referred to me as 'evil' and went on to call me 'without doubt the greatest criminal mind the world has ever known'.

Throughout the Commissioner's opening speech 80,000 people in the stands clapped and nodded, 15,000 people gasped and turned their heads away and fought back tears, and 5,000 people just sat there and didn't know what to do.

Commissioner Pizarro told the International Court of Justice and the world that God was the single greatest threat to the long-term survival of civilization. He said that I was more dangerous than a million atom bombs. He said that I had created matter nearly every day of my adult life with wild abandon and that he had personally witnessed most of my sick and depraved performances. He told the court that to cap it all, to add insult to injury, God had had the nerve, the gall, to build a perverse parody of a religion around his crime.

Commissioner Pizarro's speech was delivered in short punchy sentences uttered as his head came level with the microphone in front of him.

Before my attorney made his opening speech he told the International Court of Justice that defending me was a profound honour and the pinnacle not just of his career but of his entire life. He told them this kneeling next to God.

My attorney's opening speech was considerably shorter than Commissioner Pizarro's had been. In fact, it consisted of just one single little sentence. It went as follows:

'Do you really think, distinguished members of this court, that God would be stupid enough to have put too much matter in his own Universe?'

Throughout today's proceedings the Committee for the Scientific Investigation into Claims of the Paranormal held up placards that said, 'Astrology sucks!' 'Hermes was a fake!' 'We are not star robots!' and 'Come in, number 9, your time is up!'

THE 30TH

The planet Pluto discovered	☽ v/c 1:45 am
	☽ → ♊ 2:15 am
Rising of commune in Paris	♀ → ♒ 11:15 am
	♂ → ♈ 11:18 am
Paraguay starts war against Argentina, Brazil	☽ ✶ ♂
and Uruguay	☽ △ ♀
Japan saved from Mongol invasion fleet by	☽ △ ♆
	♀ ✶ ♂
Divine Wind	☽ □ ♃
	☽ ☍ ♇
	☽ △ ♅

Today the prosecution called its first witness, a Dr Wetering, a cosmologist.

Commissioner Pizarro asked the cosmologist to explain in layman's terms the two possible long-term fates of the Universe.

Dr Wetering said that currently the Universe was expanding. Dr Wetering went on to say that the expansion was the result of the Big Bang, the event that created the Universe something like 15,000 million years ago.

At this point God intervened, shouting, 'It's a lie! I created the Universe in 1925.'

'The defendant will in future not interrupt,' said the chairman of the International Court of Justice.

Dr Wetering said that the fate of the Universe rested on a single question. The question was this: Will the rate at which the Universe is expanding remain the same or will it decrease?

The witness went on to explain that the answer to this very important question depended on gravity. If there is too much gravity then the expansion would have to stop, otherwise the expansion would keep going for ever.

'And what exactly would happen if the expansion did stop?' asked Commissioner Pizarro.

Dr Wetering said that eventually after billions of years all the galaxies would collide and there would be a sort of Big Bang in reverse, what some cosmologists referred to as the Big Crunch.

Dr Wetering was asked what would happen to Time in such a scenario.

He said that it would simply cease to exist.

'Die?' asked Pizarro.

'In a manner of speaking, yes.'

'Let me backtrack a moment, if I may. Whether the Universe continues to expand or not is dependent on gravity, is that correct?' asked Commissioner Pizarro.

'Yes.'

'And gravity is all about mass?'

'Right.'

'So to put it another way, the fate of Time, and everything else, is dependent on mass, on how much mass there is in the Universe? On how many stars and planets there are . . . Have I understood you correctly, Dr Wetering?'

'Perfectly.'

'Very simply, Dr Wetering, the amount of matter in the Universe will determine the Universe's ultimate fate?'

'Bingo.'

'Your witness,' said Commissioner Pizarro, bouncing away.

My attorney stood up and walked over to where the cosmologist was sitting. 'Dr Wetering,' said my attorney, 'do you honestly think God would be stupid enough to have created too much matter? Do you? I mean, if you were God, do you think you'd overlook something so obvious?'

'Probably not.'

'Thank you. No further questions, your honours.'

After lunch Commissioner Pizarro questioned another cosmologist whose testimony supported that of the first; the Universe would indeed contract and Time cease if there was too much matter.

During cross-examination Mr Spillsbury asked the same question; did the witness think that God would be so stupid as to have made too much matter.

'I've never met him, so I couldn't really say,' the witness replied after a little think.

THE 31ST

Angular diameter of a star measured for the	☽ v/c 6:03 am
first time	☽ ⊻ ♅
Toilet plunger invented	☽ ♂ ♃
	☽ ⊻ ♂
	☽ △ ♆
	☽ ⊻ ♀
	☽ ⊻ ♄
	☽ ⊻ ☿

Commissioner Pizarro questioned yet another cosmologist today. During the questioning the cosmologist had a rubber sheet attached to four poles brought into Times Square. He then threw five tennis balls on to the sheet. 'This rubber sheet, your honours, is a three-dimensional representation of the four-dimensional space/time continuum,' the cosmologist explained. 'The tennis balls represent stars. Their gravity, as we can see, affects the space/time continuum by bending or warping it ever so slightly. The sheet and the tennis balls together like this are a crude model of what has been termed a Steady State Universe. In such a Universe, things can continue as they are indefinitely, Time is in no way threatened. But if there is a significant increase in the amount of matter in the Universe . . .' The cosmologist picked up a bowling ball and dropped it on to the rubber sheet whereupon the whole apparatus collapsed and tennis balls rolled all over the place.

'This relationship between matter and Time is pretty elementary, isn't it? I mean, most science undergraduates know about it, don't they?' asked Mr Spillsbury during his cross-examination.

'I would like to think so,' replied the cosmologist.

'So it stands to reason that an omniscient being, such as my client there, would also know about it?'

'I guess logically, yes.'

Court proceedings were adjourned shortly after that, when the Committee for the Scientific Investigation into Claims of the Paranormal began throwing rotten eggs.

The food in the Manhattan Correction Center is significantly better than that served to God back in Fort Knox. God, however, in his infinite wisdom, does not tell his nurse this fact.

On the down side there is no TV in here so God and his nurse missed this week's episode of *Star Trek*.

THE 32ND

✳

Birthday of Count von Zeppelin	☽ → ♎ 2:59 pm
The first Zippo lighter sold	☿ ⋎ ♃
Faraday discovers electro-magnetic rotation	☽ △ ♆
Second Sikh war starts	
Belgian Parliament approves deployment of cruise missiles	

This morning, Commissioner Pizarro called yet another cosmologist.

A tall man in a dirty lab coat took the stand. When he was sworn in he took out of his pocket a balloon. 'The Universe,' he said, 'is like this balloon, only bigger, your honours. As it expands, any two points on its surface become further and further apart.' Then he marked his balloon with two crosses and started to blow it up. Times Square was completely quiet as everyone watched him blow up his balloon.

When the balloon had been blown up the professor took it out of his mouth and held the nozzle with his fingers.

'In theory there is no reason why the Universe cannot just continue to expand, unless —'

The chairman of the International Court of Justice interrupted at this point. 'Let me guess, unless there is too much matter in which case the proverbial bubble will burst.'

'Contract back to nothing,' said the cosmologist, letting the air escape from his balloon.

'Whatever,' said the chairman.

After Commissioner Pizarro had finished questioning his witness, Mr Spillsbury asked the cosmologist, 'Would you tell the court whether you think my client, that rather large man with his hands in the air, over there, looks stupid to you?'

'I . . . I wouldn't want to say.'

'I'm asking you to say.'

'Look, I really don't know,' said the cosmologist. 'Besides I'm something of an atheist myself.'

'An atheist,' said Mr Spillsbury excitedly.

'Objection!' shouted Commissioner Pizarro. 'The witness's religious views are of no consequence to this trial, we are trying to establish the scientific facts.'

'On the contrary, they are vital,' continued Mr Spillsbury.

The International Court of Justice conferred.

'Objection overruled,' they said finally. 'The court believes that this line of questioning is relevant.'

'Professor Carter, as you were saying, you are an atheist,' said God's attorney.

'That is correct.'

'So you do not believe that my client actually exists?'

'No. I think that man over there exists but that he is not God. I also happen to believe that God does not exist.'

'So why are you giving testimony against someone you do not believe exists? You are, remember, under oath.'

'I was asked by Commissioner Pizarro to come here and talk about my understanding of the future shape of the Universe. I didn't expect to be asked about my personal views on the accused.'

'I see. So you don't personally think that my client did kill Time, do you?'

'No, no, I don't.'

ARIES

NEW YORK, THE 1ST

Start of the Ming dynasty in China	☽ ☌ ♂
Existence of black holes first theorized	☽ △ ♀
Britain joins the EEC	☽ ✳ ♇
	♀ ✳ ♇
	☽ ⊼ ♃
	☽ ☌ ☿ ☽ △ ♅
	☿ ✳ ♅ ♂ △ ♇

God Almighty took the stand today. It was frankly a relief not to have to listen to any more cosmologists.

God swore to tell 'the truth the whole truth so help me, myself, God' in front of a large mirror. Commissioner Pizarro bounced up to the witness box. Things started amicably enough.

'Zodiac Man, or should I call you Mr Fontanelle?' asked the Commissioner.

'It would be polite.'

'How about just plain old God?'

'Sure.'

'What are your feelings, God, about the Assam earthquake in 1950 which killed over one thousand people?'

'I –'

'Objection!' shouted my attorney. 'I fail to see the relevance of this. My client, as we have already established, is here on the charge of the killing of Time; his view on an earthquake that happened more than half a century ago is immaterial.'

'Objection sustained,' said the chairman. 'You will confine your questions, Commissioner, to the matter at hand.'

'Yes, your honour,' said Commissioner Pizarro. He then asked God what he thought about the Great Atlantic Hurricane that killed 25,000 people in Montego Bay on the 3rd of October 1780.

The chairman of the International Court of Justice told Commissioner Pizarro if he didn't keep to the point he would be in contempt of court. Commissioner Pizarro apologized.

'God, when exactly did you discover your remarkable, miraculous ability?'

'I realized I was God Almighty on the 28th of Leo 1945. It was a Thursday. I remember it clearly, it was the day after the end of World War Two.'

'I see.'

'That I created the Universe did not dawn on me until later. It just came to me. A classic religious experience really very much in the vein that William James discusses in his work *The Varieties* —'

'Just answer the questions, Mr Fontanelle.'

'God.'

'God. Do you, God, still maintain that hundreds of galaxies out there in space are your, how shall I put it, handiwork?'

'Not just hundreds, all of them, the whole shooting match — Milky Way included,' God said proudly.

'Are you saying, God, that you are personally responsible for all the matter in the entire Universe? I advise you to think very carefully about this in light of what the other witnesses in this trial have said so far. Are you responsible for all matter, God?'

'Is the Pope a Catholic?'

At this point all 122 electronic billboards around Times Square were turned on. 'Ooooh,' said 100,000 people including God Almighty himself.

Each of the 122 electronic billboards had the same image displayed on it; a very old black and white picture of God.

'God, would you tell the court if that is you. The picture, your honours, was taken by a photographer working for a local newspaper in Kyoto on the 21st of October 1945.'

'It is,' said God.

'And in this picture what are you doing? What do you appear to be doing?'

'God is in the process of making a million worlds.'

The image on the billboards changed. 'Here is a photograph taken in Tokyo six months later. Does it not show you in the act yet again of making another galaxy?'

'Yes indeedy.'

'Let us move on to the next picture . . .'

* * *

And so it went on all day.

* * *

Commissioner Pizarro showed dozens of images of me caught in the act of galactic genesis. God's facial expression was pretty much the same in every one of the images.

* * *

Back in the Manhattan Correction Center God had a goat's cheese salad and worked on *Chiropody and Astrology*.

THE 2ND

Deathday of Napoleon
First electric power station in England opened
Trade unions in France legalized
John Glenn orbits the Earth three times
Ice hockey played for the first time
South African police shoot at crowds

☽ v/c 11:45 am
☽ → ♐ 3:56 am

♀ ♂ ♅
☽ △ ☉
☽ ✶ ♆

Today, Commissioner Pizarro insisted on showing yet more images of God creating countless worlds. God had to sit in the witness box all day and confirm that each one was indeed of him in the act of genesis. You can have no idea how dull it was.

God spent the evening putting the finishing touches to *Chiropody and Astrology*. It is roughly thirty double-spaced pages. God intends to publish it, for the world has to know.

THE 3RD

Separation of Church and State in Portugal
First astrological phone-in service started
(calls charged at 45p per minute cheap rate, 50p per minute at all other times)
H. Ford pioneers new conveyor belt assembly techniques

☽ ⚻ ♃
☽ △ ♇
☉ △ ⚷
☽ ☍ ♅
☉ ⚺ ♄
♃ □ ♇

More fucking pictures. Nietzsche was right; against boredom the gods themselves fight in vain.

THE 4TH

Birthday of F. Castro (Communist)	☽ → ♓ 10:43 am
Eurotunnel completed	♀ □ ⚷
T. Scholl sets yodelling world record	☽ ⊻ ♆
Bruce McCandles became first man to walk in space	☽ ⊻ ☉
First showing of the film *Gone With the Wind*	☽ □ ♇

God, world leaders, the 100,000 people in Times Square, the untold millions watching the trial at home on TV and the International Court of Justice have now seen hundreds of badly taken pictures of God creating galaxies in drive-in cinemas in California, baseball fields in Boston, off the Golden Gate Bridge and the Eiffel Tower, in the Opera House in Sydney, at various locations in Africa, and on the Great Wall of China. There was even one of me back in Pearl Harbor and several showing me on the holy island of Jersey where God spent the most memorable days of his divine little life.

*

'On each of these occasions, you claim to have created approximately how much matter, would you say?' asked the Commissioner when the 122 electric billboards had been switched off.

'Oh, I don't know, it varied,' God said, my nurse patting my forehead with a hanky.

'Varied with what?'

'My mood, subject matter, lots of things.'

'But roughly?'

'Something in the region of 200 million stars, some interstellar clouds and the odd black hole.'

'No more questions, your honours,' said the Commissioner, looking very pleased with himself.

After lunch it was Mr Spillsbury's turn to question God.

'Mr Fontanelle,' he began, kneeling in front of the witness box, 'did you kill Time?'

'I had nothing to do with it,' God said, my arms up in the air as always.

'Are you capable of lying?'

'No,' God said without a moment's hesitation.

'Thank you,' said my attorney, then, still on his knees, he turned to the International Court of Justice and added, 'Your honours, the defence rests its case.'

Mr Spillsbury is the greatest legal genius the world has ever known.

THE 5TH

✴

Birthday of Michelangelo (artist)	☽ v/c 7:29 am
	☉ → ♈ 2:54 pm
Signing of the Nuclear Test Ban Treaty	☽ △ ☿
Hypnotism used therapeutically for the first time	☽ ⊻ ♆
US obtains Florida from Spain	☽ △ ♄
	☿ ⊼ ♆

In a surprise move Commissioner Pizarro called yet another cosmologist to the stand today. The new cosmologist was asked how much matter he and his colleagues believed there was in the Universe.

'Well, it's rather hard to say really. Our first attempts to ascertain the density of the local universe gave us values around 10—31 grams per cubic centimetre. This was considerably less than would be needed to create conditions for the Big Crunch.

For that to occur there would have to be a density of something like 10–29 grams per cubic centimetre.'

Commissioner Pizarro asked the cosmologist why he used the term local universe. Surely for the count to be accurate the whole Universe ought to be included.

'Ideally, yes,' said the cosmologist, 'but there's the problem of the edge of observable space.'

'And what is that?'

'Everyone knows that when you look up at the stars you are looking into the past. The further out you look the further back in time you go. Because there was a beginning to everything, the Big Bang, there is only so far we can look.'

'That must be frustrating.'

'Oh, it is, and it means, of course, that our density estimates may be unusually high or unusually low compared to the unobservable Universe. There is simply no way to know.'

'Oh,' said Commissioner Pizarro leaping at least ten feet into the air, 'but there is! The court will recall that the accused has admitted 1,034,480 counts of wilful matter creation, he has also declared under oath how much matter he created at each performance,' said the Commissioner, bouncing all over the place, 'and I quote: "Something in the region of 200 million stars, some interstellar clouds and the odd black hole." With these two bits of information the court has all it requires to calculate the actual density of the Universe and thus the fate of Time.'

Mr Spillsbury got to his feet objecting that at no point had the prosecution established the most basic requirement for convicting anyone: the motive. Without a motive God could only have killed Time by mistake, by an act of chronic incompetence which would be simply impossible for the most intelligent being in the Universe.

Commissioner Pizarro shouted that there was indeed a motive for God to have killed Time: pure unadulterated sadism. He said it was the same sadism that explained why God had made the world the way God had, full of such terrible things as earthquakes and landslides and volcanoes. Given the state of the rest of God's handiwork it should come as no surprise to find out that the entire Universe was booby-trapped.

At this point Times Square disintegrated into something close to a riot. Two windows of God's school bus were broken as the Supreme Being left to await the court's verdict down the road in the Manhattan Correction Center.

Which does a wonderful Peking duck.

Missed *Star Trek* for the second week running.

THE 6TH

✳

Birthday of George Washington (politician)	☽ ⊻ ♃ v/c 7:51 pm
Newton hit by apple	☽ ☌ ♅
Sardinia declares war on Austria	☽ ✻ ♂
	⚥ ☌ ♄
	☽ ☌ ♀
	☽ ☐ ⚷ ☽ ✻ ♄
	☽ ✻ ☿ ♃ ⊻ ♅

The chairman of the International Court of Justice said before making their ruling today that 'The privilege of holding the first trial in history for crimes against Time imposes a grave responsibility.' Then he said that he and his fellow judges were not qualified mathematicians and for this reason the court had decided that the prosecution's figures should be examined by the world's cosmologists. 'If the world's cosmologists agree that there is indeed too much matter in the Universe,' the chairman said, 'then the accused will be executed by firing squad. Thank you very much and good night.'

80,000 people in Times Square applauded the decision, 10,000 people rejected the decision out of hand and wept, 5,000 shook their heads and said, 'I'll never understand it', 5,000 people still didn't know what to do and the entire membership of the Committee for the Scientific Investigation into Claims of the Paranormal, on the count of three, inflated their orange life jackets in protest at the ruling. The inflating life jackets of the Committee for the Scientific Investigation into Claims of the Paranormal made a sssssssss noise which reminded God of the sound 50lb bombs would make as they fell earthwards in World War Two.

Before the orange life jackets of the Committee for the Scientific Investigation into Claims of the Paranormal had finished inflating, God, my nurse, my attorney, Colonel Fleming and the other Screaming Eagles were put back on their yellow school buses and were already on our way to Grand Central Station to catch the train back to Fort Knox.

There is nothing to do but wait. The story of God's life. Towards the end of World War Two, God made waiting into a fine art, a noble occupation. At the end of World War Two, God waited harder and more earnestly than any man in the history of the world. God waits again.

It's not like it will kill me.

THE 7TH

Hearing aid invented	☽ → ♏ 3:51 am
Avalanche wipes out village in Switzerland	♀ ⊻ ♃
Italian troops advance into Ethiopia	☽ □ ♆
Start of the Berlin blockade	☽ ⊻ ♇
	☽ ⊼ ♂
	☽ △ ♃

Miss Hughes said this morning that it was good to be back inside the mobile home, inside the gold vault, in Fort Knox. God wants to know how long he is expected to stay cooped up like this.

The TV networks were full of speculation today about the density of the Universe. Apparently the smart money is on 10–29 grams per cubic centimetre. Mr Spillsbury tells me if the result is more than 10–28 grams then God will be shot. Personally, God thinks it is ridiculous that his fate should rest on the silly calculations of a bunch of nincompoop scientists.

One of the TV networks has built a giant indicator which they are going to use when the result is announced. The giant indicator looks like this:

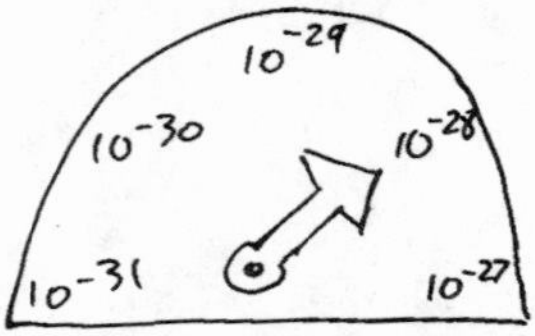

God is watching less TV than I used to.

THE 8TH

Fighting starts between Serbs, Croats and Moslems in Sarajevo	☽ v/c 5:06 am
Creation of the first insecticide	♇℞ 7:19 pm
R. Beebe descends 3,028 feet in seas off Bermuda	☽ □ ⚷
	☽ △ ♄
	☽ ⊼ ☉
	☿ ☌ ♂

The day after the Kamikaze Corps was formed Vice Admiral Ohnishi arrived at the airfield in a great big limo and we marched self-consciously from the mess house, our arms swinging loosely at our sides. We stood to attention and Vice Admiral Ohnishi (Cancer) proceeded to inspect us, his head peering out of the limo. He ordered the occasional belt buckle tightened and all shoelaces tied with double knots.

Then, swishing his bamboo cane out of the car window, the Vice Admiral addressed us.

Cancer men average 0.7 orgasms a night, never read the papers, only wear white socks and have hardly any hair.

This is what God remembers Vice Admiral Ohnishi saying:

'Boys, your country is in grave danger, grave danger. I mean, really big danger. If the Philippines fall, it's all over. Our magnificent sexy Navy is already steaming to the attack but their heroic efforts will come to nothing unless you can destroy the enemy's aircraft carriers. You know what I'm talking about, those long flat things. Japan's depending on you guys. On behalf of your hundred million countrymen, I ask of you this sacrifice and pray for your success. You are already gods, without earthly desires. You will want to know if your attacks prove successful. Well, obviously you won't be around to find out, but rest assured, I shall report your deeds to the Throne itself. So get out there and do your best.'

After that, the Vice Admiral sped off in his limo.

He left twenty-six dead men standing to attention with double knots on their shoes.

THE 9TH

✳

Sound barrier broken

Birthday of Bach (composer)

☽ v/c 11:35 pm
3rd – 11:35 pm

☽ ⊼ ♅
☽ ✱ ♁
☿ △ ♇
☽ ⊼ ♄
☽ ☍ ☉

Spent the day writing the first draft of *Teaching Your Pet to Appreciate the Zodiac*, and a little pamphlet God has been wanting to write for some time now called *Birth Control with Astrology*.

THE 10TH

✳

Birthday of Karl Marx (Marxist)

Gillette sells disposable razor for the first time

Start of the Crimean War

☽ → ♑ 1:43 am
4th – 2:38 am

☽ □ ☉
☽ ⊻ ♆
☽ ⊻ ♇
☽ ✱ ♃
☽ ⊻ ♅

My career as a kamikaze pilot, a career that God and everyone else assumed would be both glorious and short, went badly from the start: no enemy ships, let alone aircraft carriers, were sighted for three whole days.

We sat around and read magazines, studied navigational charts, sewed buttons on our uniforms, listened to the radio and played records on the corps phonograph.

God twiddled my fingers a lot and ate like a man possessed.

On the 2nd of Scorpio 1944 God took part in the first successful Japanese kamikaze attack of the war.

When the order to attack came through my unit jogged down to the command post, putting on our white gloves as we ran. We took our farewell drink from the ceremonial bowl left for the occasion by Vice Admiral Ohnishi. God must have drunk too fast because God got the hiccups. God became terrified that he was going to die while hiccuping.

We clambered into our planes. Then our group leader got out of his Zero and handed Commander Tamai strands of his hair. Seeing this, I too rushed over to Commander Tamai and threw him my toupee. It landed in the dust. Commander Tamai stepped forward, picked it up and held it in his hand as if it was a baseball mitt. Still hiccuping God ran back to my plane and we took to the skies. So long, world. We were off to die beautifully.

The heavens were thus:

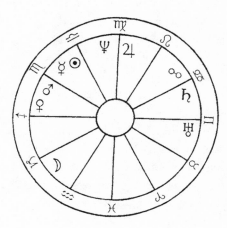

I say I took part in the first successful Japanese kamikaze attack of the war, but God was only involved in the first ten minutes of the flight, having to return to base with engine trouble.

Later, when Vice Admiral Ohnishi reported to the Emperor

that a kamikaze attack had been carried out, the Emperor asked, 'Was it really necessary to go to this extreme?'

The Emperor of Japan was born under the sign of Libra, his favourite colour was pink and his lucky sexual position was the doggy position. His best day was Friday.

My second suicide mission had to be called off because of the weather, the third and fourth because God got lost, the fifth because of engine trouble again. My sixth was cancelled when God had appendicitis, and my seventh when we got false reports that the Americans had surrendered and the war was over. The worst was my twelfth suicide mission when the US carrier God was seconds away from crashing into sank of its own accord into the deep blue sea. God was crying so badly with frustration on my way home after that mission that God had to take my flying goggles off to see where the hell God was going.

God was not, in the first few days, all that remarkable. Others returned from their one-way trips with a look of profound surprise on their faces which they never seemed to lose. But as the weeks went by God became the longest-standing member of the Kamikaze Special Attack Corps.

By July I was taking the biscuit. I was the Corps' one and only veteran. I had been on twenty sorties, each one a certain death mission.

My continued survival got beyond a joke. Statistically, pilots in normal combat units didn't last as long as I was lasting.

Commander Tamai said it was just bad luck.

My ground crew was embarrassed for me.

The other pilots shunned me, not wanting to catch whatever it was God had. God put on weight. The meals before a suicide mission were tremendously grand affairs (boiled sweet potatoes, mountains of dumplings, sweet bean jelly). I was present at dozens and dozens and I gorged myself. It was something to do besides waiting.

After my thirty-fourth failed suicide mission I weighed twenty stone and had to be helped out of my plane. God wept uncontrollably and went to see my commanding officer. Commander Tamai told me not to lose heart. He slapped me on the back and promised me another sure-fire one-way mission at first light.

During dinner that evening, we got news that God's old carrier the *Zuikaku* had been sunk in the Battle of Leyte Gulf along with what seemed like the rest of our Navy. It had been the greatest sea battle of all time and Japan's greatest screw-up. God took the news badly, ate enough food for a platoon and stripped his Zero fighter of everything non-essential, so as not to waste precious war materials when God crash-dived in the morning. I removed the machine-guns, the seat and the windscreen. I unscrewed every other spark plug and every other screw.

When day broke, my Zero and I were ready. Commander Tamai told me a scout plane had spotted a massive enemy force and that I was bound to die.

Everyone from the Corps assembled along the airstrip to see 'Zizo, the old timer' (I was twenty at the time) fly off and die heroically.

The weather was perfect. I climbed into my plane and looked over the latest intelligence reports. There were so many American carriers sighted it would be impossible for me to fail to find a target. As I plotted my course, one of my ground crew climbed up to my cockpit in which I squatted, and cleaned it thoroughly with a feather duster as he had done on all my other suicide attempts. He believed that as my cockpit was to be my coffin it was important it was clean.

From the control tower Commander Tamai gave the order for me to take off. Everyone cheered.

'For the *Zuikaku!*' I shouted and started the engine. The plane shuddered into life.

I raced down the runway, and was in the process of taking off when both wings fell off.

THE 11TH

Cholera epidemic begins in Egypt	☽ → ♍ 2:36 am
Britain annexes Punjab	☿ ✳ ♀
Birthday of Leonard Nimoy (*Star Trek*)	☽ ⊼ ♆
	☽ ⊼ ♂
Birthday of Diana Ross (singer)	☽ ⊼ ♀
Ionian Islands ceded by Britain to Greece	☽ ⊼ ☿
	☽ □ ♇ ☽ ☌ ♃

This morning after breakfast, God, Mr Spillsbury, Miss Hughes, Colonel Fleming and everyone else were taken to Times Square to hear if the world's cosmologists thought God was guilty or not of killing Time.

All the cosmologists in the world have been staying in the Guggenheim Museum of Modern Art on the Upper East Side for the last few days. All the modern art has been replaced with sleeping bags, sheets of paper, calculators and blackboards.

What they have done with all the modern art is anybody's business.

When everyone was ready a spokesman for the world's cosmologists stood up and informed the International Court of Justice that he and his colleagues had been unable to agree. Some thought that the evidence suggested that the density of the Universe was 10–29 grams per cubic centimetre but just as many thought it was considerably less. As if this was not bad enough, the spokesman said there were two radical groups who categorically believe I am innocent, one of which is made up of plasma cosmologists (who have taken over the basement of the Guggenheim) who believe that the Universe did not begin and therefore cannot end. The other group of radicals (who control the top floor of the museum) subscribe to the Oscillating Model of the Universe in which there is hypothesized a never-ending series of Big Bangs and Big Crunches. Both these groups think it is impossible that I, God, could have killed Time.

Utter pandemonium broke out in Times Square after that.

It was then, in the chaos and confusion, that an attempt was made to rescue God's fat ass. Astrologers rushed the dock with bamboo spears concealed down their trousers. Colonel Fleming ordered his men to start firing their Top Secret Weapons. The Top Secret Weapons sounded, when fired, like champagne corks popping.

It was like New Year's Eve in Times Square. Pop. Pop. Pop. Pop.

When things finally died down, 203 people (including three reporters, the King of Holland, a Presidential aide, the Treasurer of the Committee for the Scientific Investigation into Claims of the Paranormal and a member of the International Court of Justice) were dead and for some Top Secret reason all the seating in Times Square had turned fluorescent orange.

THE 12TH

Van Gogh (artist) cuts off ear	☽ → ♉ 12:01 am
First helicopter takes off	☽ □ ♆
Chernobyl nuclear reactor blows up	☿ △ ♄
	☽ ✳ ♃
	☽ ⊼ ♇
	☽ □ ♅
	☽ ✳ ☉

A man cannot wait for death all his life, God told Colonel Fleming, Mr Spillsbury and Miss Hughes at breakfast.

God had something of a breakdown after the sinking of the *Zuikaku* and his thirty-fifth failed kamikaze mission. It's possible God even went slightly mad. I'm not ruling it out.

The airfield doctor ordered I fly no suicide missions for at least a week.

Two days later Vice Admiral Ohnishi had me brought on a stretcher to his limo outside the hospital. Ohnishi told me he had read my service record with some interest. He told me he believed I was being saved for some higher purpose, and when the Admiral had sped off, I began to believe him. I began to believe him because, of course, it was perfectly perfectly true.

According to TV reports tonight, the world's cosmologists have been put on sixty-three coaches and are going to spend a few days relaxing at Disney World, Florida. They are going on the orders of the chairman of the International Court of Justice. The cosmologists have been told not to come back until they have decided unanimously if God is guilty or not.

So it looks as if God has to wait some more.

THE 13TH

✳

First showing of silent film	3rd – 5:24 pm
Hundred Years War begins	☽ ⊼ ♃
Drought in India	☽ ⊻ ♅
Serbia yields to Austria in Bosnian dispute	☽ ☍ ☉
	☽ ☍ ♄

At lunch today God told Colonel Fleming, Mr Spillsbury and his nurse all about a letter God had written back in Scorpio 1944. It was a farewell letter to my dear first wife. It had been sent to her the moment my plane had disappeared in the direction of the enemy fleet on my second suicide mission. With it were sent my toenail clippings (an old samurai tradition) and my toupee (a not so old samurai tradition). My letter went like this:

Dear Misao,

I am in good health and my spirits as always are high. Please congratulate me for I am about to crash-dive into an enemy carrier for the homeland. It is a one-way mission in case you haven't figured that out already. You see, a little while ago I became a founding member of the Kamikaze Special Attack Corps. We are a secret elite suicidal unit about to be unleashed on the Americans. It is something of a long story. Anyway, in a few moments I will put down this pen and take off on my last sortie. Due to the lack of time, I would appreciate it if you could let my friends know what finally became of me. Thanks.

I am going to score a direct hit on an enemy carrier without fail. When you listen to the reports I will have done my bit. I have to go now. Please dispose of my things as you wish. I know you will be praying for my success.

I do not want you to grieve over my death. I do not mind if you weep a bit, OK, go ahead and weep. But please remember that my death is for the best.

> *The ink in my pen is running out and anyway it is time*
> *for me to die. So long. If you should decide to have a service to*
> *commemorate me say that I died beautifully like a falling*
> *blossom from a radiant cherry tree or something along those*
> *lines.*
> Zizo.

My wife wrote back to my Commanding Officer a few weeks later asking why it was she had yet to hear of my death officially. I wrote to her again, explaining the series of freak events that had befallen me. She did not write back but sent a telegram saying that she had received enough toenail clippings to last her a lifetime.

I wrote her another letter making sure this time that it was not sent prematurely. Before every mission I gave it to Commander Tamai and after each botched mission he handed it back.

After each failed mission God would add a PS which God would always end with the words, 'Tomorrow I will plunge against the enemy without fail.'

My second letter to my first wife ran, by Sagittarius, to over 300 pages.

THE 14TH

*

Birthday of Wordsworth (poet)	☽ → ♐ 9.52 pm
Birthday of Mick Jagger (singer)	☽ ⊼ ♄
Second Burmese war breaks out	☽ ⊼ ☉
Theory of continental drift expounded for the first time	

The situation by the second half of Sagittarius was dire. Our airfield was being bombed daily (it was bombed three times on

God's birthday) and it was clear to everyone that the Americans were about to take the Philippines.

Our suicide attacks were clearly not having the intended effect. Naturally, God felt personally to blame.

On the 12th of Capricorn the invasion fleet was sighted off the coast. It consisted of over a thousand ships. Our scouts couldn't believe their eyes. They reported the entire ocean crammed full with cruisers, destroyers, carriers and landing craft.

Headquarters ordered all planes to take off and attack at once. It was, as they say, the final showdown. Our airfield had taken such a battering by this stage that there were just five operational planes with which to launch the attack. Every pilot on the base pleaded with Commander Tamai to be sent. Commander Tamai was besieged in his office by hopeful pilots. He told everyone not to be so selfish.

A little later the tannoy system came to life outside the command post. 'Would Lt. Zizo Yasuzawa please come to Commander Tamai's office.'

I had been chosen to lead the final mission. It was appropriate. It was fitting. I who had waited the longest to die for the Emperor.

'Thank you,' I said as I entered Commander Tamai's office.

'Zizo —'

'It is a great honour to lead the attack. Thank you, Commander, thank you very much.'

'Zizo —'

'I will not fuck it up this time, I feel sure.'

'Zizo, you are not going on today's mission.'

I smiled. 'You joke.'

'No joke. I received an order from Vice Admiral Ohnishi this morning. You are being transferred to the Homeland. It's a special mission, a secret mission, Zizo. High Command wants an experienced kamikaze pilot, you're certainly that, and Vice Admiral Ohnishi is convinced you have been saved all these months for a special reason. There's also the matter of landing.'

'Landing?'

'You're the only pilot on the base who knows how.'

God suddenly felt famished.

God and my nurse watched *Star Trek* tonight. Reception was terrible and God had no idea what was going on.

THE 15TH

Birthday of Charlie Chaplin (actor)	☽ ☐ ♇
Poisonous fog kills thousands in London	☽ ⊻ ♅
Hairdryer invented	☽ ⊻ ☉
	☽ ⊻ ♄
	☽ △ ⚷
	☽ ✳ ♀

It is a well-known fact, God told Colonel Fleming this morning, that men who volunteered to be kamikaze pilots at the end of WWII typically had just seven days' training. During those seven days they were taught how to take off, fly in formation, navigate and crash-dive. For obvious reasons, the training programme did not cover landings.

I flew out of Luzon two hours after the last kamikaze attack was launched from our airfield and four hours before two entire US corps hit the beaches and the largest land battle in the Pacific got under way.

Something like half a million men fought over Luzon, an island as large as Britain. When it was over, 300,000 people were dead including my old Commanding Officer, and everyone I had left on the airfield. After the fighting, the capital city of Luzon looked as if an earthquake had struck it.

Nature would have been proud of man.

THE 16TH

First flashlight photograph taken

Birthday of Rudolf Nureyev (ballet dancer)

Invention of the fork-lift truck

☽ v/c 8:59 pm

♂ ⊼ ♂
☽ ⚹ ♅   ☽ ⊻ ♃
♀ ⚹ ♄   ☿ ⚹ ♀
☽ ⊼ ♂   ☉ △ ♇
☽ ☌ ♂   ☿ ☌ ♄
☽ ☌ ☿   ☽ ☌ ♄
☽ ⚹ ♀

God's attorney, Mr Spillsbury, came by today to report that there was still no word from Disney World.

'How much longer is this going to take?' God demanded.

Mr Spillsbury said that he didn't know.

'I've got places to go, people to meet,' God told him.

When God landed at Tokyo I was welcomed like a hero. A military band was playing next to the runway. Vice Admiral Ohnishi stuck a medal on me, promoted me to Captain and told me to get in his limo.

'Yasuzawa, you must forgive me for plucking you from honourable death in the Philippines, but you can be of great service to us here.'

'Am I going to get to die in battle?'

'Sure.'

The glorious end that Vice Admiral Ohnishi had in mind for me was explained to God as we drove to an airfield near Kyushu. My fate revolved around a Top Secret weapon which High Command had been working on for months. It was called the Ohka or Cherry Blossom.

The Cherry Blossom was a piloted bomb.

THE 17TH

St Paul's Cathedral in London survives night
   of bombing during WWII

36 inches of snowfall in America

Russia invades Afghanistan

$$\begin{array}{l} \text{☽ △ ♃} \\ \text{☽ ⊻ ♇} \\ \text{☽ □ ⚥} \\ \text{♂ △ ⚷} \end{array}$$

The Cherry Blossom was designed to be carried to its target by a medium bomber. Once over the target the pilot of the Cherry Blossom was to pull the release handle and he and the bomb would hurtle earthward.

God test-flew the Ohka using something similar to a sky jump that jutted out over a lake. God very nearly drowned loads of times as I and my Cherry Blossom, after smashing through balsa-wood aircraft carriers, wobbled our way to the lake's muddy floor.

Along with a handful of other veteran kamikaze pilots from all over the empire, God was billeted in an old school building on the shore of the lake. Everything was slightly smaller than it ought to have been, particularly the tables and chairs. The windows had been blown out by air raids, and entire constellations shone through the holes in the roof. God slept on the floor with a single thin blanket to cover my considerable bulk.

It was in this school that, as God trained and waited to die, he taught himself the rudiments of English from an exercise book he found in a desk. It was something to do besides eating.

When the Americans began their attack on Okinawa Japan threw everything it had at them, including the top secret Cherry Blossoms.

With as many fighter escorts as possible, eighteen bombers, each carrying a Cherry Blossom piloted bomb, took off from our airfield. Their targets were three enemy carriers reported to the south-east of Kyushu. The stars on that day were thus:

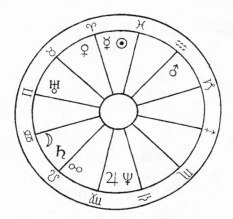

The bombers and their escorts were engaged by some fifty American fighters before anyone had sighted the carriers. One by one the bombers were shot down, their piloted bombs still attached.

Eventually all eighteen were gone. It took about ten minutes.

About as long as it normally took God to make a galaxy.

God was not sent on that ill-fated first mission because God had a most horrendous toothache, the right side of my face swelled up something awful.

Had God been well enough for the first Cherry Blossom mission there is little doubt that I would have been killed along with everyone else. So, all considered, it was a good thing God was absent. However, at the time, with my Enlightenment still weeks away, my despair was simply too great to bear.

THE 18TH

✳

Eruption of Vesuvius (volcano)

Deathday of Raphael (artist)

Birthday of Severiano Ballesteros (golfer)

☉ → ♒ 1:46 am
☽ v/c 12:57 pm
☽ → ♏ 1:35 pm
4th – 2:41 pm

☽ □ ♀
☽ △ ♂
☽ △ ♃
☽ □ ♆
☽ □ ☉
♂ ♂ ♃

God gained another four stone after the first Cherry Blossom attack and when finally I was ordered to sortie a few days later, I could hardly squeeze into the bomb's cockpit.

God took off with another seven Cherry Blossoms and headed for the waters around Okinawa. Miraculously, we avoided enemy interceptors and presently found ourselves over a number of battleships. God picked two, side by side. The ships looked like a pair of grey lips on the ocean from 6,000 feet up in the sky.

God shouted into the speech tube to the pilot of the bomber that I had selected my target.

A Cherry Blossom fell away from the bomber next to mine, the kamikaze pilot waving at me on his way down.

I looked at the sky and the ocean. I twiddled my fingers. After six months and thirty-six failed kamikaze missions I was finally on my heroic one-way trip. I had come to the end of my life. My wife would get my second letter, my spirit would nestle around the Yasukuni Shrine of the heroic dead near the Imperial Palace and, who knows, perhaps my effort would help turn the course of the war.

God looked at the release handle; it was roughly the size of my penis when fully erect.

God pulled on it with my right hand. God was wearing my white gloves.

God pulled it again.

Nothing. There was no heart-stopping descent, no hurtling seaward. Nothing.

I yanked the release handle over and over.

'Captain Yasuzawa,' came the voice of the bomber pilot out of the speech tube, 'are you still with us?'

'I'm having some technical difficulties,' God replied, shaking the lever violently.

Five minutes passed. We circled the battleships, anti-aircraft fire raced up at us, looking like tiny shooting stars.

'Captain Yasuzawa,' came the pilot's voice again, 'if you can't release we should return to base.'

'Look, just hang on a bit longer. I'll be gone in a jiffy, I promise.'

By this time three of the other bombers were spiralling out of control.

Two minutes later and despite God's protests we were heading back to Kyushu. By the time we landed, God had called the pilot everything under the rising sun.

THE 19TH

Floods in China

☽ v/c 9:06 am
☽ → ♈ 2:21 pm

☽ ✳ ☿
☽ ⊻ ♃
☽ ✳ ♆
☽ ⊻ ♂

Fort Knox was last night attacked by astrologers in hot-air balloons.

The plan, it appears, was to get God into one of the balloons and then to drift down to South America, to freedom.

Needless to say the rescue failed. The thirty balloons involved in the attempt were shot down by Stinger surface-to-air missiles and the handful of astrologers who made it to the gold vault died in a fire fight with Colonel Fleming's paratroopers.

My followers died in a way that God is not at liberty to describe. It was horrible, all the same.

During the fighting God tried to squeeze under my bed but I was too big and just had to lie on my stomach. My nurse used me as cover. It was a smart thing to do. I offered almost as much cover as a small mountain range.

When it was all over a dozen astrologers were dead in the entrance of the gold vault, two Screaming Eagles had to be taken to hospital suffering from minor cuts caused by bamboo spears and God's mobile home had, for some Top Secret reason, turned fluorescent orange.

Whaddyaknow.

What happens to you when you die is this: you move anti-clockwise around the Zodiac. It's perfectly true. If you were a Libra in this life you will be a Virgo in the next, if you were a Gemini you come back a Cancer. You also change sex, shoe size, hairstyle and taste in music. It is possible for your reincarnation to be alive even while you are. In fact, many people are friends with or even married to themselves without knowing it.

Two replacements for the two wounded soldiers arrived wide-eyed after lunch. They have come straight from boot camp. The other soldiers refer to them as FNGs. Colonel Fleming explained to me that this stands for Fucking New Guys.

God loves this country.

The FNGs have all been issued with Norwegian combat overcoats which is just as well because it is not getting any warmer in here. The FNGs stared at my mobile home as if they have never seen anything like it, which of course they have.

God waved, or rather God wriggled my podgy fingers at them through the window.

Outside the gold vault bits of balloon were picked up and security tightened. Another armoured division has been deployed around Fort Knox.

An entire corps now encircles God. Tens of thousands of soldiers with Top Secret weapons have been ordered to ensure God does not go walkabout.

God has begun sleeping badly. My nurse gives me four capsules of Nembutal every night but even so I spend the pitch-black small hours gazing at my navel or rather trying to imagine where roughly it might be. Like my penis, my navel and God have lost touch.

Apparently, last night Miss Hughes found God in the driving seat of the mobile home shouting 'Tora – Tora – Tora' in my sleep and crying like a baby. With the help of the Colonel and D Platoon she put God back to bed.

God denied the whole thing.

THE 20TH

✳

Germans seize capital of Greece	lst – 1:01 am
	Ψ → ≈ 9:49 pm
R.E. Peary reaches North Pole	☽ ⚹ ♇
Birthday of Ho Chi Minh (politician)	☽ ☌ ☉
Birthday of Elizabeth Taylor (actress)	☽ ☌ ♅
	☽ ⚹ ♄
Cellophane manufactured for the first time	☉ ☌ ♅
	☽ □ ♩
	☽ ⊻ ♀

Word spread far and wide that the pilots stationed at the old
schoolhouse were members of the Kamikaze Special Attack
Corps and were intending to pilot the Cherry Blossom bombs.
People came all at once one day as if they had collectively
finally built up enough nerve. They gathered in the playground:
children, men and women, and hundreds and hundreds of
beautiful young girls.

They came to gawp in wonder at us, they came to show their
respects, to pay us homage. Everyone left us something. They
seemed to feel they had to, so that our last hours on Earth might
be passed in some degree of luxury.

They gave us just about anything you can imagine – bicycles,
fireworks, tables and chairs, radios, fruit, eggs, pigs, chickens,
umbrellas, cows, paintings, books, crate after crate of sake, tin
cans of spaghetti and two broken Swiss cuckoo clocks.

Naturally enough, God gained yet more weight. Time
seemed to pass in direct proportion to my girth. My fat merged
with the minutes, hours and days that passed. God gained weight
as steadily and as predictably as the planets circled the Earth. I
became a sort of walking watch which measured the passing of
time in inches of blubber. God became horrendously fat, so fat it
wasn't funny, so fat that when my first little wife arrived at the
school she failed to recognize me.

That fat.

She came over to me and said, 'Excuse me, did you know a

pilot called Zizo Yasuzawa? What happened to him? Did he fly off one day and crash-dive on to an American aircraft carrier?'

God looked at my wife for a while and then said, 'That is precisely what happened to him.'

'And did it sink?'

'Did what sink?'

'The carrier, did it sink with all its planes on board?'

'Oh, yes, it sunk instantly, breaking into three pieces as it did so.'

'I'm glad to hear it.'

My wife left after that, giving me some fresh underwear which she explained had been for her late husband and a scroll she asked me to take on my own kamikaze mission in remembrance of her husband.

The underpants were far too small for God. When WWII ended local people tied them to their bamboo spears and waved them in surrender when the Americans came.

As for the scroll I opened it as soon as my wife had gone. It read:

I pray for a direct hit
— Misao

God still has the scroll here in the gold vault; it's in one of the sacred carrier bags God was allowed to bring from Jersey.

THE 21ST

MacArthur is appointed chief of Allied	☽ ⊻ ☉
Forces in the Pacific region	☽ □ ♅
	☽ ✳ ♃
Canadian Grand Trunk Pacific Railway completed	☽ ☍ ♄
Invention of the futon	☽ ⊻ ♂
	☽ ⊻ ☿
	☽ ⊻ ♄

The gifts just kept flooding in and I kept putting on weight. Cooking pots were set up in the playground and a line of pretty young women kept my mouth full from dawn to dusk.

One morning we discovered a grand piano and a 1931 Bentley had been left for us.

The fighting for Okinawa raged on. The island became littered with seven thousand shot-down planes which looked like burnt crucifixes. There were no bombers left to carry the Cherry Blossoms so we waited for replacements from the factories, only the factories had been fire-bombed so we had to wait for the factories to be rebuilt. We waited a hell of a long time. We twiddled our fingers and God gained weight. As we waited for the factories to be rebuilt so that bombers could be built to fly our Cherry Blossoms to their targets, the Americans fought their way across Okinawa and appealed to the few Japanese soldiers left to give themselves up. When the Japanese Commander on Okinawa (a Gemini) heard the appeal he found it so funny he pissed himself laughing.

Gemini men love walnuts. Their best days are Tuesdays. They hate novels.

He was still laughing when he slit open his belly with his sword and Okinawa fell to the Americans. The stars were so:

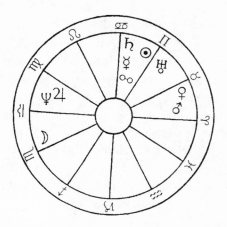

Well, shit really hit the fan after that.

When Okinawa fell, utter panic gripped Japan. The size and quality of the gifts presented to us increased and my weight problem got just plain ridiculous.

※ ※ ※ ※

It was after the fall of Okinawa that the women came at night walking across the playground like ghosts, their kimonos whispering as they walked. When I held them in my arms, and I held many, they would ask me if it was likely that I would be dead tomorrow. I assured them it was more than likely.

I made love to these women in the Bentley under the full gaze of the cosmos.

※ ※ ※ ※

Okinawa was a perfect place from which to launch an invasion of Japan proper. Everyone knew this, even the young girls that I made love to at night knew this.

Japan gripped itself for the invasion it knew had to come. Experienced pilots such as myself were removed from active service and set to teaching the rudiments of flying to anyone we could find, crippled soldiers, half-blind old men, so that they could slam into the troop ships that would soon be steaming towards our sacred home islands. Every plane in the entire empire was commandeered by the Kamikaze Special Attack Corps, every boat that could float was filled with explosives and men were told to ram them into the enemy when his invasion fleet appeared on the horizon. Every man and boy in the country was issued with a rifle or an ancient musket and women and girls were issued with bamboo spears.

Even the girls who came to the school at night carried cute little bamboo spears. It was believed that the American High Command planning its invasion of Japan was prepared to lose 100,000 men taking the beaches alone.

The whole country waited for the dead GIs from the other side of the world to wade ashore.

It never happened.

THE 22ND

✳

Invention of the spatula

Floods in China

☽ v/c 1:37 am
☽ → ♌ 2:45am

☽ ☍ ♆
☽ ⊼ ☿
☽ △ ♇
☽ ☍ ♅

Colonel Fleming told God and Miss Hughes today that everyone in the gold vault is to receive a medal commemorating the failed rescue attempt which has become known on the TV as the Battle of the Balloons. Everyone is getting a medal, that is, except the two FNGs and God Almighty.

THE 23RD

Birthday of Shaka (Zulu chief)	☽ △ ♆
Royal Academy of Arts founded	☽ ⊼ ♀
Invention of underwater photography	☽ ✳ ♇
Floods in China	☽ △ ♅
	☽ ☍ ☿

The Chaplain of the 82nd Airborne Division, who had a little white cross on his blue UN helmet, came to see God after lunch today. He said that he wanted to convert God to Christianity.

God laughed hysterically

✳ ✳ ✳

God was making love to a peasant girl on the bonnet of the Bentley when the bomb was dropped on Hiroshima.

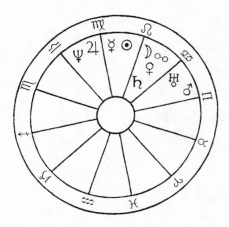

When Nagasaki was hit God, Japs Eye Fontanelle, the creator of the Universe, was fucking her sister.

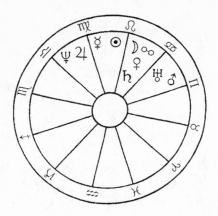

A little while later, for the first time in the history of the world, the people of Japan heard the voice of their Emperor squeaking over the airwaves. All 73.1 million of us got down on our bellies and bowed at our radio sets. This is what the Emperor said, he said:

> the war situation has developed not necessarily
> to Japan's advantage . . .

Later we realized that WWII was over and that the Emperor was no longer God.

Whaddyaknow.

THE 24TH

✳

Baby born with teeth	☽ v/c 12:30 am
Construction of the first seaplane	☽ → ♊ 10:38 am
Henry Cavendish proves hydrogen to be	☽ □ ♀
an element	☿ ☌ ♂
US bomb Tokyo	☽ △ ♆
	☽ ☍ ♇

People, as you might imagine, took the whole thing pretty badly. There were attempts to get the Emperor to become God again but he wasn't having it. People didn't know what to do. Unable to help myself I ate everything I could find.

The Commanding Officer of the airfield, Admiral Ugaki, after hearing the Emperor's speech, ordered a Zero fighter to prepare for take-off. The crazy fool was going to make one more kamikaze attack on the enemy.

When word of Admiral Ugaki's sortie reached us everyone raced to the airfield. In a frantic rush, using my now considerable bulk, I pushed the other pilots out of the way and squeezed myself into a Zero fighter and joined Admiral Ugaki on the runway as did nine other pilots.

And so it was that eleven planes took off on a suicide mission the morning the Emperor ended WWII and officially denied his own divine existence in the same breath.

God thus has the rather unique distinction of having been part of the very first kamikaze attack of the war and also the very last.

God weighed so much by this stage that my plane took longer to climb than the others. After a few moments the other Zeros were way ahead of me and I was consuming what little fuel was in the tank. I became a little frantic, a little hysterical. There I was, the longest ever serving kamikaze pilot and the war was over. My last chance to die heroically was disappearing into the distance. I screamed, I shouted. I cried, I laughed, twiddled my fingers and than miraculously I spied an American aircraft carrier.

According to Mr Spillsbury, who came to see God this afternoon, the world's cosmologists have made their decision and have already returned to New York. We will be travelling there in the morning to hear the verdict. After God was told this I, Mr Spillsbury and Miss Hughes watched *Star Trek*.

THE 25TH

Drinking water sterilized by ultraviolet rays	☽ △ ♄
Drought in China	☽ ⅄ ☿
	☽ ⅄ ♅
Birthday of Peter the Great (tsar)	☽ ⅄ ♀
Birthday of Stan Laurel (comedian)	♂ ⅄ ♆

When everyone was yet again in Times Square, a spokesman for the world's cosmologists stood up and told the International Court of Justice that there was some good news and there was some bad news. He then asked the members of the International Court of Justice if they wanted to hear the good news or the bad news first. The judges conferred for a little while before telling the cosmologist to start with the bad news.

The bad news was that science rarely produced unanimous verdicts. The cosmologist went on to explain that while fundamental disagreements remained between the various schools of cosmology a surefire way of finding God's guilt or innocence was possible. 'We need more data,' the cosmologist explained. 'What we need is a satellite able to perform what is known as "Power Spectrum Analysis", to measure the amount of background radiation in space. Such a satellite, we are all agreed, will settle the matter once and for all.'

'How long will it take to build?' asked the chairman of the International Court of Justice.

'That's the good news, your honour. The European Space Agency is planning to launch just such a satellite.'

'You don't say,' said the chairman.

The European Space Agency's satellite under construction at the moment, that will be able to perform 'Power Spectrum Analysis' and tell if God is guilty or not, has two names. It is called the Cobras/Samba satellite. Why it has two names no one, including God, knows.

THE 26TH

American Constitution drafted	☽ v/c 3:23 am
	☽ → ♍ 12:31 pm
Start of American Civil War	
Three midget Japanese submarines raid	☽ ⊼ ☉
	☽ ☌ ♃
Sydney Harbour	☽ ⊼ ♀
	☽ ⊼ ♆
Darwin begins expedition in the Beagle	☉ ⌄ ♃
	☽ △ ☿

As I put my plane into a nose-dive God never really stopped to think what an American aircraft carrier was doing bang in the middle of a rice paddy-field,

The truth was it wasn't an aircraft carrier at all, but a giant golden phallus.

The Tagata Shinto monks who were carrying the giant golden phallus as part of the Festival for an Abundant Harvest, wearing black hats and white gowns, ran in every direction as God came plummeting down from the heavens towards them.

By this stage God had realized things were not quite right. For one thing I realized the carrier was a lot smaller then it ought to have been, at around twenty feet.

God tried to pull out of my dive, failed, ploughed into the ground, sent jizzers of earth into the air and was thrown through the windscreen.

I hit the tip of the phallus and the metal plate that had been screwed to the top of my head flew off and God never saw it again. So long, *Shoho*.

Straddling the phallus, my brain case exposed to the heavens, I achieved enlightenment and then promptly lost consciousness.

That was how WWII ended for God.

Happy happy days.

* * * *

According to tonight's TV the Cobras/Samba satellite is now officially to be known as the Cobras/Samba/Fontanelle satellite. This, everyone seems to think, is better than the Cobras/Samba/He-Whose-Figure-Of-Beauty-Is-Tinged-With-The-Hue-Of-Cerulean-Blue-Clouds-And-Whose-Unique-Loveliness-Charms-Millions-Of-Little-Cupids satellite.

The satellite is to be launched 'soon'.

'How soon?' God demanded to know.

But no one in the gold vault knew exactly.

'A week? A month?'

'Your guess is as good as mine,' said Colonel Fleming.

THE 27TH

Hong Kong acquired by Britain

Opening of the Sydney Opera House

Showing of first Tarzan film

☽ v/c 11:22 am
☽ → ♒ 11:27 am
☿ ♂ ♀
☽ ⤢ ♃
☽ ♂ ♆
☉ ✳ ♇

UNCC doctors came as usual after breakfast to see if God's balls had grown back. They have not. God asked the doctors if they know when exactly the Cobras/Samba/Fontanelle satellite was going to be launched. The doctors said nothing. After they had gone the Chaplain popped by and asked if God was willing to talk about the saving grace of Jesus Christ.

God was not.

Four of the planes that took off with Admiral Ugaki on his kamikaze flight had to return to base due to engine trouble. No American forces reported any attacks by kamikazes, so what happened to the Admiral and the five other pilots remains a mystery to this day.

What seems fairly certain is that no one in the last kamikaze sortie of the war, except for me, attempted to crash-dive a giant cock near the city of Nagoya.

THE 28TH

✦

Americans attack Solomon Islands

26-letter alphabet adopted by China

♉ → ♑ 11:20 am
3rd – 12:24 pm
☽ △ ♉
☽ ⊼ ♂
☽ ♷ ☉
☽ ⊼ ♃
☽ ♷ ♀

God has spent most of today telling Mr Spillsbury, Captain Fleming and my nurse all about my enlightenment.

They were all, of course, entirely fascinated.

It had two distinct phases, the first of which occurred the moment I headbutted the golden phallus in the rice paddy-field outside the city of Nagoya. Before passing out I felt all the pain, the frustration, all the disappointment and sense of failure that had been building up inside me while in the Kamikaze Special Attack Corps disappear and in the same instant the meaning of my glorious life revealed itself to me. I saw a tremendous light, the Light Unchangeable, and in its greatness it seemed to take up all space. In this light I experienced total ecstasy. I was bathed in wonderful music, which I later realized was the music of the celestial spheres. The light, the music and I became one and I knew of the hidden meaning and significance lying behind all external phenomena. Not to make too fine a point of it, I saw the complete unity of the Universe, and how all the death and destruction I had seen didn't matter one little bit. Lying there sprawled out in the mud I saw for the first time who or what I was. I was everything that sways, breathes, opens, closes, lives. I was the underlying principle, the blazing spirit, I was that in which the world and all its creatures lay hidden. I was Life, Mind, Reality. The Monad.

I was Heaven, I was the stars, I was Everything, Primal Meaning, Undivided Unity. I was Pimander, the Divine Mind, Perfectus, Magus. I was the Fountain of All Things, the Root of

All Forms, I was Reality, the Self and Nature, the Supporter of all things and all beings. I was He Who Unfolds Himself Into Light, I was the Emanator of the Created. The Godhead, the Manifesting Spirit, the Archetypal Form, the Aeon. I was the One Being, the One Mind. I was Awo-Bam-Do-Bop-Awo-Bambo!

The world had changed for ever. What had been outside became inside. It was as if I had grown larger than the whole Universe or the Universe had shrunk inside me. Whatever it was it felt a bit like indigestion.

The scent, the sights and the sounds of the rice field, the monks screaming and kicking me, blended into a harmony so perfect it was beyond words. There was a peace that passed all understanding.

I realized that every mortal was not a lonely atom in a cold unfriendly, indifferent Universe but part of a beautiful living work of art, all of which was good and blessed. I experienced a sense of supreme exultation and an intellectual illumination quite impossible to describe and then I pissed myself.

Admiral Ohnishi, who was at that moment disembowelling himself with a sword in his study, had been right about my continued survival being something special, but not in his wildest dreams could he have guessed just how special I really was.

I was still in a state of utter joy and knowing when I lost consciousness.

When God finished describing the first stage of his enlightenment he discovered that only Mr Spillsbury was still listening. Colonel Fleming and Miss Hughes were watching TV.

God told Mr Spillsbury that in 1975 a sign was erected in that rice paddy-field which said in thirty-two different languages:

Captain Zizo Yasuzawa,
also known as He-Whose-Figure-Of-Beauty-Is-Tinged-
With-The-Hue-Of-Cerulean-Blue-Clouds-And-Whose-Unique-
Loveliness-Charms-Millions-Of-Little-Cupids
or Japs Eye Fontanelle struck a 20-foot gold penis on this spot
at the end of WWII and came to the realization
that he was God.

Down the road a little way from the rice field my followers also set up a tea house and souvenir shop which sold among other things cups, table mats, shower curtains, jumpers and bumper stickers with my holy birth chart printed on them.

God told Mr Spillsbury that God had no idea if the sign, the tea house and souvenir shop are still there or whether the UNCC or the Japanese Government have bulldozed the lot.

The Committee for the Scientific Investigation into Claims of the Paranormal were shown on TV later still wearing their dumb-ass life jackets, waving their anti-astrological placards and insisting that whatever the final fate of the Universe turns out to be I, God, have nothing to do with it.

THE 29TH

---

*

Fidel Castro takes over Cuba	☽ v/c 9:25 am
S.S. *Titanic* sinks	☽ → ♉ 10:53 am
Germans surrender in Stalingrad	☉ ✶ ♅
Deathday of Dame Margot Fonteyn (ballerina)	☽ □ ♆
First X-ray photograph taken	☽ □ ♀
	☿ ✶ ♃
	☽ ⊼ ♇
	☽ □ ♅

The second phase of my enlightenment was more gradual than the first and began two days later when I regained consciousness in the Osaka City Hospital head injuries ward. Upon awakening I saw across the room Captain Fuchida, the Hero of Pearl Harbor. Holding a safe and completely covered in foul-smelling soot, he was talking animatedly with a patient whose head was covered in bandages. While he talked Captain Fuchida kept pointing at the ceiling and then at the safe he was carrying.

After a little while the man whose head was covered in bandages told Captain Fuchida to go away.

Captain Fuchida looked around the room and then came over to me.

He looked at me for a while, then said, 'There is a hole in the top of your head.'

'Yes,' I said. Captain Fuchida peered in.

'Captain Fuchida, I served under you in '41,' I said, smiling.

'Really?' he said, still peering into the hole in the top of my head.

'I flew with you at Pearl Harbor,' I said.

He stepped back and looked at me, trying to recognize me.

'You're a pretty big guy for a fighter pilot,' the hero of Pearl Harbor said.

We talked about the war. I told Captain Fuchida about my horrendous career as a kamikaze pilot. He nodded sympathetically and laughed all the way through, the way

Capricorns do. I decided not to tell him about my discovery in the rice field that I was God.

When I had finished my account of my war experiences, Captain Fuchida peered into the hole in the top of my head a second time.

'Where were you when Hiroshima was destroyed?' he asked, still looking into the hole on the top of my head, as if talking to my brain directly.

'In a playground making love to a girl on the bonnet of a Bentley,' God said.

Then Captain Fuchida told God what had happened to him when the bomb had been dropped on the city of Hiroshima. God would hear the account a number of times as the years went by.

When the bomb had detonated Captain Fuchida had been sixty miles away flying to an Army-Navy liaison conference being held in the city. A funny-looking cloud was over Hiroshima when he got there. Fuchida called the airport's control tower but there was no reply. As he flew closer he saw that Hiroshima was not there any more, there was just a pile of burning rubbish. He had no conscious memory of landing his plane but must have done because the next thing he remembered was walking towards the airport exit. Black spots were falling all the time on his white uniform.

When Captain Fuchida walked out of the airport he was confronted with hell. That is the only word for it. The dead and the dying were piled up on the streets, others were floating down the river, the whole city was just a mound of bodies. Survivors, black, burnt crispy people, their flesh following them like shadows, wandered about politely asking for water. Captain Fuchida made his way under the funny-looking cloud to where Hiroshima Castle had been and there the Hero of Pearl Harbor found a series of little black lumps stuck to the parade ground in rows. He counted them. There were 2,322 lumps in neat little rows. They had been soldiers at 8.16 that morning standing to attention as their Colonel carried out his morning inspection. By 8.17 they were a series of little black lumps. It took Captain

Fuchida an hour to find the remains of the Colonel and his stallion. You'll never guess where he found them. He found them in a crack in the ground.

* * * *

Whaddyaknow.

* * * *

After finding the Colonel and his stallion in the crack, Captain Fuchida had something of a breakdown. He ran screaming all over the place. He ended up on the outskirts of Hiroshima where the buildings were only partially destroyed and it was there, in the ruins, that he found a slightly charred but still legible book.

The book was *Star Sign Secrets* by Humphry Barnard and, as Captain Fuchida would say over and over again, 'It changed my life.'

When Fuchida had finished his account of the bombing of Hiroshima he took out of his safe the slightly burnt holy paperback.

The cover showed a picture of a beautiful sunrise over which were superimposed the following words:

THE ULTIMATE ASTROLOGICAL LIFESTYLE GUIDE

STAR SIGN SECRETS
USE THE LOVE-HATE CHART TO FIND
YOUR IDEAL PARTNER

*

Discover How You Get Your Looks and Physique

*

Find Out Your Best and Worst Qualities

*

Check Out Your Preferences on
HOMES * CARS * FOOD * HOLIDAYS * DRINKS * SPORTS
PASTIMES * WORK * PEOPLE

HUMPHRY BARNARD

The Hero of Pearl Harbor asked God when he was born.

'17th of November 1925,' God told him.

He told me that I was a Scorpio and that as a result I liked cress, the colour green and was ruled by my sexual organs.

He told me my lucky number was the value of pi, 3.14159, etc., etc. . . .

Captain Fuchida turned to page 41 of *Star Sign Secrets* and pressed the book into my hands. I read all that Humphry Barnard had to say about people born under the sign of Scorpio as I lay in the head injuries ward of Osaka City Hospital in the aftermath of WWII, my family convinced I was dead, and the Hero of Pearl Harbor sitting by my bed, radioactive as all get out.

When I had finished I cried. I wept tears of joy. Captain Fuchida, crying as well, grabbed the book from my hands and put it back in the safe. He then, with tears running down his blackened face, told me that he was convinced that astrology was the only true hope for Japan, for the world. Captain Fuchida, pointing at the ceiling then at the safe, told me he had decided the day the bomb was dropped on Hiroshima to tell as many people as possible about the noble science of astrology.

The Hero of Pearl Harbor and God talked late into the night, then, when the nurses were threatening to physically throw him out, Captain Fuchida put the safe on his shoulder and left.

✳ ✳ ✳

The second phase of my enlightenment had begun and the ward was filled with little bits of what had once been Hiroshima and its populace. Hiroshima, thanks to Captain Fuchida, was a city on the move.

I collected some of it up and when no one was looking sprinkled it into the hole on the top of my head, then fell fast asleep for the very first time in years.

✳ ✳ ✳

God and my nurse watched *Star Trek* after dinner.

Above: Kyoto Naval Academy
  Class of '41. God is 3rd from
  right, second row.

Right: God on board the carrier
  Zuikaku before the raid on
  Pearl Harbor.

Below: God and other kamikaze
  pilots being addressed by
  Admiral Ohnishi (out of view).

Above: God (second from right) and other pilots being briefed the night before first kamikaze attack of WWII.

Right: God receiving his kamikaze sortie orders.

Below: God taking off on his third suicide mission.

Above: God returning from ninth suicide mission
(note increase in weight).

Below: An Ohka piloted bomb.

The atomic cloud above Hiroshima, 6th August 1945.

Above left: Golden Phallus being carried by Shinto monks, similar to the one God crash-dived into thereby achieving his enlightenment.

Above right: The Great Humphry Barnard.

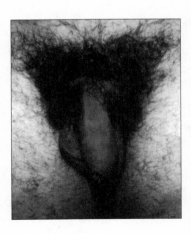

God's genitals.

Illustration of Hermes, the Thrice Great One, Siena Cathedral.

Right: Captain Fuchida meeting evangelist Billy Graham.

Below: Dr Hultcravitz about to attach two magnometers to God's testicles.

Right: Kirlian photograph No. 10,432.

Above: Life-support machine for God's left (possibly right) ball.

Below: United States Marines storm St Quen's Bay
on the Holy Island of Adocentyn.

The Cobras/Samba/Fontanelle satellite.

The Launch of Diament 'E' rocket from the Guiana Space Centre
with Cobras/Samba/Fontanelle in nose cone.

♉ TAURUS

Fort Knox, the 1st

Turkey signs armistice with Bulgaria

First motorway opened

Birthday of Genghis Khan (politician)

2nd – 9:19 am

☽ ♂ ♄
☽ ✱ ♂
☽ □ ☉
☽ ⊼ ♅
☽ △ ☿
☽ ✱ ♃

The Chaplain called around again today. God told him I was far too busy to see him. God said I had a million and one things to do. This wasn't strictly true but the Chaplain left anyway.

While the doctors and nurses on the head injuries ward waited patiently for the hole in my head to close Captain Fuchida and God read *Star Sign Secrets* from cover to cover. We learned that for people born under the sign of Gemini the important thing is to think and talk; we learned that Taureans are all basically gardeners, that Arians' lucky number is 547 and Aquarians' best colour is blue. We learned that fire signs lack subtlety while Leos are natural winners. We discovered that Librans cannot function without friends and that Geminis get bored chewing their food, that Sagittarians are normally medium to tall in height and that a Scorpio never moves more than is strictly necessary. We were told that Virgos aren't the sort of people to make a fuss of their car and Capricorns are ideal dentists if not fluent talkers. We read that Arians have short memories, Pisceans often own pubs and that my sign is the most likely to have leather furniture.

When we had read avidly the whole of *Star Sign Secrets* we read it again. It was just too much.

God was interrogated by members of the United States Strategic Bombing Survey on the 22nd of Libra 1945. A naval officer and a United Press news correspondent stood beside my bed. The American naval officer kept asking whether some form of compulsion had been used to get me to volunteer for the Kamikaze Special Attack Corps.

'Nope,' I said. Then I asked him what star sign he was.

He wanted to know how long I had served in the corps. When I told him I had been one of the founding members he was taken aback. If I had told him I was God Almighty he could not have looked more astonished.

THE 2ND

Flashlight invented	☽ v/c 10:54 am
	☽ → ♓ 1:09 pm
F.W.A. Argelander completes the Bonn	☽ ⊻ ☿
catalogue of stars	☽ ☌ ♃
First moving escalator turned on	☽ ⊻ ♆
	☽ ☌ ♂

In hardly no time at all Captain Fuchida and God quickly mastered the art of casting birth charts. There was an appendix at the back of *Star Sign Secrets* devoted to the subject. We calculated the birth charts of the former Emperor, MacArthur,

and the President of the United States of America. We calculated the birth charts of 452 dead kamikaze pilots. Then we drew
up my own birth chart.

It was not so much a chart of an individual ego, as the
focus-point of truly mighty cosmic forces. It was really
remarkable. Its symmetry, its elegance were, well, breathtaking.
It was quite simply the most beautiful thing we had ever seen,
even if I do say so myself. Captain Fuchida and I knew we had
stumbled on something important, something historic. Together
we pondered the beauty of my chart in silence then Captain
Fuchida told me I was touched.

God began consulting the stars after that on a regular,
religious basis, performing what is known as Electional
Astrology, choosing, by astrological principles, the most
auspicious moment for any given deed. In hardly no time
God became obsessed with Electional Astrology, drawing up
horoscopes for all manner of things: when to bathe, what side of
the bed to get out of, when to have breakfast, even when to have
bowel movements. Everything was recorded in God's very first
astrological diary, filled with the minutiae of my life and the
grand celestial motions of heaven.

THE 3RD

German troops invade Denmark	☽ → ♒ 8:02 am
Britain agrees to US Polaris missiles sites	☽ ☌ ♆
Birthday of St Teresa	☽ ✳ ☉
Toaster invented	☽ ✳ ♇

To this day God does not know how Captain Fuchida got hold of
another seminal astrological text on the black market. The work

was entitled *The Emerald Tablet* and the first time God read it the heavens were thus:

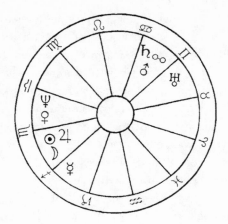

The opening of *The Emerald Tablet* encapsulates the work's central principle, the key mystery, the very essence of the whole of astrology.

The opening of *The Emerald Tablet* goes like this:

> *It is true, without falsehood, certain and very real*
> *That that which is on high is as that which is below*
> *And that which is below is as that which is on high.*

THE 4TH

Wallpaper invented

Turkey recognizes Bulgarian independence

Deathday of Charles Darwin

☽ v/c 3:45 pm
☽ → ♋ 7:43 pm

☽ ⊼ ☉
☽ △ ♃
☽ ☍ ☿
☽ ⊼ ♆
☽ ⊼ ♀
♀ ☌ ♆

Absolutely nothing has been done about the heating in here.

The Emerald Tablet, the oldest, wisest, greatest book the world has ever known, was written by one Hermes Trismegistus.

God told Miss Hughes my nurse, Captain Fleming and Mr Spillsbury today that Hermes Trismegistus wrote a total of 20,000 books, each containing the secrets of the Universe. God told them that to Roger Bacon, Hermes Trismegistus was the 'father of philosophers'.

Known as the Thrice Great One; he was the greatest astrologer, priest and king ever to be.

Hermes Trismegistus built the Great Pyramids of Egypt in four and a half hours one afternoon with a bucket, a spade and the intimate knowledge of the stars.

When God stopped speaking about Hermes Trismegistus Mr Spillsbury, kneeling nearby, shouted 'Happy happy days' over and over.

Miss Hughes asked if he was all right.

God assured her he was fine.

THE 5TH

First crossword puzzle published

Paris postal workers go on strike

2nd – 3:41 am

☽ □ ☉
☽ ⚹ ♄
☽ ⚻ ⚷

Went on and on today about the glory and brilliance of Hermes Trismegistus: how Hermes Trismegistus had been the very greatest of the Egyptian priests, and how Hermes Trismegistus had been without doubt the fountain from which all philosophies of the ancient Greeks flowed.

After lunch, God explained how Hermes Trismegistus had named the Zodiac and given the planets and stars their powers.

Mr Spillsbury, who has heard all this before, shouted 'Happy happy days' over and over.

THE 6TH

Deathday of Mark Twain (satirist)

E. Wigton performs 225 different magic tricks
    in two minutes

☉ □ ♆
☽ ⚹ ♂
☽ □ ♇
☽ ⚺ ☿
☽ ⚺ ♅
♀ ☌ ♃
☽ △ ⚷

Hermes Trismegistus was the founder of astrology, the religion of the Egyptians, the ancient science. When *The Emerald Tablet* was rediscovered during the Renaissance, it single-handedly started the revival in astrology that has continued to this day. It is fair to say that the whole edifice of modern Western astrology rests on the holy teachings of Hermes Trismegistus the Thrice Great One.'

Mr Spillsbury was about to shout out happy happy days when there was a knock on the door of the mobile home.

Miss Hughes answered it. It was the Chaplain.

'I'm not in,' whispered God.

'Where the hell else are you going to be?' whispered Colonel Fleming.

'Everywhere,' God whispered.

THE 7TH

E. Judson invents zip fastener	☽ v/c 1:22 pm
	☽ → ♊ 2:42pm
General strike in Belgium ends	☽ □ ♃
Invention of the microwave oven	☽ ⊼ ☿
	☽ △ ♆
	☽ △ ♀

No one said anything at breakfast this morning, so God, trying to make conversation, said that Hermes Trismegistus had invented language.

'You don't say,' said Miss Hughes.

God was still going on about Hermes Trismegistus when I was told that it was time for *Star Trek*. Tonight's episode was about aliens who only had one word for coat-hanger and bachelor and could therefore not tell the difference between them.

THE 8TH

Armistice in Mexican Civil War

Carmelite order of nuns founded

Push bike invented

♀ → ♑ 14:04 pm

☽ ☍ ♇
☽ △ ♅
☽ ⚹ ♄
☽ ⊼ ⚷
☽ △ ♂

After lunch God read out a sacred passage from *The Emerald Tablet*, the cornerstone of astrology.

> *The macrocosm has animals, terrestrial and aquatic; in the*
> *same way man has fleas, lice and tapeworms. The macrocosm*
> *has rivers, springs and seas, man has intestines. The macrocosm*
> *has winds, man has flatulence. The macrocosm has sun and the*
> *moon; man has two eyes; the right related to the sun, the left*
> *to the moon. The macrocosm has twelve signs of the zodiac,*
> *man contains them too from his head, namely from the lion to*
> *his feet, which correspond to the fish.*

After that God told everyone how, back in post-war Japan, God and Captain Fuchida became Hermes Trismegistus's biggest fans. It being much later that God realized Hermes Trismegistus was an aspect of himself.

Captain Fuchida and God would spend the afternoons in the park outside my hospital introducing ourselves to strangers as the Hero of Pearl Harbour and a retired kamikaze pilot. We told them about Humphry Barnard and the Thrice Great One and how astrology would change their lives for ever and ever.

THE 9TH

Boer War begins	☽ ⅄ ♄
Thirty Years War ends	☽ ♑ ☊
Switzerland declares neutrality	☽ ✳ ☿
Russia declares war on Turkey and invades	
Romania	

God's Total-Complete-Supreme-Enlightenment occurred on Libra the 11th 1945.

Captain Fuchida and I were in the park trying to make the world a better place by telling people about astrology when we met Professor Asda.

I asked the very old and very small professor if he had heard of a Humphry Barnard, the most important Western thinker alive. 'Are you familiar,' I asked, 'with the principle that Universal Sympathy unites Heaven and Earth? That, as the Thrice Great One brilliantly put it, "That which is on high is as that which is below"?'

I went on to tell him that Japan would have won the war if astrologers had been assigned to Imperial Headquarters.

'Bullshit. Your midwife exerted more gravitational influence on you at birth than all the stars and planets put together,' said Professor Asda.

I told him this was blatantly untrue.

Whereupon he stuck out his tongue and said it was utterly irrational to see human existence determined by stars. He said it was the stupidest thing he had ever heard. God told him he was flat wrong and showed him my birth chart to prove it.

We went on arguing for hours. Eventually the professor insisted we come back with him to his lab so that he could show us various studies on astrology that proved it was a complete joke and a total waste of time. Confident we could refute all such studies and after I had drawn up a quick horoscope showing our prospects of converting the professor were fair to good, Captain Fuchida and I agreed to come along.

The professor's lab was such a mess that he had some problem finding the papers he was looking for. While we waited Captain Fuchida noticed a strange-looking contraption in one of the corners of the room. It looked like a sort of gramophone. He asked the professor what it was.

'That,' Professor Asda said proudly, 'is my Death Ray.'

'Oh,' said Captain Fuchida.

Professor Asda then stopped looking for the studies on astrology and proceeded instead to tell us about his life during the war.

Little Professor Asda had, after the raid on Pearl Harbor, joined the Japanese Navy's nuclear weapons programme just as everyone realized that to build a bomb you needed plutonium, and plutonium was not something the Japanese empire had any of.

Asda turned his attention to other things, radar and proximity fuses, mostly. But by 1943 it was clear to him that to win the war a truly awesome secret weapon would have to be invented. So Asda sat down and invented one. By the end of 1943 he had built an early prototype which, when fired, caused a laboratory rat great discomfit at a range of six inches. By the middle of 1944 he was able to agitate a pig halfway across the lab. Asda perfected his Death Ray on the 3rd of Leo 1945. 'One blast from it would take out an aircraft carrier at two nautical miles,' he said.

'So why didn't Japan use it on the Americans?' God asked.

'I was due to give a demonstration that very afternoon when I received a telegram from Imperial Headquarters ordering me to travel to Hiroshima to investigate reports that the enemy had dropped some sort of new weapon on the city. You don't argue with a telegram from Imperial Headquarters so I set off for

Hiroshima. When I came back I sent a telegram to Imperial Headquarters. The telegram went: "All Gone. Stop.'"

Captain Fuchida told Professor Asda he too had been in Hiroshima hours after the bomb had been dropped.

'It's a small world,' said Professor Asda.

God then told Professor Asda how he had been making love to a peasant girl on the bonnet of a Bentley when the bomb had been dropped on Hiroshima.

'But not that small,' said Professor Asda.

Captain Fuchida went on to tell Professor Asda how the bombing of Hiroshima had introduced him to astrology.

'So what happened to the Death Ray?' God asked when Captain Fuchida had finished.

'The generals who knew of its existence all committed hara-kiri when Japan surrendered. It's been sitting here ever since,' said Professor Asda. 'Can I get you some tea?'

While we waited for the water to boil Professor Asda explained how the Death Ray worked. Captain Fuchida found it all fascinating. God asked where the toilets were.

'Down the corridor on the left,' Professor Asda said.

Famous, famous words.

Professor Asda had left a copy of the journal *Astronomy Now* in the toilet. God picked it up and started to flick through it after I had written in my astrological diary the precise time and place of my bowel movement and calculated the position of the stars, which were so:

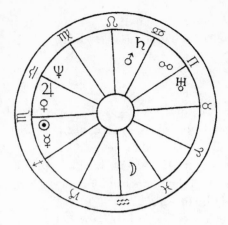

God came back to Professor Asda's lab a few minutes later, my trousers around my ankles, my astrological diary in one hand, *Astronomy Now* in the other, telling Captain Fuchida and Professor Asda what I had discovered in the toilet. Fuchida got down on his knees and called God the 'Thrice Great One' and Professor Asda went very pale.

God discharged myself from the head injuries ward that night, the hole in my head very much still there, and with Captain Fuchida carrying his safe, Professor Asda carrying his Death Ray and God clutching my astrological diary and *Astronomy Now*, we flew to Sydney.

THE 10TH

Birthday of Hitler (politician)	♉ → ♓ 5:22 am
Opening of first public pay phone	☽ ☌ ♇
The element scandium discovered	☽ ⚹ ♆
	♉ ⊻ ♆
Freud publishes *Totem and Taboo*	☽ △ ♄
US declares war on Spain	☽ ⊻ ♅
British Museum opened	

Everyone knows the fantastic details of the second stage of God's enlightenment. How God flicking through an article in *Astronomy Now* on the toilet, read about a group of Australian scientists who had discovered a number of new galaxies, and how God had felt that the dates and times of the discoveries of the galaxies were somehow familiar, and had taken out my astrological diary and discovered that at precisely the moments the Australian scientists had been finding galaxies in the blackness of space God had been in bed in the head injuries ward quietly masturbating under the sheets!

Everyone knows, God told Colonel Fleming and Miss Hughes at lunch, how God had stumbled back into Asda's lab crying, laughing, twiddling my fingers and uttering the following holy words over and over: 'My spunk is full of stars!'

And it was perfectly perfectly true.

'Every man I've ever met thinks his balls are something special,' said Miss Hughes at this point.

'Ah,' said God, 'but in my case it happens to be true.'

THE 11TH

✳

Birthday of Shakespeare (playwright)	☽ v/c 5:26 am
	☽ → ♐ 8:56 am
Deathday of Lao-tzu (Taoist)	4th – 10:27 am
Lennon (singer) and Ono (artist) begin	☽ □ ☿
'bed-in for peace'	☉ ⊻ ♆
	☽ □ ☉
Clashes occur on the Chinese-Soviet border	☽ ✳ ♆
	☽ □ ♃

The Chaplain called by today. God again refused to see him. Miss Hughes said that she thought this was mean. When she had finished telling me off God told her how on the flight to Sydney God had informed Captain Fuchida and Professor Asda about my experience in the rice field with the giant phallus at the end of WWII and how Captain Fuchida on hearing this got out of his seat and kissed my feet, getting into a lot of trouble with the air hostesses for taking off his safety belt.

In Sydney God demanded to speak with a Dr Frank Drumon, the man who had led the team of scientists that had discovered the new galaxies. We waited outside his office for nearly two hours. Captain Fuchida said this was no way to treat God and God was inclined to agree with him. Professor Asda wanted to use the Death Ray. God suggested patience.

When Dr Drumon finally agreed to see us I introduced my colleagues and then drew Dr Drumon's attention to the entries in God's astrological diary at the time of his discoveries, declared myself the Creator of the Universe and suggested a joint press conference be held right away in his office.

Dr Drumon called security saying he was surrounded by Japs driven crazy by the war.

God asked him if this meant the joint press conference was off.

We were ejected from the astronomy department of Sydney University by the entire complement of campus security guards on account of my bulk and Captain Fuchida's considerable martial arts skills.

The cops showed up, as did a local TV camera crew. We were arrested for disturbing the peace. It would not be the last time God found myself in trouble with the law. As we were bundled into a police van God announced to the world that I was God, that I had created the entire Universe with my genitals and that they had not seen the last of me.

THE 12TH

Invention of Morse code	☽ v/c 11:21 am
Birthday of Tammy Wynette (singer)	☽ ☍ ♂
Start of Babylonian excavations	☽ ⊼ ♄
	☽ ⊼ ☿
	☽ ✳ ♇
	☽ △ ♀
	☿ □ ♇
	☽ ⊼ ☉

We were flown back to Japan on the next available flight. From Tokyo we took an overnight train to Kyoto, city of eight thousand shrines and God's home town.

At 8 a.m., with Jupiter in conjunction with Mars, the three of us got out at Kyoto Station and made our way on foot to a public square not far from where God had grown up. There were maybe thirty or forty shoppers and stallholders in the square.

'My friends and I have travelled all night from Tokyo with wonderful news. I am God. I have created the eternal filament with my balls,' I shouted.

Some people laughed, some people ignored me, some people looked worried.

'I Zizo Yasuzawa did not die in the war though I tried my

very best to do so. I did not die I know now because I am terribly important, I am God. I will demonstrate.'

And I did. Right there in the square. The people in the street, neighbours who had known me as a child, couldn't believe it. There was a flash of light which only God saw and the heavenly spheres began to make their music, which only God heard. I moved beautifully in time with the music. Humming the tune no one else in the history of the world had ever heard before, my arm got tired but I kept at it, out of love for the world.

The whole Universe was quivering, shaking.

And then God came. Stars flew. The Universe rejoiced; jism was everywhere.

When God had finished everyone was looking up into the sky.

The police arrived moments later.

'It's all right, officers,' I said. 'I'm God and I was just making a galaxy.'

THE 13TH

✳

The Institute of Propaganda founded by the	☽ ⊻ ♇
Roman Catholic Church	☽ ☐ ♅
First hot-air balloon built	☽ ✳ ☿
Deathday of Mussolini (politician)	☽ ⊼ ♄
First human cannon ball fired; goes 6 metres (woman)	

'After my very first public performance God was committed to an asylum. There are hundreds of such places in Kyoto, the mystical capital of Japan,' God explained at breakfast today. A month later I was released and reunited with Captain Fuchida and Professor Asda. Together we set up the Astrological Institute, where I gave lectures about my enlightenment, my balls and the wonderful influence astrology could have on people's lives.

The Astrological Institute was a back room in a bar and I freely admit that to begin with my followers were freak heads, wackos and kooks. Most were alcoholics still getting over the war and capable in their despair of believing anything.

'From the beginning of Time,' I would say at the start of my lectures, 'the greatest philosophers have wondered where the stars come from. Now we know,' and then I would point.

After the war, everyone in Japan had problems of one sort or another and astrology was their only real hope. After my lectures, I would conduct personal sessions with dozens of people. God would draw up their birth charts and tell them what to do. God remembers telling lots of people to get into the dry-cleaning business.

God soon had another run-in with the authorities, being charged this time with public indecency, for since leaving the asylum, except for a short time when I sported a white jumpsuit with jewels sewn on it, God had gone around completely naked. The magistrate (Cancer) asked me why I refused to wear a loincloth. To which God famously replied 'To cover what with what?' thereby expressing the essential oneness of reality.

Cancer males apologize at climax, wear shoes that are too small for them and like it when it rains. Their most unlucky number is 97832.1

When released again, with money donated by my followers, I bought a nine-inch telescope which we carried with us as we wandered through the streets guessing people's star signs and telling them the wonderful news that I was God.

During our marches through the streets of Kyoto we would

inform people that I, God, was going to create a galaxy that very night. I would jump around, my arms waving in the air like some heavyweight boxer and shout, 'Yes indeedy.'

I told Captain Fleming and Miss Hughes that my nightly performances in Kyoto were held in the garden behind the Astrological Institute.

They would begin with me rushing out of the rear door, a lit sparkler inserted in my urethra (surprisingly not as painful as it sounds). I would run around for a bit, my sparkler swaying in front of me, then I would climb up into the branches of a bo tree that grew at the end of the garden. Able to see with the light of the sparkler, I would read from either *The Emerald Tablet* or *Star Sign Secrets* until the sparkler fizzled out. Then I would grab my organ and to shouts of encouragement from the hundreds of spectators, and to the accompaniment of a hand cymbal played by Captain Fuchida, I would begin the process by which stars are made, having removed the sparkler with the aid of an oven glove kept in the bo tree especially for the purpose.

'Me! Me! Me!' God would shout.

'You! You! You!' the crowd would shout.

After God had spanked my monkey, people would break into applause and my bodily fluid would be carefully collected by Captain Fuchida using a silver teaspoon and put into little glass vials. These were then labelled with the word 'stars'.

People would then form an orderly line to the roof of the Astrological Institute where, watched over by Professor Asda, they would peer through the nine-inch telescope at a distant galaxy. One after the other, the people would sigh as they looked through the telescope. Some prayed, some cried, some smiled, some chuckled, some would say, 'Who would have thought it possible?', some cursed as they squinted up at my glorious handiwork, my sublime creation. Before making their way back to the stairs, they would lean over the side of the building and stare down at me reclining against the trunk of the bo tree, and make gracious bows.

God would normally at such times be smoking a cigarette and dabbing a tissue on my sacred organ.

In the *Nippon Dokusho Shimbun*, a copy of which God has here in one of his carrier bags, the headline read:

MAN SHOWN TO CREATE STARS WITH BALLS.
DISCOVERY IS HAILED AS EPOCH-MAKING.
JAPANESE SCIENTISTS CALL THE FINDING
ONE OF THE GREATEST OF HUMAN
ACHIEVEMENTS.

Space, the paper said, would never quite feel the same again. One renowned scientist was quoted as saying that, '*The implications are shocking and nearly completely incomprehensible*', while others reported feeling quite, quite queasy.

One enthusiastic columnist wrote that, '*Zizo Yasuzawa has appeared in the aftermath of the chaos of WWII. He brings with him a message of a new order to the universe . . . His testicles are sacred . . . He fulfils two profound needs in man, the need to know and the need not to know but to believe. In this time of uncertainty Yasuzawa represents order. Someone has to be making all the stars so why can't it be this guy?*'

The other religions in the city differed in their treatment of me; the Shintoists rejected me out of hand as did the Christians, but some Buddhists begrudgingly accepted that God might be a truly Enlightened One.

Some people (Virgos mostly) were outraged by my '*full frontal assaults*' and concluded that God was in the grip of a most terrible bout of narcissism. They said God was overweight and overwrought, hysterical and capable of thinking only of my organ. One reporter wrote '*Woe to a country that can spawn such a man as Zizo Yasuzawa*' and other things in that vein.

Other social commentators decided God was confused but happy.

THE 14TH

Birthday of Charles Chaplin (comedian)	☽ v/c 2:33 am
	☽ → ♑ 8:05 am
Torrential rain in Brazil leaves 100,000 homeless	
Journal of Egyptian Archaeology published	☽ △ ☉
	☽ ⋎ ♆
Aeronautical map of France published	☽ △ ♂
	♀ ⋎ ♅
Russia declares war on China	☽ ⋎ ♇
	♃ △ ☊

Nearly two months after realizing that I was the Creator of Everything, and as attendance at my nightly meetings had risen into the thousands, Captain Fuchida came to see me.

I was in the back room casting the horoscope of a well-to-do lady. When I had predicted she would have her hair cut and advised her to go into the dry-cleaning business, Captain Fuchida stepped forward and said, 'Oh, Thrice Great One, something has been troubling me.'

'Emm?'

'I can see how you create distant galaxies, but when exactly did you create this particular galaxy, the Milky Way?'

God did not answer Captain Fuchida, having fallen asleep suddenly due to the physical exertion brought about by my earlier orgasm.

I answered him a few days later, moments before lighting my sparkler and stepping out the back door of the Institute for another of my performances. 'The Milky Way was created when

I was three, produced by my earliest unconscious sexual urges,' God explained.

Captain Fuchida was troubled by this explanation. He nitpicked; how could I have been conceived if the Milky Way had yet to be formed? How indeed could I be, as I claimed, the reincarnation of Hermes Trismegistus who lived thousands of years ago, if the Milky Way was less then one hundred years old?

'You are limited by the way your mind has been taught to think,' God told him. 'I am the great singularity. When I come I travel faster than the speed of light. This has been proven. My balls hang outside the space/time continuum. For God anything is possible. You cannot catch me out, Fuchida. Effect can come before cause for God. Try to remember this.'

'And what of the galaxies catalogued before 1945?' asked the Hero of Pearl Harbor.

'Do you not think that God was being productive during his adolescence?'

'I see.'

'It's about time.'

Professor Asda was given the task of providing the scientific evidence of my Godhood. This was a daunting task given the bigotry of the scientific community. At the beginning of my rise to fame Asda had been described by the newspapers as '*arguably Japan's most imaginative wartime scientist*' and was quoted as saying things like he was '*One hundred per cent certain Zizo is making galaxies*' and that my '*powers had been completely proven by science*'.

But despite the best efforts of Asda, the scientific establishment wanted nothing to do with God. They thought me nothing more than a charlatan.

Watched *Star Trek* tonight with my nurse.

THE 15TH

Potato introduced to Britain	☽ v/c 3:41 am
	☽ → ♓ 11:42 pm
French troops invade Tunis	☽ ✳ ♄
Birthday of Rudolph Valentino (actor)	☽ □ ⚷
Man reaches the South Pole	☽ ⊻ ♂
	☽ ⊻ ♀
	☿ ⊻ ♅

God is just terrible with names. Some of my followers used to joke that this was because of the blow to the head God received at my Enlightenment. To overcome my poor memory for names God would often give my followers new astrological names each time I saw them.

I renamed my nurse this morning when I couldn't think of her name. 'You are to be called Jellybaby-Daughter-of-Jupiter,' I told her. She laughed and said I was mad.

* * *

Occasionally, a follower of God would deny that they were the star sign I guessed they were. I would tell them they were mistaken, God was omnipotent, therefore he always guessed correctly. A few brought me their birth certificates to prove their date of birth and thus their star sign. God would say there had been a terrible mistake and tear up their silly little birth certificates.

It never ceases to amaze God just how many people get their star sign wrong.

THE 16TH

Deathday of Salvador Dali (artist)	1st – 12:26 pm
P. Müller invents DDT	☽ ⊻ ♆
Creation of Premium Bonds	☽ ☌ ♃
Start of the Boxer rebellion in China	☽ ☌ ☉
	☽ □ ♇
	☉ □ ♇
	☽ ⊻ ♅

I had by this stage a fair number of business clients who sought my advice on the influence the Zodiac had on the world of trade and commerce. Even to this day many people are unaware that God and the ancient science of astrology were the sole cause of the economic boom of post-war Japan.

In 1947, God went on his first nationwide tour. I travelled all over the Home Islands performing every night the stars came out. Turnouts were mind-boggling, enormous. Japan quickly acquired more telescopes then any other country in the world. The police and civil authorities got off my back about public indecency, my lawyers arguing that for me masturbation was a religious act and that to prevent me from doing it in public would have been religious intolerance, which was a big no-no at the time.

I performed at night and during the day I did consultations and wrote star-sign predictions for various newspapers. They were read by an estimated two million people and broadcast from the roof of the Astrological Institute via loudspeaker.

I set up my nine companies that manufactured all sorts of astrological merchandise, slept with whatever girl I chose (when I found the energy) and decided to spread the word of my coming to the rest of the world. Astronomically, it was the right time to do this, what with Mercury in Virgo. Rather than go myself I sent Captain Fuchida, who was continuing to ask awkward questions. Fuchida was the very first Astrological Missionary; in time hundreds of Japanese would follow him, searching the Earth for people who did not know what star sign they were and what they were missing. Fuchida was reluctant to go until I showed him how it was astrologically vital. Captain Fuchida took his old Zero fighter with him, thinking that it would help him get people's attention. He took off from Kyoto airport, one of my pubic hairs, a sacred relic if ever there was one, clasped in his right hand.

After waving Captain Fuchida off, God boarded another plane and flew naked to Hiroshima, where I attended that year's reunion of retired kamikaze pilots and got completely smashed on sake.

THE 17TH

✳

Birthday of Noël Coward (playwright)	☉ → ♓ 3:55 pm
Birthday of Boris Becker (tennis player)	☽ ⊼ ♄
Prussians invade Denmark	☽ ☌ ♃
Book of Common Prayer published	☽ △ ♂
	☽ ⁎ ♀

Captain Fuchida flew all over the Far East bringing news of my existence and the power of astrology. He was a brilliant shining comet. Within months my horoscopes were appearing in papers in Singapore, Borneo and India and reports of new galaxies being discovered came from as far away as Oman.

I was interviewed a number of times on TV and appeared on several religious talk shows with the leaders of new religions and representatives of the older faiths. Once during one such talk show, a scuffle broke out between God and a Catholic nun and the poor woman managed somehow to knock herself unconscious. While we waited for the ambulance I created a galaxy live, on TV.

More missionaries were sent out. In no time at all, God had followers in every continent.

As my message spread, I demonstrated my divine power with more and more gusto, performing in the gleaming new baseball stadiums that were springing up all over the place. Tens of thousands of people came to see me every night.

After dinner God showed nurse a copy of my best-selling book *The Darn Truth* that had first been published in the spring of '48. It explained how, through the interconnectedness of the Universe, of the small with the large, the Microcosm with the Macrocosm, I was able to do what I did. It also explained just how the Zodiac worked and what awesome influences it had over people.

The Darn Truth gave a summary of the twelve personality types, their likes and dislikes, their fashion senses, favourite food, typical height and body weight. It explained the influence the stars had on a host of human activities: tennis, roller hockey, flower arranging, washing clothes, small talk, interior decorating, gardening and dancing. It argued that people needed to consult an astrologer at least once a day, worship my genitals and prepare for the Age of Aquarius.

In *The Darn Truth* I showed without a shadow of a doubt that I was the reincarnation of Maitreya or Miro Buddha, the Buddha of the future who would soon institute the Age of Justice. God also explained in *The Darn Truth* how astrology can allow one to quadruple one's income. *The Darn Truth* showed clearly that I was the real Emperor of Japan and the supreme Shito Dama, astral spirit.

In the penultimate chapter of *The Darn Truth* I claimed to be the Messiah Christians and Jews had been waiting for and that the Japanese were the missing tribe of Israel, deported by Sargon of Assyria on the fall of Samaria in 721 BC.

In the final chapter of *The Darn Truth* I came to the inescapable conclusion that I was the reincarnation of the Thrice Great One, Hermes Trismegistus.

Every other page of *The Darn Truth* had a picture of my beautiful sublime birth chart. I read a few passages of *The Darn Truth* out to my nurse and then showed her all the highly astrologically harmonious reviews the book had received:

> 'His Divine Grace Zizo Yasuzawa is doing valuable work,
> and his book is a significant contribution to the salvation of
> mankind.'

> 'Very sad not available 200 years ago.'

> 'Words fail to describe this book.'

> 'The height of scholarship and divinity is manifest in
> The Darn Truth. *Our future generations will definitely find
> a better world to live in thanks to Mr Yasuzawa.*'

> 'The book by Zizo Yasuzawa is not only deeply beautiful but
> also highly relevant to our times as we as a nation search for
> new cultural patterns for our way of life.'

> 'The most concise informative information ever read.'

> 'Should be required reading for anyone who can . . . well . . .
> read.'

And God's personal favourite:

> 'Giving The Darn Truth *to my son instead of sending him
> to college.*'

THE 18TH

Gibraltar taken by the Moors

New Zealand proclaimed a British colony

Presence of hydrogen discovered in a glass
   of water

First mechanical dishwasher

☽ → ♎ 9:05 pm

☽ ⊼ ♄
☽ ⊼ ♂

God's nurse asked me this afternoon exactly how I had met my
second wife. God told her it was all thanks to Professor Asda and
a conference he organized at the Astrological Institute called
'Exploring God's Genitalia'.

    Here is the horoscope for the conference which, as you can
see, clearly suggested that progress would be made:

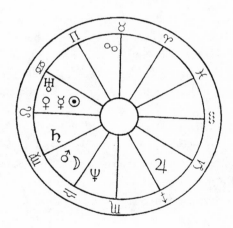

During the three-day conference a number of hypotheses were
put forward to explain my remarkable ability. One speaker
thought that there was a teeny-weeny black hole in either one
or both of my balls. Another spoke for many hours about the
butterfly effect, where something seemingly insignificant, like a
butterfly flapping its wings, could cause something massive, like

a hurricane, to occur the other side of the world. Perhaps, the scientist suggested, I was the ultimate example of the butterfly effect. At this point I flapped my arms and everyone laughed.

Other theories were proposed, to do with ectoplasm chambers, unconscious teleportation, ouija boards, UFOs, tarot cards, crop circles, wormholes, the 5th, 6th and 16th dimensions, my diet and something, God forgets just what, to do with dolphins.

The truth was, of course, that no one really knew how I did what I did. Even so 'Exploring God's Genitalia' was a great success, perhaps the most important scientific conference of all time.

When it was over, Professor Asda introduced me to each of the scientists who had taken part. This was how my second wife, Dr Hultcravitz, and God met. She was wearing red, her astrological colour, and like most Capricorns was very tall with striking cheekbones. Her lower lip was absolutely perfectly formed. In fact, God had never seen anything like it before. I introduced myself in English and welcomed her to Japan. She said she had been waiting to meet God for ages. She then asked permission to hold my right finger by the middle joint with her right thumb and index finger. God agreed. She did this for about a minute. Then for about ten minutes she told God someone else's life story with utter precision. She then predicted a rosy future for this unknown person. God realized after this extraordinary display of psychic power that Hultcravitz was an incredibly gifted woman.

I asked her what star sign she was. Her lower lip was just too much.

'Capricorn.'

'Have you ever thought of becoming a dentist?' I asked, smiling.

'I . . .'

Professor Asda changed the subject. 'Dr Hultcravitz has been working on a number of fascinating paranormal case studies in the US.'

'And do any claim to have made the Universe with a series of flicks of the wrists as I do?'

'They don't even come close, Mr Yasuzawa,' she said and smiled.

God felt the stirring of a galaxy.

'Please call me Japs Eye Fontanelle, Dr Hultcravitz. It is the name I and the Zodiac have decided I should be known by in the West. It has a nice ring to it and is easier for people in the West to say than Zizo Yasuzawa. Alternatively, you may refer to me as He-Whose-Figure-Of-Beauty-Is-Tinged-With-The-Hue-Of-Cerulean-Blue-Clouds-And-Whose-Unique-Loveliness-Charms-Millions-Of-Little-Cupids.'

'I think I'll call you Japs Eye Fontanelle.'

'You will be at my performance tonight?'

'I wouldn't miss it for the world,' Dr Hultcravitz said.

And she didn't.

THE 19TH

Röntgen discovers X-rays	☽ v/c 12:01 pm
	☽ → ♒ 10:10 pm
Henry Ford produces Model Ts	☽ □ ♄
Anarcho-Communists riot in Chicago	☽ ✳ ⚷
President Bush is taken ill while out jogging	☉ ☌ ♃
Work on the Panama Canal begins	☽ ✳ ♂
	☽ ☌ ♀
	☽ ☌ ♆

God spent several days with Dr Hultcravitz, discussing my powers and what they meant for mankind. Dr Hultcravitz was determined to try, with God's help, to overturn the entrenched mechanistic philosophy of the twentieth century. She was

determined to alter man's concept of himself and his relationship to the rest of the cosmos, a concept that had suffered so
drastic a change for the worse with the emergence of
Copernicanism and Darwinism.

God agreed. I was completely taken by her lower lip. It was
too much.

'Darwinism is bullshit,' God told her, after I had looked the
word up. 'How can man be the centre of the Universe, how can
he be the Microcosm, if he evolved from an amoeba?'

'You're so right, Japs Eye.'

'I am, aren't I.'

THE 20TH

Greenwich Observatory opened	☽ → ♌ 9:57 am
Guernica bombed in Spanish Civil War	☽ ☍ ♆
Deathday of Napoleon I	☽ ⚻ ♃

'We cannot go on being told that there is no meaning to life,' Dr
Hultcravitz shouted in the Ryoanji, 'Temple of Heaven Peace', a
Buddhist landscaped garden built in the fifteenth century and
made of just raked sand and a few rocks.

'No,' God said and, getting down on the ground, made a
hole in the sand with my finger and easing my sex organ into it,
started to move rhythmically.

'We can't go on believing the lie that life is a crazy by-
product of chemical reactions.'

'It's silly.'

'Back to the ideas of the Middle Ages.'

'To the ideas of the Middle Ages.' Dr Hultcravtiz held God's
hand.

THE 21ST

✳

R. Bannister runs a mile in 3 mins 59 seconds

Lebanese Government resigns

☽ → ♈ 10:49 am
♉ ℞ 2:37pm
1st – 10:14 pm

☽ ✳ ♆
☽ ☌ ☉
☽ △ ♇

Playfully, God and Dr Hultcravitz would chase each other through the shrines and temples of Kyoto eating ice cream.

'We must make your sexual organ a bulwark,' Dr Hultcravitz would say.

'A what?'

'A bulwark, a wall.'

'A wall?'

'Against the black tide of mechanistic philosophy.'

'Yes. A bulwark.'

'This far and no further.'

✳ ✳ ✳

After dinner, the Chaplain called by yet again. God felt sorry for him and invited him inside the mobile home. Miss Hughes made the Chaplain a coffee and offered him a doughnut. As he nibbled on the doughnut the Chaplain told God about the saving grace of Jesus Christ, of his death on the cross, resurrection and all that jazz.

God, of course, had heard it all before.

When the Chaplain had talked for about half an hour there was a moment of silence then God told my nurse to turn the TV on as it was time for *Star Trek*.

THE 22ND

Sierra Leone, Gambia and the Gold Coast are	☽ △ ♆
taken over by British Government	☽ ⊼ ♃
H. Helmer makes a record 427 omelettes in	☿ ⋎ ♀
half an hour	

When Dr Hultcravitz had been in junior high, her gym teacher had explained to her that man was nothing but a collection of chemicals, a fancy-ass machine. Life itself, her gym teacher had said, was really nothing but a rather bizarre oxidative process, a strange sort of combustion. To live, the gym teacher said, was to burn.

All of life, all the creatures in the world, were only so many different kinds of fireworks the gym teacher said.

If all that were true Dr Hultcravitz asked her gym teacher, what possible meaning could life have? 'To burn the brightest,' the teacher told her, then he blew his whistle and told her to get out there and play.

The episode had affected Dr Hultcravitz deeply. She fervently believed that life had meaning and that people were more than fancy-ass fireworks.

THE 23RD

Margaret Thatcher elected Prime Minister	☽ v/c 6:25 pm
of Britain	☽ → ♈ 11:42 pm
Shipwrecked Spaniards settle on the	☽ ⋎ ♄
Sandwich Islands	☽ △ ⚷
	☽ ☌ ♂
	☽ ✳ ♀

One evening, as Dr Hultcravitz and God were criticizing the mechanistic philosophy of modern science, we got into some difficulty understanding each other. She said it was due to the language problem.

'What is language problem?' God asked.

When Dr Hultcravitz had explained several times what a language problem was, God absolutely denied that they were having anything of the sort.

Had a second meeting with the Chaplain today. It lasted a lot longer than the first. When he was comfortable God asked the Chaplain what star sign he was. He said he was an Aquairus.

'That explains it then, doesn't it,' God said.

'Explains what?'

'Why you're a Christian. All Aquarians are.'

'Really?'

'Why, of course, don't tell me you haven't noticed.'

After that the Chaplain told God about the Holy Ghost and Jesus Christ.

'You Christians are pretty screwed up when it comes to sex,' said God.

God asked the Chaplain what had happened to the Corinthian Christians who were so sure Jesus was coming back at any moment that they abstained completely from lovemaking.

'I don't know,' said the Chaplain.

'They died out,' said God and laughed hysterically.

THE 24TH

United Nations founded

The biro invented

Improvements in fluorescent lighting

☽ v/c 1:08 pm
☽ → ♑ 5:30 pm
☽ □ ♂
☽ ⊻ ♀
☽ ⊻ ♆
☽ ✳ ♅
☽ ✳ ☉

Today the Screaming Eagles played baseball here in the gold vault. It was Colonel Fleming's idea. He said it would be good for morale.

A Platoon beat B Platoon and C Platoon beat D Platoon.

God did not get involved.

Dr Hultcravitz refused God's suggestion that she experience the phenomenon of stellar formation directly. God could not understand this. I told her that we had talked enough and that it was time for action. She agreed and suggested I fly back with her to America. I told her this was too far to go for sex when we could do it back at the Astrological Institute around the corner.

For the second time she brought up the language problem, saying we were talking at cross purposes. God stormed off in a huff. I came back a little later and said I applauded.

'You mean apologize?'

'That's it, yes, that's what I mean, apologize,' said the creator of absolutely everything.

THE 25TH

✸

Invention of sewing machine

Birthday of Marlon Brando (actor)

☽ v/c 1:06 pm
☽ → ♉ 9:09 pm

☽ ⌴ ♃
☽ ⌴ ♀
☽ ♂ ♄

When we weren't rubbishing empiricism and the modern mind set, Dr Hultcravitz and God talked about her lower lip. God would tell her she had the prettiest lower lip I had ever seen and Dr Hultcravitz would normally become embarrassed and say, 'I used to suck my thumb a lot when I was a child. My mother was worried my lip would be, you know, deformed.' God would then tell her that her mother had had nothing to worry about and that she could trust me because I was God, and everything.

THE 26TH

✸

Minnesota becomes US state

Invention of the vacuum cleaner

T.S. Eliot finishes *The Waste Land*

☽ ⊼ ♂
☽ ✳ ♆
☽ ♂ ♇
♂ □ ♆
☽ □ ♀
☽ △ ☿
☽ ✳ ♅   ☿ ⌴ ♀

'Did you and Dr Lips get married in Japan?' Miss Hughes asked while making breakfast.

'No,' God said. In the end Dr Hultcravitz took several photographs of my penis and flew back to America. Much to God's surprise we did not make love. Needless to say, though, we were astrologically perfectly suited.

175

After dinner, Miss Hughes and God watched *Star Trek*.

THE 27TH

China becomes a republic	☽ ⚹ ♆
Birthday of Frank Sinatra (singer)	☽ ⚺ ♃
US Marines land on Okinawa	☽ △ ♇
	☽ ⚹ ☉
	☽ ⚹ ♅

As the months went by, my following grew and grew. Astrology became a buzzword in Japan. Everyone was reading their horoscopes in the papers and seeking my guidance. People poured scorn on the idea that the Earth went round the Sun. It was a wonderful time. Indians in the jungles of Brazil and Eskimos were being told what star sign they were and what sort of car best suited their sign. Tribesmen in Africa born under the sign of Pisces were being told to stay away from spicy food. Virgo Australian Aborigines were given clothes the colour of which did not clash with the cosmos.

In Japan itself, well over half the population could, when shown a picture of my testicles, name their owner. There were Astrological Institutes all over the country and God's birthday effectively became a national holiday.

On my fortieth birthday, Professor Asda presented me with an astrolabe, an astrolabe being an ancient scientific instrument for calculating the precise position of the stars and the planets.

The astrolabe given to me by Professor Asda was unique, as far as God knows, being intended to be worn on the head. It meant I could, at a glance, see what was going on in heaven. My astrolabe looked like this:

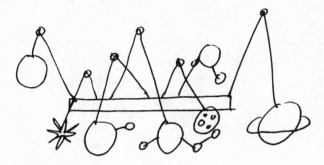

God soon wondered how he had ever coped without it.

God also received, on my fortieth birthday, two million birthday cards from all over the place and two letters. They both came from the United States of America. One was from Dr Hultcravitz asking, as she had been for months, for me to come to America for tests. The other letter God received on his fortieth birthday was from Captain Fuchida telling God that he had found Jesus.

THE 28TH

B-25 bomber crashes into the Empire State Building	☽ ⊻ ♄
	☽ □ ♂
	☽ ☍ ⚷
US declares war on Mexico	♂ □ ⚷
	☽ △ ☉

Some scientists were on TV this morning saying that they were confident that the Cobras/Samba/Fontanelle satellite would soon be ready. The reporter interviewing them asked how they felt about God's belief that the Sun in fact goes around the Earth. One of the scientists said he thought God really ought to know better, another one nodded in agreement. The scientists were then asked how they felt about my fate resting on the measurements made by their satellite once it got into orbit.

'I've never really been a very religious guy,' one of them said.

'That's right,' said another scientist. 'You know, we just work here.'

THE 29TH

First atomic tests are held in the New Mexico	☽ □ ♇
desert	☽ ⊼ ♅
	♀ ♂ ☉
Birthday of Florence Nightingale (nurse)	☽ ⊼ ♄
Two groups of researchers discover rings around	♀ ⊻ ♃
Neptune	☽ ⁎ ♅

Captain Fuchida had lost faith in me and had written a book called *No More Pearl Harbors*, a copy of which he had included with his letter. He was touring the US in his Zero fighter, baptizing people and handing out bibles, with an organization called Sky Pilots of America International.

In his letter Captain Fuchida begged me to become a Christian and let Jesus into my life. He said all the masturbation and sex had to stop, that it was a sin. He also said I had to confess to being a false prophet. As a penance for my ludicrous behaviour, he suggested eight years of fasting on bread and water. He said that if anything this was pretty lenient given what I had been getting up to. It wouldn't hurt, he added, for me to lose some weight anyway.

He went on for four or five pages about all the sins that were attached to sexual acts of various kinds.

It was in this long and rambling letter that Fuchida informed God that Japan's crushing defeat at Midway had been caused by the divine intervention of Archangel Gabriel. Fuchida also wrote that the dropping of the A-bomb on Hiroshima had saved his soul. It had been dropped, not by the crew of the B-17 *Enola Gay*, as most people think, but by Jesus Christ. Fuchida ended his letter by saying that he felt personally to blame for my terrible sins, having been the person who had introduced me to astrology in the first place. He said that he knew he would have to answer for this on the Great Day of Judgment, which he added, was any day now, as Christians never tire of telling God.

THE 30TH

National Geographic published for the first time	☽ ☌ ♅
Geneva Convention bans poison gas	☽ ✳ ♀
Bakelite invented	☽ □ ♃
National bankruptcy in Portugal	☽ □ ♂

After breakfast my nurse did a spring-clean of the mobile home. God did not see the point.

Above the sound of the vacuum cleaner, God told Colonel Fleming and Mr Spillsbury that in the foreword of *No More Pearl Harbors* Captain Fuchida had dedicated the work '*To all pastors, Sunday school teachers, public school teachers and all governmental agencies as well as all organizations that are seeking the solution for peace on Earth and good will among men, to the end that all mankind may seek — as this man sought — Jesus Christ, the Way of Peace.*'

God also told Colonel Fleming and Mr Spillsbury how Captain Fuchida referred in *No More Pearl Harbors* to Jesus Christ as his new Commanding Officer.

II

GEMINI

Fort Knox, the 1st

Invention of toilet paper

H. Geiger and W. Müller construct Geiger counter

Toothpaste invented

☽ △ ♄
☽ □ ⚷
☽ ☍ ♂

Chapter One of *No More Pearl Harbors* begins:

When the Prince of Peace, the Lord Jesus Christ is seated in Authority in the Assembly of the United Nations, the deceitful darkness of men's hearts will disappear, dispelled by the glory of Him who said 'I am the light of the World. He that followeth me shall not walk in darkness but shall have the light of Life.' Having met the Prince of Peace Mitsuo Fuchida is no longer an emissary of hate but an ambassador of love.

No More Pearl Harbors ends:

When I was appointed to train five hundred men for two months prior to bombing Pearl Harbor I remember that I gave my all effort to preparations for that attack. Now I pledge myself to the Lord and the members of my Sky Pilot Missionary Board to give my all effort to train the men and boys of America to become loyal Christian people, living in love, joy and peace with one another and the whole wide world.

In the middle of *No More Pearl Harbors* was a picture of Billy Graham giving the right hand of fellowship to Captain Fuchida upon his acceptance of Christ.

At the back of the book was an application form.

APPLICATION FOR MEMBERSHIP

I wish to join Sky Pilots of America International as an active member. Please send application.

Name _____

Address _____

State or Country _____

I desire to be a supporting Sky Pilot member. My monthly contribution of $_____ enclosed for the period of _____ to _____

Name _____

Address _____

State or Country _____

I desire to contribute $_____ monthly to the support of General Mitsuo Fuchida and the work of Sky Pilots in Japan and Orient for a period of five years. Enclosed is check for $_____

Name _____

Address _____

State or Country _____

I desire to contribute $_____ monthly to the support of Sky Pilots of America International to reach the boys of U.S.A and the world. Enclosed find check or sum of $_____

This enclosed check is to go to General Mitsuo Fuchida's Helicopter Fund. $_____

Name _____

Address _____

_____

State or Country _____

Please send me the *Sky Pilot News*.
Please detach this sheet – Fill out and mail to:
SKY PILOTS OF AMERICA INTERNATIONAL
45 E. Julian Street
San José, California

THE 2ND

Steamboat invented	♂ ⚹ ♅
Valium discovered	☽ ☌ ♇
Germany annexes New Guinea and the	☽ □ ♃
Bismarck Archipelago	☽ ⚹ ♅
	☽ △ ♂
	☽ ⚹ ♀

God thought he had heard the last of Captain Fuchida. But two months later God got another crazy-assed letter from the Hero of Pearl Harbor in which he said that God had been appointed the Commanding Officer of the Japanese Sky Pilots Missionary Movement.

The whole thing infuriated God, astrology wasn't even mentioned. God wrote back to Captain Fuchida as follows:

> *Captain Fuchida,*
> *Have you forgotten what God has revealed to you? Have you forgotten the great teachings of Humphry Barnard, of Hermes Trismegistus the Thrice Great One? Where is your loyalty? your sanity?*
> *You have forsaken your God. You are a nincompoop, a scoundrel. Astrology is better off without you. Take your stupid Christianity and stuff it where the stars do not twinkle!*
> *Yours sincerely,*
> *God.*

THE 3RD

✳

Birthday of Stevie Wonder (singer)	☽ □ ♀
Deathday of Marcelin Berthelot, first man to	☽ □ ♅
	♂ ⊻ ♃
produce organic compounds synthetically	☽ ⊼ ☿
Invention of the shopping basket	☽ ☌ ♅
	☽ ⊼ ♄

The UNCC doctors examined God again. They still refuse to tell me their star signs.

When the doctors had gone God told my nurse how God had announced, on the 4th of Gemini 1965, with the Zodiac in perfect alignment, that I was standing for election to the Japanese Diet, and how I would be advocating radical astrological reform for the entire country. My followers were overjoyed.

God ejaculated at rallies up and down the country, and had loudspeaker cars drive through the streets blaring my campaign promises – eternal bliss and harmony with the Universe.

God guessed people's star signs as they opened their doors, tapped babies on their heads in front of cameras and handed out copies of my fantastic birth chart and *The Darn Truth*.

Over three million copies of my birth chart were nailed to trees and street lights in Kyoto alone by my followers.

Still refusing to wear clothes, God made quite a contrast to the grey-suited politicians I was competing against. We would appear on TV together and they would dismiss me as a crank. Every time I was called mad by the mainstream politicians my position in the polls would shoot up.

As the election date got nearer my seminal emissions increased and my followers took to the street with huge papier mâché phalluses and stars singing my election song, which was written by God and went like this:

Zizo, Zizo, Zizo, Zizo, Zizo Yasuzawa,
Zizo, Zizo, Zizo, Zizo, Zizo Yasuzawa,
He's great, he's God — he knows what's best,
He's the cause of the stars and all the rest!

THE 4TH

Birthday of President Truman (politician)

First aeroplane flown by the Wright brothers

Britain annexes the Tonga islands

First Peace Conference

☽ ☐ ♇
♀ ✳ ♄
☽ ⊼ ⚸

Here is an extract from God's election manifesto. My nurse found it in one of God's carrier bags today:

If we allow unzodiacological energies to increase, it will be extremely difficult to prevent large-scale male impotence and all-out nuclear war. For these and other reasons God has decided the time has come to transform Japan. God's plan is without equal in its scope, and will bring the whole of Japan into line with the ancient science of astrology.

Wouldn't you like to help build a society based on Truth? Wouldn't you like to be better in bed? Wouldn't you like to help the world avoid disaster and build a future of happiness? Let us, people of all star signs, join together and bring about the great plan of God, He-Whose-Figure-Of-Beauty-Is-Tinged-With-The-Hue-Of-Cerulean-Blue-Clouds-And-Whose-Unique-Loveliness-Charms-Millions-Of-Little-Cupids.

The plan to transform Japan into a zodiacological paradise is only the first step towards making the whole world perfect. Your participation in this plan will bring you untold joy and sexual virility.

Night after night my followers danced in the streets with their papier mâché dicks and stars telling people to vote for God. When election day came I went with my followers and cast my vote. God was confident as only the Supreme Being can be. Afterwards, we threw a massive party at the Astrological Institute and awaited the results. Professor Asda released a hundred thousand off-white balloons into the air as the votes were counted. I was so excited I came four times and had to sit down.

Then the results were announced. I had won just .01% of the vote. The stars were thus:

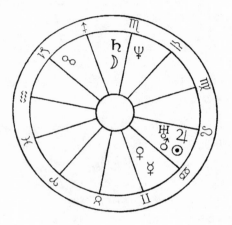

THE 5TH

Start of the Children's Crusade	☉ → ♐ 7:34 am
Typewriters mass-produced	☉ ⁜ ♆
The Japanese island Unsen blows itself to pieces	☽ ⊻ ♀
	☽ ⊻ ♇
	☽ ⊻ ♅

God's defeat came as quite a shock to me, being omniscient. My followers took it badly as well, demanding a recount. This was refused. There was then a sort of small-scale riot which God in no way encouraged. Political analysts blamed my poor results on a sudden bout of sanity in the electorate of Japan. '*Mr Zizo Yasuzawa is entertaining but the vast majority of people cannot take him seriously*,' one commentator said. The real cause of our defeat was, of course, a poor alignment between Saturn and the Sun which we had failed to notice. I did not play with myself for an entire week and gained weight.

Following God's electoral humiliation my followers left in droves, joining all kinds of loony religious movements. Hundreds went over to a Tokyo stockbroker (a Capricorn) who claimed he was the reincarnation of Socrates and had set up a College for Research into Human Happiness which predicted that the end of the world was coming and only a few square feet of Japan, roughly the size of a basketball court, would survive. A lot went into Chinese astrology which is so far off the money it isn't even funny. A few joined the following of a flower arranger and master meditator, who, it turned out, had been dead for years. A lot became Moonies, or went into things like numerology. (God has never understood people's interest in numerology, the whole thing simply does not add up.) Some started to worship a farmer's wife (a Leo) who said she was the Sun Goddess.

The press went for me with a vengeance, kicking God when I was down. They described God as a conman and a wanker. They had a number of established scientists state that no causal relationship had been established between God's ejaculations and the discovery of galaxies. They had a psychologist say on prime-time TV that in his opinion God was an egomaniac and newspapers published a letter by Dr Daisetsu, an Aquarius and noted authority and proponent of Zen Buddhism, which said God was an embarrassment to the country. Four national papers stopped running my predictions.

Aquarius males' lucky number is 9,000,000. They like the colour blue, don't mind paying for sexual favours and have a passionate interest in the uniforms of the Napoleonic wars.

Defiant, God came on the top of Mount Fuji. Deep down, though, God took such criticisms badly. In fact, God became very depressed. My libido went right down and I hardly slept at all. Studying the astrolabe I decided it was time for God to take a holiday. I and an entourage of around three hundred astrologers went off and toured India.

God had another little chat with the Chaplain of the 82nd Airborne Division tonight.

'Why do you Christians have such terribly fucked-up ideas about sex?' God asked.

'What do you mean?' the Chaplain asked.

'For two thousand years your theologians have been debating whether or not Mary's hymen was broken when the Holy Ghost entered her, as if it somehow mattered. Since the first century AD you've tried to hide the fact that Jesus had brothers and sisters, changing the wording of the Bible so they become cousins, all this in order to keep Mary's vagina a cock-free zone. Why? As for the idea that Jesus himself might have actually had sex, that fills you with utter terror. Why is that?'

The Chaplain didn't say anything for a while then read a few passages out of the Holy Bible that were absolutely no help at all and then he left.

THE 6TH

※

Birthday of Wagner (composer)

Roller skates invented

♂ → ♎ 5:10 am
☽ v/c 7.56 pm
♆ → ♒ 8:09 pm

☽ □ ♇
☽ ⊻ ♅
♂ △ ♆
☽ □ ♀
☽ □ ☿
☽ ♂ ♃

During my visit to India I climbed on to the sacred seat where Buddha found enlightenment, pulled out my shalong and stroked it lovingly.

'It's all right,' I told the head priest of the temple who started shouting at me to put it away and get down, 'I'm God and I'm just making a galaxy.'

Later I had an audience with the Dalai Lama during which I drew his attention to my male member. The Dalai Lama was visibly surprised and this was captured wonderfully on film by Professor Asda.

Thinner, tanned, refreshed and feeling my time in India had been well spent, God returned to Japan to find that the police had a warrant for my arrest. It seemed that at least two hundred and twenty Librans had taken their own lives after reading their horoscope predictions for the 14th of Aries 1966 in the newspaper *Yomiuri*.

God had written at the end of the horoscope, published in English: 'Avoid red and if at all possible now is a splendid time to die.' God had meant to write 'diet' but had left off the 't'.

THE 7TH

✶

Famine in Scotland

Portuguese explore Africa

Very first Jane Fonda workout video goes on sale

☽ v/c 5:11 pm
☽ → ♏ 5:42 pm
☽ ⊻ ☄
☽ ⊻ ♂
☽ ⊻ ☉
♀ ⊼ ♄
☽ ☍ ♄
☽ ⊻ ♀
☽ □ ♆

God was arrested outside the airport.

For three days and nights I explained to the police that it had all been a terrible mistake that could have happened to anyone. I hired the very best lawyers in town and on the fifth day I was released on bail but told not to leave the country and to put some clothes on. God had Professor Asda buy me a transparent raincoat.

Those followers who remained were overjoyed at my release; however, hundreds, thousands had renounced astrology after the 14th of Aries 1966 suicides and what they saw mistakenly as my fallibility.

The next day, as rumours spread that the police were coming to take God away for further questioning, a huge truck pulled up outside. The driver insisted I sign, in person can you believe, for the delivery. God did so suspecting the whole thing some sort of police trap. Inside the truck was a Zero fighter in perfect working order.

Here is how God signed for the delivery.

THE 8TH

✳

Building starts on the Taj Mahal

Elizabeth Taylor (actress) has facelift

London dockers go on strike

☽ v/c 3:33 am
☽ → ♒ 3:43 am

☽ △ ♂
☽ ☌ ♆
☽ ✶ ☉
☽ ✶ ♇
☽ ✶ ♀
☽ ☌ ♅

It was Captain Fuchida's plane. He had bequeathed it to God in his will. On the windscreen was a note:

> *Zizo,*
> *This is the plane that led the attack on Pearl Harbor.*
> *This is the plane that started World War II for Japan and*
> *America. My dying wish is that you will renounce your silly*
> *idea about being the creator of the Universe and use this plane*
> *as I have done, spreading the Loving Word of Jesus Christ.*
> *Captain Fuchida.*
>
> *PS Stop playing with yourself and think of your glorious*
> *saviour.*

The next day God was summoned to appear in court. God did not go. When the police came for me my followers fought them in the street with the papier mâché cocks and stars made during my disastrous election campaign. While this was going on God and Professor Asda readied Captain Fuchida's plane for take-off in the backyard.

In the cockpit were hundreds of stupid Christian artefacts, crosses, prayer beads, hymn books and yellow newspaper clippings reporting on Captain Fuchida's outdoor Christian meetings in the midwest of America. God climbed into the cockpit and then Professor Asda thrust his Death Ray into my lap. He said it might come in handy.

'Contact!' God shouted.

The professor climbed down from the side of the cockpit, raced over to the propeller and yanked it with all his strength. It hardly moved.

'Put your back into it!' God ordered.

The professor yanked the propeller again and then promptly keeled over dead. The engine started.

Chased by screaming policemen, I ploughed my way over Asda's lifeless body, through neighbours' gardens, shredding bamboo fences and destroying clothes lines, until I reached a road long enough to allow me to get into the air.

Here is Professor Asda's deathday chart:

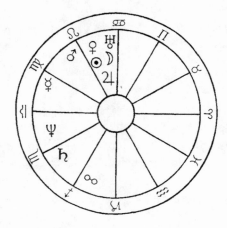

THE 9TH

Birthday of Lawrence of Arabia

First showing of the film *Lives of a Bengal Lancer*

Invention of the cash machine

☽ v/c 8:52 am
☽ → ♌ 9:33 am
☽ □ ♄
☽ ☍ ♆
♀ ⁎ ♂
☽ △ ♇

After flying over Mount Fuji, weeping at my misfortune and taking my own name in vain, God flew to the Philippines. From there God flew to the Marshall Islands and then to Hawaii and finally San Francisco. God had come to America.

While flying over the Pacific Ocean, God read a number of the newspaper clippings about Fuchida in the cockpit. It seemed that on many occasions the people of the Midwest were not exactly overjoyed to listen to the man who had effectively brought them into a war that had cost them over 900,000 casualties. From the clippings it seemed as if poor Fuchida had been given a beating on a number of occasions and was very nearly lynched outside Kansas City.

At customs God declared my balls as the two most powerful objects known to man. For some reason the customs men ignored them and searched my suitcase instead. 'What's that?' said one of them, pointing at the Death Ray which I carried under my arm.

'This is the greatest weapon of mass destruction ever invented,' God said matter of factly.

'You're a pretty funny guy,' one of the customs men told me, then he suggested I put some clothes on. I put on my raincoat and that was that.

In the arrivals lounge were several reporters. Taking off my raincoat God denounced the Japanese Government as Cosmically Unharmonious. A reporter asked me what I thought of America. 'I like the place and I've only been here a few minutes. Americans say they "trust in God" which is nice considering most of them haven't met me.'

God then gave an impromptu speech, calling on America to embrace astrological teachings. And then God spied Dr Hultcravitz's lower lip in the crowd. God had written to her from the Philippines informing her of my plan to come to America. God was like the shipwrecked sailor who, floating on his back, thinks of his sweetheart, ties his handkerchief to his resulting erection for a sail, puts his thumb up his ass with his palm for a rudder and sails safely home to port. Dr Hultcravitz was my port and of course God had flown from Japan rather than sailed but you get the idea. Dr Hultcravitz and God shook hands then talked over coffee in the airport café. She insisted on holding my index finger again. God informed her that I was willing to undergo examination at the Stanford Research Institute.

When we had finished our coffees, I flew Dr Hultcravitz and myself the thirty miles to the Institute. It took longer then it should have done because I was unable to see where I was going due to the position of the model Saturn on my astrolabe and my need to constantly stare at Dr Hultcravitz's wondrous lower lip.

When we had landed in the car park I was introduced to Dr Green, Dr Hultcravitz's assistant. Dr Green had lost $3,000 at a game of dice in 1934 and had become an ardent believer in PK or psychokinesis, the mind's ability to move objects at a distance. As we headed to the main building Dr Green asked me to roll a pair of dice. God refused, quoting Albert Einstein, '*God does not play dice with the Universe.*'

God and my nurse watched *Star Trek* after dinner.

THE 10TH

Plague comes to Europe	4th – 7:29 pm
First mobile phone on sale	☽ ☌ ♅
Napoleon is crowned King of Italy	☽ △ ☿
End of American Civil War	☉ △ ♃
	☽ ⊼ ♃
	☽ □ ☉
	☽ ⊻ ♂

Dr Hultcravitz and Dr Green showed God around the Stanford Research Institute, introducing him to the other subjects under examination. There was a man from Britain who claimed to influence the behaviour of single-celled creatures by merely shouting at them very loudly. Another subject believed he could read the minds of various types of fungi.

There was a retired Hungarian naval officer called Oskar who believed he could heal people with the aid of a bath plug he claimed was from the *Titanic*. Dr Hultcravitz's most celebrated experiment with Oskar had involved mice. The experiment had been inconclusive but everyone had agreed that the mice had been cute.

A Mr Fiddleston claimed he could increase the growth of fingernails by mind power alone, while a Mr Cruickshanks claimed he could hear plants telling him to grow. Another subject swore food he swallowed disappeared from his mouth only to reappear later in his stomach, completely bypassing his throat. Also staying at the Institute were thirteen Catholic nuns from Georgia who were believed to have been blessed by what Dr Hultcravitz termed Invisible Stigmata.

The star subject of the Institute when I arrived was, however, David Brown, nicknamed John Doe by Dr Hultcravitz and her colleagues. John Doe, Dr Hultcravtiz explained excitedly, had, since arriving at the Institute, failed every single test that had been devised for him.

'That's good?' God asked.

'Nothing John Doe has ever done here has been even slightly above average.'

'Ask him to guess at dice and he gets the answer right once every six goes,' added Dr Green.

'But that's normal.'

'*Too* normal,' said Dr Hultcravitz, her lower lip looking fantastic. 'His results are *consistently* average. He never gets lucky or unlucky. He's supernaturally average. Everything about him — his ideas, his sense of humour, his clothes, his haircut, his taste in music, his home, his car, his family, it's all average. Spooky, isn't it.'

'What star sign is he?' I asked.

Even his star sign was average.

When God was introduced to him John Doe smiled and said, 'Hi.'

'Bless you,' God had replied.

THE 11TH

Japanese annihilate Russian fleet in the	☽ v/c 5:59 am
	☽ → ♈ 6:27 am
Tsushima straits	♉ → ♐ 11:03 am
Man balancing on tightrope falls off after 205 days	☿ ⊼ ♄
	☿ ✶ ♆
Birthday of Nat King Cole (singer)	☽ ⊻ ♄
	☽ ✶ ♆
	☽ △ ☿ ☉ □ ♅
	☽ △ ♇ ☽ ✶ ♅
	☽ ⊼ ☉ ☽ ⊼ ♀

After dinner today God worked on *Hairstyles: the Astrological Way*.

After being shown around the Institute God was introduced to a Major Applebee, a Virgo and former astronaut. Major Applebee was a close friend of Dr Hultcravitz (they had met after hailing the same cab to go to the same paranormal conference). Major Applebee was introduced to God as a man with an open mind and one of my biggest fans. He took God to one side and told me that he had been the first man to masturbate in space and that he had loved my book.

THE 12TH

Nobel invents dynamite	☽ v/c 9:58 pm
Birthday of Andy Warhol (artist)	☽ △ ♂
90-year-old couple get divorced	☽ ☍ ☿
	☽ □ ♃
	☽ ⊼ ♀
	☽ ⚹ ♄

The first thing Dr Hultcravitz, Dr Green and Major Applebee did was see if God possessed any other, more common psychic powers. 'You will take this blank pad and pencil and go into the next room,' Dr Hultcravitz had told God. 'I will stay here with a pad and pencil. When you hear me shout "Go" I will write down three digits and at the same time you will write down the first three digits that come into your mind. Is that clear?'

'Yes, God understands,' God said and took my pad and pencil and went next door. A little later God heard Dr Hultcravitz shout 'Go' and without thinking God wrote down 6, 3, 1 on his pad. Dr Hultcravitz had written 8, 12 and 6. After three days of this Dr Hultcravitz decided to try something else.

God was given a spoon and asked to make it bend solely with

the power of my mind. 'This is silly,' I said. 'I am God, I make entire galaxies before breakfast and you ask me to bend a teaspoon? What sort of psychic power is that anyway?'

Dr Hultcravitz and her colleagues shrugged in agreement and took the spoon back to the cafeteria.

After that we began more serious research. First we tried to establish if there were any unusual physical properties to my reproductive organs.

Tissue samples were taken. The atmosphere was relaxed, even playful at times. God's private parts were photographed from every conceivable angle, my blood was analysed, my balls X-rayed. My sperm was sent off to be studied by seven independent labs across the country.

The results of these early tests showed nothing unusual. 'From my initial investigation you have a perfectly normal set of sexual organs,' Dr Hultcravitz told me when the test results came back.

'That is what they all say,' God joked.

'Except for the sperm. They are catatonic, they have no tails. They're just lumps.'

'Globular clusters,' God said.

'Comatose,' Dr Hultcravitz went on. 'They have no movement at all. Your testicles have checked out as normal and there's no indication of infection or trauma. Given the unusual state of your sperm there is a very good chance that you will never be able to conceive children,' Dr Hultcravitz told God.

God had suspected something like this for some time. As a Sex God I slept around in Kyoto with literally hundreds of female astrologers (on their birthdays) and yet not one had ever got pregnant as a result.

'You have lovely lips, Doctor,' God said.

THE 13TH

✳

Plague breaks out in India	☽ → ♉ 1:05 am
Wisconsin becomes US state	☽ □ ♆
Cosmopolitan magazine first published	☿ ✳ ♂
Man climbs Mount Everest	☽ △ ☉
	☽ ⊼ ♇
	♀ ✳ ♃

While our research continued Dr Hultcravitz and God had long meaningful conversations in the grounds of the Institute about the errors of the modern scientific outlook and man's need to be appreciated. While we agreed on just about everything there was disagreement over the question of free will. For her it was crucial that man lived in a non-deterministic world. God, of course, laughed at this idea. For how can man have free will if the glorious Zodiac influences every single human activity? God told Dr Hultcravitz again and again that man had as much free will as an eggplant.

THE 14TH

✳

Invention of brown paper bag	☽ ☍ ♃
Birthday of Cortés (captured Mexico)	☽ ✳ ☉
	☽ ☌ ♂
	☽ ✳ ⚷
	☽ ✳ ♀

In the weeks that followed more elaborate tests on God were conducted. God's balls were wired up to an EEG machine used to monitor brain waves; nothing unusual was detected. God's balls were thinking about as much as your average dead guy. God's balls were examined thoroughly for two hours by an electron microscope which found nothing unusual. Individual sperms were dissected, again nothing unusual was found. God's balls were checked for gamma, alpha and beta radiation emission. There was nothing. Not a squeak. Zip.

God was taken to a Particle Accelerator in Nevada where sub-atomic particles were collided with my scrotum. Dr Hultcravitz was theorizing that God's balls might be made of anti-matter, which would go some way towards accounting for the incredible amounts of energy that God must be expending to create whole galaxies in seconds. Again the tests proved negative.

As the days went by more tests were conducted. God's organ was placed in a vacuum chamber and presently turned blue, which was apparently normal. God's left ball was then heated to 150°C for reasons that were never adequately explained to God. A magnometer was strapped to God's inner thigh to register any sort of magnetic fields; none were detected.

After staying with Dr Hultcravitz for nearly a month, and having God's genitals exposed to every test known to science, she, Dr Green and Major Applebee were forced to conclude that God's balls were, physically at least, unremarkable.

It was clear that they were disappointed; Dr Green threw his dice with less gusto than he had when we had started our research, and Major Applebee was quiet and withdrawn, talking to himself about the problems of going to the bathroom in micro-gravity.

God, however, was not in the least bit downhearted by the lack of findings, arguing, as I always had, that my ability was somehow beyond the physical.

We decided to take a three-month break. During that time God went on a tour of the US publicizing my book, *The Darn Truth*.

It was a gruelling schedule — twenty cities in twenty-five days, and involved what seemed like hundreds of interviews for magazines and television. My interview on the *Today Show* was a complete disaster. Miss Walters, who was supposed to ask me about my book, couldn't stop laughing. This made God uncomfortable. You would be surprised how often God provoked this response in the mortals he meets. She would try to get serious and say something like, 'I'm sorry about that . . . Now in your book you claim —' then she would be laughing again.

Some studios insisted God wear at least a dressing-gown while being interviewed. When God refused, bowls of well-positioned fruit appeared on the coffee table between God and the camera. One studio in Chicago absolutely demanded God wear a pair of boxer shorts during transmission. God found myself distracted and put off by the odd sensation of wearing underwear for the first time in decades. I lost my concentration repeatedly and wriggled all over the sofa.

God was sorely tested in other ways: on at least two occasions God lost my luggage and found out the hard way that it was technically impossible anywhere in the States to hail a cab when one has renounced the custom of wearing clothes.

The Chaplain of the 82nd Airborne Division called around today at six and we continued our discussion on Christian unease about sex.

God asked if it was true that Christians were not supposed to fuck on Sundays, over Christmas or on any saint's day.

'No,' the Chaplain said, 'that used to be the case but it's not any more.'

God laughed and said it was frankly remarkable the whole of Europe had not gone the way of the Corinthian Christians.

'And what about changing position?'

'What about it?'

'Is it still a sin for a Christian couple to change position during sex?'

'I'd have to check,' the Chaplain said.

'And people say *I* have confused and deranged ideas about sex,' God said.

God knows all these things about Christianity from Captain Fuchida's letters back in the sixties begging me to join his stupid Sky Pilots of America International.

THE 15TH

The electronic computer invented	☽ v/c 5:28 am
Royal Navy destroys Chinese fleet	☽ → ♉ 6:12 am
Start of French Madagascan war	☽ ♂ ♄
Birthday of Michelangelo (artist)	☿ □ ♆
	☽ ⊼ ☿
	☽ ⊼ ♇
	☽ □ ♅

After my book tour I was God in Residence at Washington University in Missouri for a week. God spent most of the time there watching Woody Allen movies, God preferring his early work. That was followed by a spell in Las Vegas and then a short stay with Alcoholics Anonymous.

Hollywood, where God travelled next, was just as God expected it would be; a succession of glamorous stars and starlets trekking to God's motel room where they got a horoscope, tea and a sympathetic ear.

One of God's greatest pleasures is to see or hear about people I guided years ago going on to make so much of their lives, such as the former Lieutenant-Governor of Jersey who wrote to me today to tell me he is thinking about taking a Bachelor of Arts degree as part of the Pentonville Prison Education Programme.

When three months had passed, God returned to the Stanford Research Institute and Dr Hultcravitz, Dr Green and Major Applebee turned their attention to the actual process of galaxy making. God's balls and penis were covered in temperature sensors, electroncephalographs, EEG wires and galvanic skin detectors. It was impossible to see what was underneath it all and it proved impossible for God to become aroused until well over half of the stuff had been removed.

God masturbated four times a day under rigorous scientific conditions while Dr Hultcravitz and her colleagues looked frantically for the energy source that somehow spawned worlds.

The weeks at the Institute went by and the number of followers outside grew. Some days God was provided with pornographic magazines, other times God was instructed by Dr Hultcravitz to watch videos. Occasionally God was given nothing but a tissue. During this time God's feelings for Dr Hultcravitz and her lip grew. It was perhaps an unusual setting for two people to fall in love but this Universe of mine is a wonderful place and fall in love was what Dr Hultcravitz and God did.

It is important to point out that a strong motivation, even love, is not necessarily incompatible with a strictly scientific approach to the subject matter of any inquiry. Some of the greatest scientists have been emotionally involved in their work to a very high degree, Pavlov and his dog, for example, and probably all are to some extent, whether they recognize the fact or not.

After dinner God and my nurse watched tonight's episode of *Star Trek* which was about a world that did not have small talk.

THE 16TH

Birthday of Lord Byron (poet)

Birthday of James Dean (actor)

Safety razor blades invented

☽ v/c 4:29 am
☽ → ♊ 5:11 am

☽ ⊻ ♄
☽ △ ♆
☽ ☍ ☿
☽ ☍ ♇
☽ △ ♅

It has to be said that Dr Hultcravitz and her team met with absolutely no success at all and after nine months Dr Hultcravitz, Dr Green and Major Applebee abandoned any hope of demonstrating what Dr Hultcravitz had termed ESP (Extraordinary Spermal Propagation).

The atmosphere at the Institute became depressed and God found it hard on occasions to get an erection, something that had never happened to me before in my entire life, ever.

When rumours of our singular lack of progress came out we became the laughing stock of the scientific community.

THE 17TH

Invention of stainless-steel cutlery	☽ ✳ ♂
China grants Russia the right to operate a	☽ △ ♇
railway in North Manchuria	☽ ☍ ♅
First skycraper built	☽ △ ☉

Dr Hultcravitz, despite our lack of success, announced our preliminary findings at a press conference during which Dr Green rolled four sixes in a row, the odds for which were twenty-four to one against. Dr Hultcravitz told reporters that while she had so far failed to isolate the physical process by which God generated galaxies she had no doubt that God's powers were genuine.

A paper was published in the magazine *Nature* under the title *Seminal Ejaculations and Galactic Formations*. It was only the second parapsychological research paper to appear in a major scientific publication, the first being on Uri Geller, a Capricorn; whom God has always suspected is a fake.

Capricorn males are patronizing, slimy, greedy, they have absolutely no sense of rhythm and suffer from a profound lack of imagination.

Nature had accepted the paper for publication only after a panel of esteemed scientists had concluded that it was of serious scientific merit.

Reports that arose later that the scientists on the panel had taken the paper to be an April Fool's joke and had played along were, of course, entirely false.

THE 18TH

✳

Birthday of Allen Ginsberg (poet)

Inca civilization wiped out

Implementation of apartheid in South Africa

☽ v/c 3:06 pm
☽ → ♍ 5:38 pm
☽ □ ♀
☽ □ ♅
☽ △ ♄
☽ ⊼ ♆

While *Seminal Ejaculations and Galactic Formations* had failed to impress the scientific world, it created a tremendous stir in the media. The paper was seized upon by the science editor of the *New York Times* who gave it a favourable review and before long many of the popular magazines carried articles on my testicles. ESP soon became a household word, and a number of TV documentaries appeared on Hermes Trismegistus, the Thrice Great One, founder of astrology, and God was asked to write predictions for just about every paper in the country. God's following began to surpass what it had been even in my heyday in Japan.

THE 19TH

✳

Israel invades Lebanon

Velcro invented

US Marines land in Cuba

☽ v/c 2:22 pm
☽ ⊼ ♂
☽ ⊼ ☿
☽ ✳ ♃
☽ △ ♀
☽ ⊻ ♄

After the publication of *Seminal Ejaculations and Galactic Formations* hundreds of thousands of people sought an audience with God at the Stanford Research Institute; housewives, film stars, politicians, all wanting to know if it was astrologically OK to neuter their cat, move house, murder their business partner, wear shorts, and a million and one other things.

There was a downside, however, to all of God's popularity, for it brought God to the attention of the Committee for the Scientific Investigation into Claims of the Paranormal, and this would have far-reaching consequences for God's sex life and the Universe in general.

THE 20TH

P. Kapitza publishes paper on the state of	☽ v/c 7:42 pm
helium at –456°F	☽ ☍ ♂
Deathday of Buddha (Buddhist)	☽ □ ♀
Deathday of Benny Hill (comedian)	☽ ⊻ ♃
	☽ ♂ ♄
	☽ ⊼ ⚷

While the Committee for the Scientific Investigation into Claims of the Paranormal began their hate campaign against God and astrology, rumours spread that the US Government was planning to take legal possession of God's balls and slap a patent on them. When this rumour hit the headlines there was an international outcry, but no application for patent was ever made, no secret agents accosted God in dark alleyways or anything like that.

There was also a half-baked idea to use my balls to send messages to Advanced Extraterrestrial Life. Some officials from Nasa's jet propulsion laboratory came to see me about it. The idea was to use my remarkable ability to send messages in Morse code. A galaxy would be a dot, an empty bit of space a dash.

Nasa was working on the content of the first message when the House Appropriations Committee reduced the proposed expenditure for the project and the Senate, realizing success was thus jeopardized, deleted the item entirely from its agenda.

THE 21ST

Suntan lotion invented	☽ v/c 2:09 pm
	☽ → ♌ 6:56 pm
Famine in China	☽ △ ♃
Birthday of Charles Dickens (author)	☽ ⊼ ♀
Synthesis of Sulpapyridine	☽ △ ♪
	☽ □ ♄
	☽ ☌ ♆
	☽ △ ☿

There were, as might have been expected, a lot of copycats, young men who claimed their seminal emissions were causing airplanes to crash, or influencing the weather, or affecting which ads came next on their televisions, or the President's dress sense. Paraspermologists diligently studied these individuals who were all, of course, nothing but nutcases.

THE 22ND

Detergent invented	☿ D 1:24 am
	☽ v/c 11:31 am
Birthday of Placido Domingo (opera singer)	☽ → ♎ 11:44 am
	♀ → ♑ 1:33 pm
World somersault record set	☽ ⚹ ♪
	☽ ⊼ ♄
	☽ □ ♀
	☽ △ ♆
	☉ □ ♃
	☽ ⚹ ☿
	♀ ⊻ ♆

In 1967 Dr Hultcravitz published another paper, *Spermatic
Galactic Genesis and the Inverse Square Law*, in which she argued
that the evidence so far accumulated on Japs Eye Fontanelle
could best be explained by assuming that ESP obeys an inverse
²⁄₁₆th law. She showed this was the case using complicated
statistical analysis. God didn't understand any of it but loved
her for it all the same.

God and my nurse watch *Star Trek* after dinner.

THE 23RD

Rubber band invented	1st – 5:42 pm
	☽ v/c 5:50 pm
Deathday of Jules Verne (novelist)	☽ → ♑ 11:55 pm
Brittany acquired by France	☽ □ ♃
	♀ ⊻ ♇
	☽ ♂ ☉
	☽ △ ♄
	☉ △ ♄
	☽ ⊻ ♅

A third paper followed shortly after called *Paraspermology and
the New Scientific Revolution* in which Dr Hultcravitz suggested
it would be sensible to stop thinking in terms of cause (God's
climax) and effect (galaxy) and merely regard the two events as
psychically linked occurrences in a fifth-dimensional superstring
space-time continuum.

THE 24TH

✳

Deathday of Michael III of Serbia

The game Scrabble goes on sale for the

   first time

Birthday of James Joyce (novelist)

☽ → ♏ 12:17 am
☽ □ ♆
☽ ⊻ ☿
☽ ✳ ♀
☽ ⊻ ♇
☽ ⊻ ♂
☽ □ ♅

In 1968, the first chair in paraspermology was established, not in America where so much of the groundwork was being carried out, but in Holland, at the University of Utrecht. Its first occupant was Dr W. C. Tenhaeff who had seen God come, under laboratory conditions, innumerable times during trips to the US.

THE 25TH

✳

Frisbee invented

End of Civil War in Afghanistan

Birthday of Humphrey Bogart (actor)

☽ v/c 10:56 am
☽ → ♓ 4:45 pm
☽ ✳ ♄
☽ □ ♅
☿ ✳ ♅
☽ ⊻ ♆
☽ ✳ ☉

In 1975, the Paraspermology Association was formed to meet the needs of the growing army of professional research workers all over the world who were obsessed with my reproductive organs and the wonderful things they did.

THE 26TH

Cultural Revolution begins in China	☽ v/c 4:33 pm
Yo-yo world record set	☽ △ ♃
Birthday of O.J. Simpson (actor)	♂ △ ♅

God has been working today on *Mercury; The Planet of Electrical Beauty Gadgets*.

In the paper *Seminal Ejaculations and Galactic Formations* Dr Hulcravitz stated that she had evidence that the sort of galaxy God created was in some way dependent on the sort of woman God was thinking about at the time of climax. Girls with black hair produced typical spiral galaxies. Brunettes produced what are known as 'peculiar' galaxies. Redheads elliptical galaxies, while blondes produced what are termed 'barred spirals'. It was also hypothesized in *Seminal Ejaculations* that irregular galaxies were formed when God lost his line of thought and proto-galaxies were the product of premature ejaculations.

A few reporters noted that Dr Hultcravitz had black hair and that way over half of the galaxies God had made while staying at the Institute were spiral.

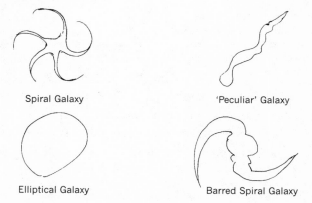

Spiral Galaxy   'Peculiar' Galaxy

Elliptical Galaxy   Barred Spiral Galaxy

THE 27TH

Pope reaffirms opposition to contraception	☿ ♂ ♇
Birthday of Josef Goebbels (politician)	☽ ✳ ♇
Arkansas becomes US state	☽ ✳ ☿
	☽ ♂ ♅
	♀ □ ♂
	☽ △ ♂ ☽ ⅴ ♀
	☉ ⅴ ♆ ☽ ⅴ ♃

Following *Seminal Ejaculations and Galactic Formations*, Dr Hultcravitz suggested she try taking Kirlian photographs of God while I masturbated. The technique, named after the Soviet scientist (Sagittarius) who had invented it, involved pressing the object to be photographed against a photographic plate. An electrical current was then sent through the plate and the film was developed in the normal manner.

Using this technique, Dr Hultcravitz hoped to capture some 'emanations' travelling from God's penis at climax out into space.

※ ✳ ※

Sagittarian men get turned on by a shared shower and like to make out in the back of cars. They do not like fried foods, Tuesdays or rhetorical questions.

※ ✳ ※

God agreed readily to the idea of capturing on film what had proven so elusive to every other test of modern science and eagerly entered the darkroom with Dr Hultcravitz.

It took Dr Hultcravitz nearly an hour to assure God, once she had shown him the procedure, that neither God nor my balls would be electrocuted in the process. After this was cleared up there began a long series of trials all of which were failures.

The months passed and still we failed to capture the elusive 'spurt of energy'. Then one afternoon we developed photograph number 10,432.

We had found the first hard scientific evidence that God was indeed the creator of the Universe. We had also, corny as it may sound, found love. In the darkroom, as God, day after day, sighed and panted, we had grown ever closer. When we showed Major Applebee and Dr Green negative number 10,432, Dr Hultcravitz and God were holding hands.

GALAXY SEEN COMING OUT OF GOD'S PENIS! read the headline of the *New York Times*.

THE 28TH

H. Winctler leads archaeological expedition to	☽ → ♐
North Cappadocia	☽ ⚺ ☉
A. Kumar sets world record for balancing on	☽ ⚻ ♄
	☽ ☌ ♅
one foot	☽ ⚹ ♆
Start of civil war in Afghanistan	☽ ☌ ☿
Discovery of the neutron	

The Kirlian photograph appeared all over the world and did more for astrology than even *Seminal Ejaculations and Galactic Formations* had. My followers took it as proof absolute of my claims. Sadly though the scientific community did not, Kirlian photography being dismissed by them as a mere pseudo-scientific technique. The spokesman for the Committee for the Scientific Investigation into Claims of the Paranormal insisted that the so-called galaxy on the photograph was in fact just a bit of dust.

We did not get embroiled in the arguments over the Kirlian photograph. Instead Dr Hultcravitz, Dr Green, Major Applebee and God travelled to another particle accelerator in Nevada to carry out more tests.

At midnight on the 13th of Leo we spent the night outside the accelerator. Dr Green and the Major were asleep, Dr Hultcravitz and God were lying next to each other under Indian blankets looking up at the sky. When Venus was properly aligned with Jupiter God turned to Dr Hultcravitz and whispered very quietly: 'Would you like to help me make a million suns?'

We embraced. We rolled around in the desert, the planets and constellations of my astrolabe banging into one another. 'What about scientific impartiality?' Dr Hultcravitz said, breathing heavily.

'It's shot to hell already and we both know it,' God gasped.

God told her to lie back and think of the Universe and we made love under this wonderful face of the Zodiac:

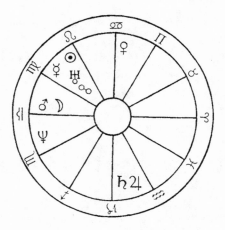

Dr Frida Erra Correlia Hultcravitz reminded me that night of why God had brought the Universe into existence in the first place.

'How was it for you, Doctor?' God asked, my quivering body covered in sweat. 'It was nice,' she said, lying next to God Almighty, holding my hand.

Now you need to understand that no woman had ever said sex with God was nice. My lovers in Japan, both before and after God came out as God, had used terms like divine, sublime, awesome, never merely nice.

'A galaxy has materialized on the edge of the Universe as a result of what we just did and all you can say is that it was nice?'

'Japs Eye, I'm sorry but . . . I'm a scientist. I have to report things as I see them.'

God forgave her and we hugged.

Miss Hughes and God Almighty watched *Star Trek* after dinner.

THE 29TH

The Berlin Wall comes down	☽ v/c 3:18 am
	☽ → ♒ 9:17 am
Automatic railway coupling invented	☉ → ♑ 8:56 pm
Linoleum invented	☽ ☐ ♄
	☽ ✳ ♇
Deathday of Col. Custer (politician)	☽ ⊻ ☉
Dunlop invents pneumatic tyre	☽ ♂ ♆

Six weeks later Dr Frida Erra Correlia Hultcravitz and God were married in a San Francisco registry office. The main reason was, of course, our deep love for each other, but another was the threatening letters I had started receiving from Immigration. John Doe was our witness.

The stars were so:

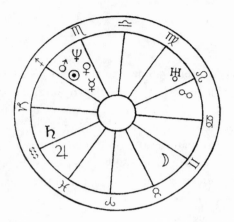

SEX GOD MARRIES PARASPERMOLOGIST read the headline of the *San Francisco Herald*.

After the legal ceremony we held an astrological wedding in a nearby park. Astrologers posed as the various heavenly bodies and danced around us. My wife, decked out in garlands and ornaments, held in front of her a giant cardboard cut-out of her birth chart. There were holes for her eyes so she could see where she was going. God held a similar cardboard copy of my own remarkable horoscope.

Together we stood on an eight-petalled lotus flower and studied each other's birth charts.

Afterwards, God used the Love-Hate Chart in chapter four of *Star Sign Secrets* to establish our relationship score. It was 1, the best possible, almost too easy according to the great sage. Then thirty-two astrologers with trumpets played heavenly music. Our birth charts touched. We jumped up and down, a symbolic attempt to get closer to the stars, and we were married.

We were married under the full gaze of the Zodiac and the approval of the entire cosmos, not counting God's first wife.

After we were married the 15,000 astrologers and other guests in the park clapped and threw confetti over us in the shape of the signs of the Zodiac.

We then went off in Captain Fuchida's Zero and consummated our marriage on the island of Hawaii. Experts agreed that the group of galaxies known as M123 were the tangible result of our wedding night.

On our return to California God brought my wife the painting by Man Ray called *Observatory Time – The Lovers* from the William N. Copley collection for a great deal of his followers' money.

It was a picture of a pair of bright-red women's lips hovering in a grey sky. God gave it to his wife and told her that he loved her and that her lower lip was even more beautiful than the one in the painting, and it really was true.

Soon after that we toured the country together. My wife gave lectures on my power and her attempts to understand it before God appeared, sparkler alight.

For nearly twenty years my wife and God were on the road, or rather in the air, criss-crossing America in Captain Fuchida's Zero fighter, to which we attached a banner that fluttered behind us and looked like this:

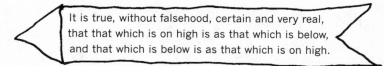

It is true, without falsehood, certain and very real, that that which is on high is as that which is below, and that which is below is as that which is on high.

Everywhere we went we spread the good news of astrology, the ancient science and my remarkable power. It was, if God is honest, one of the best periods of my life.

CANCER

Fort Knox, the 1st

J. Dewar elucidates the composition of air	☽ → ♊ 2:22 am
US declares war on Britain	☽ ☍ ♉
Birthday of Leon Trotsky (politician)	☽ △ ♆
Deathday of Noël Coward (playwright)	☽ ⊼ ☉
	☽ ☍ ♇
	☉ ⊻ ♇

Astrologically, the end of 1970 was just perfect for God to make a world tour. My wife encouraged the idea but felt she ought to stay in the States to work on yet another scientific paper concerning God's balls and the creation of the cosmos. And so God set off on my world tour alone in my Zero fighter, Professor Asda's Death Ray where my beautiful and brilliant second wife would have been.

The next time God would return to America I would be a prisoner of the United Nations and due to stand trial for the killing of Time.

It's funny how life turns out, even if I do say so myself.

THE 2ND

Krakatoa, volcanic island near Java, blows itself up   ☽ ☐ ☉

Birthday of Nostradamus   ☽ △ ♇

Invention of the personal stereo   ☽ ✳ ♅

       ☽ △ ☿

At breakfast today God announced his idea for a new book. It will be called *Planning a Dinner Party with the Help of Astrology*. Only Mr Spillsbury seemed at all interested. He had come by to tell God that the Cobras/Samba/Fontanelle is going to be launched 'really soon'.

'How soon is that?' God demanded. When Mr Spillsbury confessed that he didn't know God had something of a fit.

God phoned my wife every day as I flew from country to country on my world tour. Everywhere God performed I received standing ovations.

While in northern Dahomey, Africa, the Somba tribe presented God with a penis-sheath made from a long thin gourd which, when tied around one's waist, gave the impression of a constant erection. God has worn my penis-sheath often, even since my castration. God's nurse has to put it on for me now, and extra bits of gourd have had to be added as God has put on more and more weight.

In Paris, God did it from the top of the Eiffel Tower.

Everywhere God went I was a runaway success. When God took off from Paris, thousands came to wave me goodbye. God was due to land at Heathrow; the Supreme Being was planning to spend a few days at Oxford University's newly set-up Religious Experience Research unit. God was also hoping to meet the legendary Humphry Barnard, author of *Star Sign Secrets*. God never made it.

THE 3RD

✳

28,000 villages in India are washed away	☽ ☐ ♇
in monsoons	☽ ⋎ ♅
The silicon chip invented	☽ ☐ ☿
West Virginia becomes US state	☽ ⊼ ♂
Italy declares war on Austria	☽ ✳ ♀

Halfway over the English Channel God experienced engine trouble; black smoke started to seep out of the Zero's air vents. Quickly God cast a horoscope then swung westward and in a few minutes made out an island in front of me that looked remarkably like the Hawaiian island that had a naval base on it called Pearl Harbor. The island was Jersey.

THE 4TH

✳

Electric battery invented	☽ v/c 6:11 pm
Kodak develops 16mm colour film	☽ ⊼ ♃
First photograph of a comet taken	☽ ✳ ☉
	☽ ☍ ♄
Queen Victoria's Golden Jubilee	☽ ⋎ ⚷

There is only one airport on the island of Jersey. As God made my way towards it at 5,000 feet the engine died altogether. God's left wheel hit the ground first, the plane banked, then the right wheel made contact with the ground. Sirens blared and the stars were composed thus:

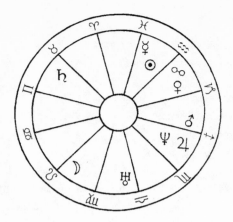

Seconds later ambulances and fire engines were all around God. A team of paramedics helped me from the plane and asked if God was all right.

'Of course,' God said, looking around approvingly, 'I'm God.'

God then fainted and was taken to Jersey General Hospital in St Helier, the main town on the island.

The next day God awoke to find reporters at my bedside.

'Why have you come to Jersey, Mr Fontanelle?' one reporter asked.

'The same reason God does anything; it is in the stars.'

'How long will you be staying?'

'That, as always, young man, depends on Mercury.'

God discharged myself from the hospital that evening, squeezing through a sizeable crowd of people that had gathered outside to see me, jumping up and down en masse in an attempt to gaze into the hole in the top of my head, and booked myself into the most expensive hotel on the island, Longueville Manor.

God's phone rang incessantly. The people of Jersey wanted astrological guidance on every aspect of their lives. God decided to stay on the island for a few days, ordering engine parts for the Zero from a company based near Hiroshima, but telling them that there was no rush.

Then God had 50,000 flyers printed. They looked like this:

Famous Japanese/Egyptian
Astrologer/God
has come to Island!

Japs Eye Fontanelle
MASTER OF THE ZODIAC

The Universe Cares!
Witness a Miracle!

All Welcome
8 pm St Helier sports field tonight
100% Satisfaction Guaranteed
Things will be good for you

The turnout that night was fantastic. God had to fight my way to the spot. As God built up to the climax the model planets hanging from his astrolabe collided with each other and wooshed around in beautiful wide arches.

When God had done the crowd went wild. They arched their heads back into the night sky and clapped for what seemed like hours.

The next night God did my thing in the Parade Gardens to an even larger audience and received a standing ovation.

God phoned my second wife and told her of my runaway success on the little island. 'They really love me here,' God said.

As soon as God put the phone down there was a knock on my door. God opened it. 'With Venus due any minute to go retrograde it is inadvisable to discuss matters astrological until tomorrow morning,' God said solemnly. The two policemen seemed to agree and arrested God for indecent exposure.

* * *

Venus went retrograde.

THE 5TH

Birthday of Sophia Loren (actress)

ECC governments vote against economic

    sanctions against Poland and USSR

Invention of the automatic door

Israel rejects peace plan

Invention of the long-playing record

☽ ⊻ ♀
☽ ☌ ♇
☽ ⁎ ♅
☽ ⁎ ♂

While waiting for my case to come to court, God was held in a clifftop prison on the north side of the island where the views of the celestial canopy were simply magnificent. God masturbated and waited. God masturbated and hired the best lawyer on the island who was born under the sign of Libra. Then God masturbated and wrote voluminous letters to my second wife, and two treatises, one on astrological accounting and the other on the effects of the Zodiac on horticulture.

News of my arrest was announced to the world and God received hundreds of letters of support from astrologers all over the place.

Great crowds of people gathered outside the prison, picnicking and shouting out questions to God behind bars and thanks to the bribing of a number of guards God was still able to send my horoscopes every week to various papers around the world.

God's incarceration came to an abrupt end when, with Venus and Jupiter in stations of power, guards came into my cell one morning, put a hood over God's head and bundled me outside. God was put in a car and driven for about half an hour. God was then pushed out of the car and taken up some stone steps, through a series of echoing halls or corridors until the hood was removed and God was swaying slightly in the private study of the Lieutenant-Governor of Jersey who was standing by the window wearing a blue seventeenth-century hooped skirt, a headdress and was holding a fan.

The hood had been removed with such force that Jupiter and Saturn were pulled from their position around God's head and fell to the floor, bouncing twice as they did so. Cursing, God bent down to pick the two planets up, one the size of an orange, the other the size of a walnut. Or rather God tried to bend down, it being, like so much else due to my ever increasing size, an anatomical impossibility for me. God huffed and puffed. God's face became quite red. 'They were made by the greatest scientific minds in Japan,' God said by way of explanation.

The Lieutenant-Governor fanned himself.

'You are a Virgo,' God said. 'A Taurus?'

'Sorry,' said the Lieutenant-Governor, shaking his head.

'Zodiac Man only kids, he always knows a person's sign.'

'You are wondering why it is that I am dressed in this manner, Mr Fontanelle, are you not? Most people do.'

'God was slightly curious, yes.'

'It's perfectly obvious really,' said the Lieutenant-Governor, staring out of the window, his fan behind his back. 'I represent the Monarch on this Island, the Queen, a woman. I simply feel it is my duty, my obligation to do so as faithfully as is humanly possible without recourse to surgery.'

'Sure,' God said, attempting to retrieve Saturn and Jupiter, perhaps the two most important planets of them all, by squatting down. This proved impossible and on trying to straighten up again God fell on to my sizeable behind.

Still looking out the window the Lieutenant-Governor said,

'May I ask you a question, Mr Fontanelle?'

'Of course,' said God, on my behind, still searching with my hands for the two lost planets.

'Do you really in all honesty think you made the Universe and all that's in it? Do you really, really, really, think you're God Almighty?'

God laughed. 'I have no choice,' God informed the Lieutenant-Governor, groping around frantically, smiling up at him from the floor. 'The evidence is overwhelming, the facts speak for themselves. I survived the war –'

'Others did that as well.'

'True, but how many headbutted a golden phallus in a paddy-field outside the city of Nagoya? There is no possible alternative explanation: my spunk are stars and I'm God.'

'I suppose,' said the Lieutenant-Governor, 'you could be right, though I always imagined God would be, well, taller, frankly, and in better shape.'

The Lieutenant-Governor then turned from the window and walked briskly up to God, picking up his skirt in order to do so.

'Mr Fontanelle, I want you to know that this meeting has been arranged by my adoring wife. She is one of your biggest fans on this island, she reads your horoscopes all the time. We copulate only when your horoscopes advise it, in fact.'

'It is the sensible thing to do,' God said, having located Jupiter.

'She talks of little else apart from astrology. At dinners and functions we attend all you can hear her saying is "And what star sign are you?" She puts great stock in the whole thing, which is why you are here. Mr Fontanelle, I have, for reasons that escape me, agreed to my wife's request for you to cast my horoscope. If it impresses me sufficiently I will have all charges against you dropped and you will be free to leave Jersey. If, however, you turn out to be a charlatan, as part of me suspects you are, then it's back to prison with you. How does that grab you?'

'Fine,' said God, Saturn now also safely in my hand, confident of my success as only a true God could be. 'Just get someone to stand me up.'

After dinner God and my nurse watched *Star Trek*.

THE 6TH

British ship hit by Exocet missile near Falklands	☽ v/c 6:23 am
	☽ → ♈ 10:04 pm
Japan defeats Russian Navy at Tsushima	☽ ☌ ♃
Evacuation of Gallipoli completed	☽ ⚹ ♄
National Gallery opened in London	☽ △ ♅
	☽ ⚹ ♆

The predicament God faced with the Lieutenant-Governor of Jersey was not unlike that the astrologer Thrasyllus had been in with the Roman Emperor Tiberius. It was not identical for various reasons; for one thing Thrasyllus did not, as far as we know, have a weight problem as bad as God's.

Emperor Tiberius had been going around demanding every astrologer in the land cast their own horoscope for him to inspect. Being an amateur astronomer himself, Emperor Tiberius would decide if the astrologers' predictions for themselves were up to scratch. If they weren't the astrologer would be put to death. When he was brought before the Emperor, Thrasyllus, cool as a cucumber, drew up his own chart, oohed and aahed then declared that he was presently in a great deal of danger. The Emperor made Thrasyllus his personal astrologer.

Vertical again, God was given some paper and a pen and told to sit at the Governor's desk.

'These things are not necessary. I, Japs Eye Fontanelle, am so in tune with the cosmos, with the Holy Zodiac, that it is possible for me to find out all there is to know about you standing here. I merely require some glue with which I may fix mighty Jupiter and sublime Saturn to their rightful places about my head.'

Some glue was duly sent for and without too much bother the planets were back where they belonged. After waiting for the glue to dry, God said I was ready to begin.

'Just remember, Mr Fontanelle,' said the Lieutenant-Governor, pulling up his skirt and climbing on to an exercise bike in the corner of the room, 'I'm very sceptical.'

I grabbed my crutch with my right hand and my astrolabe in my left.

'When born please?'

'February the 4th 1935.'

God fiddled with the astrolabe.

'Where?'

'Middlesex Hospital, London.'

'Postcode?'

'I couldn't tell you.'

God fiddled again with the astrolabe.

Then God did some fine tuning. Then God oohed and aahed and then said finally, 'You are very sceptical.'

THE 7TH

✳

Invention of the radio	☿ ☌ ♀
Napoleon invades Russia	☽ △ ♎
Jesuit monks expelled from Germany	☽ ⊻ ♄
	☽ ✳ ♆
	☽ ☍ ♂

God went on to tell the Lieutenant-Governor that he was intelligent, open-minded and deeply spiritual, a born leader, sharing his star sign with Ronald Reagan, Franklin D. Roosevelt and even Abraham Lincoln.

God went into tremendous detail. It was perhaps the most in-depth reading of a horoscope God had ever carried out with the exception of my own, of course. By the time God had finished the Lieutenant-Governor had pedalled thirteen miles, the sun was nearly coming up and the birds were singing in the trees outside Government House.

God told the Lieutenant-Governor that his nativity was remarkably akin to that of Winston Churchill and that he was destined to do great things, as indeed he was. Saturn dropped off God's astrolabe at this point. Instead of God floundering around trying to find it as before, the Lieutenant-Governor picked it up himself and glued it back in place.

The Lieutenant-Governor's wife came in at this point and grovelled around on the floor in front of me, tears of joy in her eyes. She had been listening at the door the entire night. 'Isn't he marvellous?' she said to her husband. Who, in reply, dragging his wife back out of the room, said, 'He's very fat and quite short but totally on the money. Now leave us, my dear, while I find out more,' and he slammed the door shut behind his applauding wife.

We could hear her shouting 'bravo', saying 'quite so' and clapping in the hallway.

All other business was cancelled for the day as the Lieutenant-Governor and God engrossed ourselves in the ancient science of astrology. God explained to the Lieutenant-Governor the great and very true concept of Cosmic Sympathy, of how the stars influence all manner of things. I lectured him on the magical relationship between the Microcosm and the Macrocosm, which explained how my balls could influence the size and shape of the Universe. I told him in great detail about my own horoscope and its meaning for the modern world. I quoted Hermes Trismegistus, allowed him a brief examination of my genitals and drew up nativities for his wife and cat.

We had lunch when God suggested it was the right time to do so and afterwards walked together in the grounds outside Government House. It was there that God explained to the Lieutenant-Governor how helpful astrology could be to the running of an island such as Jersey.

God showed the Lieutenant-Governor a copy of God's old political manifesto. He asked if he could keep it.

'Sure. Now God is a little pooped, Your Majesty.'

The Lieutenant-Governor was fanning himself furiously thinking hard. 'What? Yes, of course.'

'Am I to be escorted back to my cell?'

'What? I gave you my word, Mr Fontanelle. You are a free man, or God rather.'

'The Universe thanks you.'

'Does it really?'

'Profusely.'

God left the Lieutenant-Governor in the garden, mulling over what I had said. I moved in again to Longueville Manor.

God got a call a few hours later from the Lieutenant-Governor asking me what he ought to have for dinner. God suggested broccoli.

'You know,' said God's nurse after I had lectured her on some aspect or other of astrology, 'whenever you mention astrology, whenever you go on and on about Cosmic Sympathy, about the magical correspondence between things, do you know what it sounds like? It sounds like, well, like really bad poetry.'

God did not dignify this with a response.

THE 8TH

Birthday of Marilyn Monroe (actress)	☽ v/c 5:49 am
	☽ → ♐ 6:13 am
North Carolina introduces prohibition of alcohol	☽ ⊼ ♄
	☽ ⚹ ♆
Baby born weighing just 280 grams	☽ ☌ ♀
	☽ ☌ ♇

Word of my release was welcomed across the globe. Grown astrologers wept openly with joy. To celebrate my release, God organized another public masturbation in the Main Hall of the Fort Regents Leisure Centre.

The Lieutenant-Governor and his wife greeted God when I arrived outside the Leisure Centre. The two of them were wearing identical evening dresses and sat in the front row when God came on stage a little later while talking about the Oneness of the Universe.

Afterwards, God's two most devout identically dressed followers told me they had never seen anything like it in all their days. I grunted and came very close to dozing off, as God is prone to do at such times.

God said God would go back to Government House for one drink and a little chat before heading to the airport and my Zero fighter, to continue the last leg of my world tour.

God ended up staying years on Jersey and becoming King.

Whaddyaknow.

After lunch today, God had another discussion with the Chaplain. The topic of conversation was oral sex and how traditionally it had been seen by Christian leaders as on a par with premeditated murder.

God, not for the first time, asked the Chaplain of the 82nd Airborne Division to explain to him Christians' fucked-up attitude towards sex.

When the Chaplain said nothing, God told him that God had a pet theory of my own that explained why Christianity was so screwed up when it came to sex.

The Chaplain did not want to hear God's pet theory and left.

THE 9TH

Deathday of Claude Lévi-Strauss (anthropologist)	♀ △ ♃
First heart transplant	☽ △ ☉
Mussolini founds Fascist Party	☽ △ ♃
	☽ △ ♀
	☽ ✳ ♂
	♉ ✳ ♅
	☽ △ ♵

The Lieutenant-Governor of Jersey and his wife quickly became two of the most devoted followers God ever had. They sought my guidance and approval for everything they did, bless them.

God accompanied the Lieutenant-Governor and his

identically dressed wife everywhere, dined with them often, told them the story of my remarkable life several times and gave them private performances of my ability to create entire galaxies, after which the Lieutenant-Governor would exclaim 'Extraordinary!' and his wife would shout 'Bravo!'

The Lieutenant-Governor and God discussed matters astrological every day and little by little we began applying astrological principles to the running of Jersey. The very first thing we did was change the opening hours of the libraries on the island to coincide with the movements of Mercury, the planet associated with knowledge. At first the reason all libraries were opened only once every eighty-eight days (the time it takes little Mercury to orbit the Sun) was not explained to the public in terms of astrology but as part of necessary cutbacks.

Next we had the street lights turned off so that the majestic stars could be seen more clearly and their influence become more pronounced. The crime rate rose as a result and driving at night became slightly more dangerous, but seeing as the speed limit was a mere 35km per hour God argued no one would get too seriously hurt.

THE 10TH

Ayatollah Khomeini (politician) returns to Iran	☽ ⊻ ⚷
from exile in Paris	☽ □ ♂
	☽ △ ♄
Power handed over to army in Chad	☽ ⊻ ☉
General election in Britain	☽ ⊻ ♆

God then insisted the Lieutenant-Governor instigate a wide-ranging shake-up of all government departments. It was imperative, God told him, for the island to have each office astrologically harmonious. People with signs that didn't interact well should not have to work together (for example Virgo and Aquarius, Capricorn and Sagittarius). This would improve productivity tenfold. The changes were carried out and some hundred or so government employees were moved to new posts without any explanation. God and the Lieutenant-Governor became more and more confident, egged on by these early successes, and more open about the role astrology was playing in our reforms.

We faced our first serious opposition when we tried to reorganize rubbish collection along zodiacal principles. Pisceans and Sagittarians had their rubbish collected on Thursday, astrologically their best day, Aquarians and Capricorns on Saturday, Scorpios on Tuesday and so on. The refuse collectors made a song and dance about the new system, saying it was silly having to go down the same street collecting different people's rubbish just because of their birthdays. They threatened to strike. God told the Governor that their unrest was because of Mars. In fact, the day the refuse collectors were due to hold their ballot over strike action was astrologically identical to that of the battle of Crecy in 1346. God told the Lieutenant-Governor that he had to act resolutely. He marched into the workers' meeting just as the ballot was being taken, walked up to the podium and gave a speech God had written for him challenging in the strongest language possible the belief that collecting people's rubbish according to their star signs was silly. He then, as God insisted he had to, sacked every single one of the refuse collectors.

We hired Virgos (earth signs famous for their tidiness) and there was no more complaining about the refuse collection system on Jersey.

The confrontation with the refuse collectors showed that the Lieutenant-Governor and God meant business and other council employees were less willing to oppose our ideas after that. No one questioned, for example, why building work could only commence when it was astrologically advisable and that those buildings that had been erected while the Moon was void had to be taken down with all haste.

Government House, erected at a horrendous astrological moment, was one of the many buildings on Jersey dismantled and then put back together again on the same spot. Opening hours of all public buildings got later and later and running water was available on the island only when the Sun was in a water sign. A number of people left the island in protest at these changes and as more reforms were carried out, such as banning any non-Leo from making a living as a hairdresser and encouraging any non-Sagittarian teacher to take early retirement, the Assembly, the governmental mechanism on the island, became concerned. In their narrow-mindedness they failed to see that things would be good for Jersey thanks to the astrological genius of Japs Eye Fontanelle.

THE 11TH

---✳---

Death of Herbert I of Italy, assassinated   ♀ → ✗ 4:06 pm
  by anarchist   ☽ ⅄ ♇
Zola Budd becomes British subject   ♀ ✳ ♅
Bread riots in Tunisia   ☽ □ ♅
French lorry drivers block roads

God demanded today to know when exactly the Cobras/ Samba/Fontanelle satellite was going to be fired into orbit.

'Very soon,' Colonel Fleming said.

A month to the day after my arrival on Jersey the Lieutenant-Governor asked me if it was a good time, astrologically speaking, to make a significant announcement. God fiddled with the astrolabe and said that it was.

The Lieutenant-Governor told God I was to be Jersey's first Minister of Astrology. God fiddled again with my astrolabe, climbed on to the Lieutenant-Governor's exercise bike, wept with joy, thanked the stars and fondled my star-spangled balls.

God's appointment as Minister of Astrology was witnessed by my wife, her lip, Dr Green, Major Applebee, 200 other leading paraspermologists and 25,000 astrologers who came from all over the globe, and the entire population of Jersey. It took place under this favourable position of the heavens:

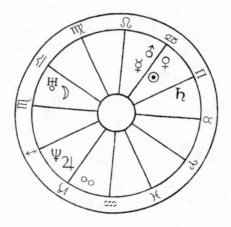

For the occasion, the Lieutenant-Governor wore a beautiful cocktail dress as did his wife. Afterwards, with tears rolling down my face, God read aloud part of the introduction of *Star Sign Secrets*, overcome with emotion and pride.

> *People love finding out about themselves through astrology, and the two questions which are asked most frequently are 'What am I like?' and 'Who is best suited to me?'*

God paused and all 25,000 astrologers, 200 paraspermologists and the residents of Jersey shouted out 'What am I like?' and 'Who is best suited to me?' again and again. When they had finished, God went on reading from the introduction of *Star Sign Secrets*:

> *This book will answer both those questions, and it will answer a lot more besides. It will tell you not only the person best suited to you but also the person most likely to piss you off.*
>
> *Appearance . . . cars . . . music . . . teeth . . . gullibility . . . sense of humour . . . investments . . . hair loss . . . holidays — all these things are influenced by your birthday. It's all in here; everything you could ever possibly want or need to know about yourself, and more.*
>
> *So dip in, and get to know yourself!*

'Dip in, and get to know yourself!' screamed the astrologers, the paraspermologists and the residents of Jersey, 'Dip in, and get to know yourself!'

> *After you've read* Star Sign Secrets *people will wonder where you get all your new perception from when you begin to unmask their real natures. In fact, understanding the 12 Sun signs will literally change your life. You're on your way to understanding deeply people you've never even met! You'll soon feel closer to strangers, as well as to friends and isn't that really, when you stop to think about it, rather wonderful?*

'It sure is!' everyone screamed.

Miss Hughes, God's nurse, says that 'Dip in, and get to know yourself!' and 'What am I like!' are expressions God sometimes shouts in my sleep here in the Gold Vault, along with 'Tora Tora Tora!'

God was provided with an office just down the hall from the Lieutenant-Governor's private study at Government House and God was also given a limo, to which I attached a pennant depicting my birth chart. God's driver was a Sagittarius. As Minister of Astrology God would offer my divine guidance on all manner of things at meetings of the Assembly. Some members of the Assembly found God's contributions cryptic and unhelpful and said so to God's face. God persisted. A few also objected to the way I grasped my gonads for emphasis while talking.

On hearing of my appointment in Jersey, the Committee for the Scientific Investigation into Claims of the Paranormal released a statement which said that the credulous man is father to the liar and the cheat and that it was always wrong for anyone to believe anything upon insufficient evidence. People, the Committee said, had a moral obligation to everyone else not to believe in dumb ideas like astrology. Dumb ideas like astrology were very dangerous things, the Committee said, a million times more dangerous than smart ideas.

The statement finished by calling yet again for a warning to accompany all of God's horoscope predictions. The new warning the Committee for the Scientific Investigation in Claims of the Paranormal suggested in their statement was shorter then the two earlier versions had been and did not mention midwives. It went like this:

Grow up!

The media as you might expect went wild about God's appointment and God was headline news for days. On every TV station there were heated debates between sceptics and astrologers. God made a number of Godlike appearances, totally destroying my critics with brilliant arguments and astrological insights into their personalities.

The British Government expressed incredulity over God's appointment and the Lieutenant-Governor was summoned to London. As his personal astrological adviser as well as an appointed Minister, God went along. In fact, we flew into Heathrow in God's repaired Zero fighter.

We met stone-faced high-ranking civil servants to whom God explained as simply as I could the principles of astrology and how God believed it could aid civil institutions. God gave them signed copies of my book *The Darn Truth* and even offered to read their horoscopes. They were not terribly impressed and it was decided that the Lieutenant-Governor and God ought to undergo psychiatric assessment.

God had hoped that I would have time, while in London, to visit the great Humphry Barnard, but yet again God was thwarted as the psychiatric assessments took so long we had no time to spare. We returned to Jersey, putting a brave face on events, insisting that any problems with the mainland had been ironed out, which was something of a white lie.

Later that day the Lieutenant-Governor and God prohibited anyone not born under the sign of Scorpio from being involved in the undertaking business and legislated that only Cancerians were allowed to work in the island's libraries, on the rare occasions when they were open.

THE 12TH

Term quantum mechanics first used	3rd – 12:18 am
Birthday of George Bush (politician)	☽ ☌ ☉
Serbia declares war on Turkey	☽ ☌ ♀
Gyro-Compass invented	☽ △ ♂
	☽ ⚹ ♃
	☽ ☌ ♄

This morning, during breakfast, God exclaimed loudly:

'All space is jism! We are living on an outwardly expanding explosion, the Great Pan-Galactic Spunk Explosion, the Wave Crest of my Sexual Emissions. Praise be to me!'

The Lieutenant-Governor soon relied so heavily on God's astro-logical views for the day-to-day running of the island, that he became nervous and on edge if God left his side for the briefest of periods. It got so bad I had to hold his hand while he pissed and afterwards tell him it was astrologically wise for him to wash his hands.

After dinner God and my nurse watched *Star Trek*.

Tonight's episode was about some aliens whose paintings were so beautiful the crew of the Enterprise had to wear welders' masks when they looked at them to avoid crying for ever and ever.

THE I3TH

✳

Birthday of Barbra Streisand (singer)	☽ ☌ ♂
Electrolysis discovered	☽ ✳ ♇
Deathday of Sultan Mahmud II	☽ △ ♅
	♂ ✳ ♇
	☿ ⅄ ♀
	♄ ⊼ ⚷

When the meddlesome Assembly became too much of a hindrance the Lieutenant-Governor, after a careful consultation with the stars and their maker (me), invoked powers not used since WWII and declared a state of emergency. Thirty-two of the thirty-three members of the Assembly were removed from office on the grounds that their horoscopes were not 'conducive to good government'.

The British Government requested the presence of the Lieutenant-Governor in London to explain this 'unprecedented' action. He declined the invitation, informing them that he and his astrological adviser (me) were tied up with local matters.

No longer hindered by the Assembly we pulled all the stops out. Patients in the island's hospitals were taken in their hundreds to the roof so that the wonderful influence of Venus could heal them more effectively. It is true that many such patients died of pneumonia and ten or so fell off the roof to their deaths but there were several well-documented cases of miraculous cures. Cures that confounded modern science. Then the Lieutenant-Governor and God published twelve new newspapers, catering exclusively for the needs of each star sign. The horoscopes in these papers were some of the longest and most detailed the world has ever seen. The papers consisted of one very very long horoscope prediction and a tiny little corner of the back page devoted to actual news. On one occasion seven pages in one paper were devoted to what would happen to Leos before they got out of bed the morning of the next day.

Everything was covered, absolutely every aspect of life. Nothing was seen by God to be too mundane or too trivial not to be of importance to the stars. When was the best time to visit the bathroom was clearly stated as was how many sheets of toilet paper were to be used, when to get dressed, what item of clothing to put on first, what direction you ought to be facing, whether to brush the top row of teeth or the bottom row first, when to watch TV and what channel, what to say to your husband or partner and children, what novels to read, when to go to bed and what position to have sex in, if it was astrologically the right night for sex and how to say no it was not. It was all there, clearly laid out.

God normally finished my horoscopes on Jersey by telling the entire population of the island when they were to turn off their bedside lights the next night.

We completely revolutionized the retail food industry on the island as well. Each restaurant was ordered to specialize in catering for people of a single star sign. This had its drawbacks, people having to travel to the other side of the island to get something to eat. The benefits, however, were incalculable.

Only hot spicy dishes were served in restaurants for Scorpios and the longest dessert menus were in Libran restaurants on account of their sweet tooth caused by their birth under the planet Venus. Virgo restaurants were entirely vegetarian whereas Leo and Arian restaurants served nothing but meat. Cancers ate only smooth things like mousses and patés.

There were obviously no restaurants for Geminis for whom food is not the most important thing in their lives and who quickly get bored of chewing.

Pubs were segregated by star signs too and were given suitable astrological names. In pubs for Geminis only fizzy drinks were served. Arians were allowed to drink only Bloody Marys, because of its Arian red. Cancers drank exclusively White Russians on account of its smoothness; Martini was the drink best suited to the Virgo temperament, and the only one they were permitted; Leos with their close affinity with citrus fruits drank Tequila Sunrises. Taureans, who rarely like to go out and are more the sit-at-home type, were not allowed into any pub or nightclub, entirely for their own good.

For the first time since ancient Egypt and Hermes Trismegistus, man and his cosmos were at peace. There was order, there was predictability. People knew where they stood in relation to everything. Everything had its place and things were in perfect harmony.

Curiously, a number of residents decided to leave the island during this time. But for every local that wanted to leave there were a dozen astrologers pulling their hair out to come and stay.

While all this was going on, Government House phones rang day and night with civil servants from London asking to speak urgently to the Lieutenant-Governor. God spoke to a number of such functionaries asking them their star sign and telling those who were not born under the influence of Capricorn to seek alternative employment or come to Jersey and live in harmony with the stars.

THE 14TH

Nuclear tests off Bikini Atoll begin	☽ ⌄ ♆
Invention of plastic cutlery	☽ ⌄ ♅
Peace between Prussia and Denmark	☽ ⌄ ♇
Montenegro declares war on Turkey	☉ ⌄ ♅
	♀ ⌄ ♅
	☽ ⌄ ♅
	☽ ☌ ♀

Schools on Jersey had their curricula changed to incorporate the ancient science of astrology and twelve-year-olds were taught to draw up simple horoscopes and recognize my handiwork in the night sky.

Atomic clocks, which kept time perfectly to a fraction of a fraction of a second, were installed in the maternity wards and operated by former Olympic referees, so that we could find out the precise time of birth and thus ascertain the influences of the stars with even greater clarity.

Buying your star sign newspaper became compulsory on Jersey, it was, after all, in everyone's interest to know how to harmonize one's life with the stars. The police would ask people to present yesterday's paper to show that they were where they astrologically ought to be. Not to be seen avidly reading your paper was frowned upon. Everywhere people went, on the buses, in cars, they kept their head firmly in their papers reading about their futures.

Of course often people were so engrossed with what they would be doing tomorrow according to the stars, they would bump into each other, sending their papers flying into the air. There were some pretty nasty accidents caused this way. Each week outside Government House the person who had been admitted to the roof of a hospital with the most serious injuries caused while reading their paper was presented with a medal by God himself. The medals were based on my Pearl Harbor medal, which God hardly ever wore, having nothing to pin it on.

THE 15TH

Tornado hits Waco, Texas	☽ → ☾ 1:22 am
Double glazing invented	☽ ⊼ ♆
Deathday of Mahatma Gandhi (politician)	☽ □ ☿
Creation of NATO	♀ △ ♄
	☽ ⅄ ♂
	☽ □ ♇
	☽ ⊼ ♅

On the 28th of Leo a delegation of high-ranking officials, including the Home Office Minister, attempted to land at Jersey Airport, which God had renamed Humphry Barnard Airport. The delegation was told by ground control that with Jupiter in the cusp of Virgo landing permission was denied.

The plane circled the island three times then landed on Guernsey, an astrologically backward island twenty miles away.

The very next day the officials arrived in St Helier Harbour, recently renamed by God the Hero of Pearl Harbor Harbor, on board a Royal Navy minesweeper. (Captain Fuchida was remembered as God's First Apostle, his defection to Christianity having been sufficiently explained away as the influence of Mars.)

The minister and his aides were kept at the passport office for several hours on God's orders. They were then segregated according to star sign, shown all the progress that had been made on the island, given VIP seats at my performance that night at the Fort Regents Leisure Centre, renamed the Temple of God's Illustrious Gonads, and sent back to their minesweeper with two vials labelled stars (one for the Queen, one for the PM) and told to come again.

An hour later they left.

THE 16TH

Birthday of Ian Fleming (writer)

Fatal gas leak in Bhopal, India

General Bignone installed as President of

   Argentina

Britain, France and Italy guarantee the

   Independence of Abyssinia

☽ v/c 8:02 pm

☽ ⊼ ♃
☽ □ ♂
♀ ⊻ ♂
☽ △ ♀
☽ △ ♄

People on Jersey no longer paid taxes according to their income, an absurd idea, but according to the positions of the planets on their day of birth. Airplanes and ferries full of devout astrological pilgrims came to the island from all over the world singing:

> *That which is on high is as that which is below.*
> *And that which is below is as that which is on high*

while waving *Astronomy Now* and banging hand cymbals.

They came to witness me perform my creations of matter, which took place every night at the Temple of God's Illustrious Gonads, one of the very few places on the island where people with different star signs were still allowed to mix together.

In a further measure to help us unify the population of Jersey with the cosmos, God decided it would be a good idea if everyone wore badges clearly showing their star sign. Virgo badges were blue, Sagittarius purple, Cancer white, Leo gold, Gemini yellow, Taurus green, Aries red, Scorpio black, Libra pink, Capricorn grey, Aquarius indigo, Pisces turquoise.

Many people were reluctant to wear their badges for some reason and one or two 'instances' occurred with the police in St Helier and in some of the smaller communities inland.

On the 3rd of Libra the Lieutenant-Governor and God made it illegal for astrologically incompatible couples to continue in their doomed pointless relationships. Over 1,260 were nullified by the state. This step was taken in full accordance with chapter four of *Star Sign Secrets*.

Those who were affected by this law were installed in more astrologically harmonious relationships.

On the 10th of Libra the British Government announced that the Lieutenant-Governor of Jersey had been fired and that a woman, a Mrs O'Shaughnessy, would be arriving shortly to take over the running of the island. An hour after we heard this news the former Governor of Jersey walked into my rooms in Longueville Manor wearing a pinstriped suit and asked if it was a good time, astrologically, for Jersey to officially declare itself independent.

Five minutes later, Jersey was renamed Adocentyn after the fabled city Hermes Trismegistus the Thrice Great One, wisest of the wise, highest of the Egyptian priests, philosopher-magician and lawgiver, had founded some time in antiquity, either just after the Flood or around the time the Israelites left Egypt; no one, not even God, knew when for sure.

Adocentyn's flag was my birth chart and everyone on the island swore allegiance to the stars.

There were a few public demonstrations against the move to independence and calls for the matter to be put to the vote. Such demonstrations were put down by our police force, made up by this time entirely of Scorpios, who are the perfect people for such work.

When Mrs O'Shaughnessy (Taurus) arrived on Jersey she was thrown into the boiler room of the Temple of God's Illustrious Gonads.

Taurus females go on self-catering holidays, enjoy seafood, have the finest voices in the Zodiac and have huge nipples. Their lucky letter is h.

Those citizens born under the water signs were relocated near to the sea. Some people were reluctant to move even though it was clearly astrologically sensible and God had to go to trouble spots myself and shout at the top of my voice, 'Things will be good for you!' and play with my penis to calm things down. Similar changes took place with air signs, who had, by law, to live above the ground floor.

Throughout these heady days of change and progress the slightly burnt copy of *Star Sign Secrets* by Humphry Barnard was by God's side at all times.

Cars on Adocentyn were redistributed according to the principles of astrology. Leos, Sagittarians, Taureans and Capricorns were given fast, expensive cars, the rest were given to coastal dwelling water signs. The air signs, who had never really been terribly interested in cars anyway, were encouraged to use public transport.

Then Japs Eye Fontanelle turned my attention to the legal system. This God completely overhauled. A person's innocence or guilt of any crime was determined by God spending a few minutes studying their birth chart. It was simple, quick and absolutely foolproof. God was astonished it had apparently never been used before. For some reason civil rights groups got upset by these momentous improvements.

THE 17TH

Invention of the microwave oven	4th – 12:54 pm
Venezuela becomes independent	☽ □ ☉
Birthday of Cecil Rhodes (politician)	☽ ☍ ♃
Invention of the first hairspray	

On the 22nd of Libra, everyone on Adocentyn had a two-inch circle of hair removed from the tops of their heads, and wore platform shoes. This was so the glorious Zodiac could influence them all the more.

THE 18TH

First Laurel and Hardy film	☽ ⚹ ☿
Deathday of Dalai Lama (politician)	☽ ⚻ ♃
J. Hinckley acquitted of attempted assassination	♂ ⚹ ♅
of President Reagan by virtue of insanity	☉ ☌ ♅
	☉ ⚹ ♂

You should have seen the stink in the British press when it was found out that God was encouraging parents on Jersey not to have children on certain days of the year. The reason for doing this was clear: people born on certain days were going to be so horrendous it would be better for everyone, including them, if their lives never happened. So God outlawed births on these days. Every effort was made to induce birth a day or two early, and if that didn't work doctors tried everything they could to keep the baby from coming out until the poor conjunctions had passed.

On his first birthday on Adocentyn God was made King with tremendous pomp and ceremony. My second wife was made Queen.

It was the happiest day of God's wondrous life as anyone with an understanding of astrology can see in the position of the heavens at the time:

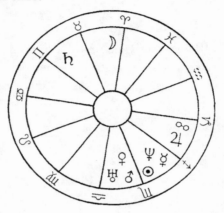

After dinner God and my nurse watched *Star Trek*.

THE 19TH

Bombs in London underground stations kill 13

US spy plane shot down over Russia

Man found in Queen's bedroom in Buckingham Palace

☽ ⊼ ♂
☽ ⌄ ♃
☽ ⊼ ♄

The day after my coronation a declaration was read out all over the island of Adocentyn. It went like this:

The King of Adocentyn, the Zodiac Man, the Thrice Great One, Creator of Everything, sex symbol extraordinary, Shiva, Buddha, Jesus, He with the Magical Phallus has decided, this day, with

Mars in ascendant, that the Ancient science of Astrology is to be this island's state religion. No other faiths, misguided as they are, are to be permitted.

As of today all churches belong to Japs Eye Fontantelle and his followers. We will all be better off as a result of this change. It was in the stars.

Those priests unable to see the sense of this step or who fail to see me as the One True God are advised to leave the Holy Isle by noon.

Yours,

God.

A week later when the churches on Adocentyn were opened again their spires had been replaced with state-of-the-art telescopes. On Sunday nights priests, dressed as ancient Egyptians, would say things like 'And if you look into the telescope you will see M1132 which King Fontanelle brought into being at lunchtime on the 14th of Capricorn 1948 while in Japan, the moon in retrograde. Praise be to God.'

At points like this the congregation were expected to shout, 'Wow!' and 'What am I like?'

'You can also see M323 nearby, which was made exactly eighteen minutes after M1132 with the help of King Fontanelle's girlfriend at the time, a fashion model called Zuiho. A fine catch. Praise be to God.'

And 'Wow! What am I like?' shouted the congregation again.

After that passages were read out from *Star Sign Secrets* or *The Emerald Tablet* or *The Darn Truth*. These readings would be interspersed with songs and further star gazing.

On the first of each sign the inhabitants of Adocentyn celebrated their own form of Eucharist. The ritual would start with a priest saying, 'Let us give thanks to the Lord for the mystery of the wondrous Zodiac.'

At which point the congregation would shout, 'Holy holy holy!'

A vial with the label 'stars' on it was then opened and its contents added to a few gallons of God's holy bathwater. This mixture was ladled out to every man, woman and child on the island with dessert spoons, while everyone prayed aloud, 'Grant that we who are nourished by God's holy boom boom seed may be filled with his sublime majesty and brought closer to the stars. Happy happy days!'

'For the first time in two thousand years,' I told Colonel Fleming and my nurse at dinner, 'people felt that they mattered, that the Universe was not vast and cold but warm and intimate. People felt that they were part of some giant cosmic process, the centre of things again. They asked the question, "What am I like?" and I furnished them with an answer. I, God, gave man self-respect. Was that so bad? Was that so wrong?'

'You gave man self-respect by making him drink your sperm?' Miss Hughes said.

'Yes,' God said, 'and what did God get in return? I got castrated and, more than likely, will be shot by firing squad.'

THE 20TH

✳

First pair of sneakers worn at Olympic trials	☽ v/c 7:10 am
	☽ → ♓ 11:14 am
North Vietnamese troops mount big offensive	2nd – 7:22 pm
in the South	☽ □ ⚷
Value Added Tax introduced in Britain	☽ ✳ ♄
Greece declared a republic	☽ ⊼ ♂
	☽ ⅴ ♆
	☽ □ ☉

Occasionally God would make an appearance at the various churches on Adocentyn during services. God would be escorted on such visits by God's Happy Women of the House of Joy and members of the Zodiac Guard, formally known as the police. It was around this time that God, my wife and God's Happy Women of the House of Joy appeared in *Hello!* magazine.

The heavens were thus:

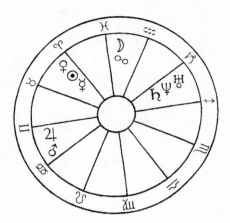

God's Happy Women of the House of Joy were what we would call in Japan geisha or courtesans. There were 345 Happy Women of the House of Joy. I was 79 and having the time of my life. God's wife had always accepted that what with me being a sex god, there were always going to be other women. She also, bless her, endured God's long-standing interest in hard-core pornographic videos.

THE 21ST

Birthday of Ham (first American monkey
   to be sent into space)

Start of Spanish Civil War

Start of Arab-Israeli War

Chewing gum invented

☽ ⊼ ♄
☽ △ ♆
☽ ⁎ ♇
☽ △ ♆

It was absolutely freezing in here last night.

Paraspermologists from all over the world came to the island to study my remarkable little balls.

By Capricorn the 2nd, the entire government administration on Adocentyn was run by Capricorns, the ideal employees for any large organization.

It was also in Capricorn that God decided to divide Adocentyn up into the twelve signs of the Zodiac.

THE 22ND

Birthday of De Gaulle (politician)

America stops bombing Cambodia

State of emergency declared by Mrs Gandhi

Iran demands £10,000m for release of
   American hostages

Plastic garden furniture goes on sale

☽ ⁎ ♆
☉ ⊼ ♄
☽ ☌ ☿
☽ □ ♃

The amount of concrete we used was stupendous and twelve people accidentally gave their lives turning Adocentyn into one big horoscope. They did not die in vain.

It took a little over two years to completely divide the island formerly known as Jersey into twelve equal segments. When the last section of concrete was left to dry God threw a party and when the party was over everyone was loaded on to buses and taken to their star sign.

It was a truly wonderful day. God told reporters present for the occasion that it was God's wish that the concrete walls should reach across the sea and in time cover the entire planet so that everyone could find peace and harmony with the cosmos.

Around the same time that people headed to their star signs, God had animals released into the appropriate segments. There were 1,500 deadly poisonous scorpions in Scorpio, 34,000 goats in Capricorn, 15,000 tiny red crabs in Cancer, 50 African lions in Leo, 10,000 bulls in Taurus, 5,000 rams in Aries and 10,000 goldfish in 10,000 goldfish bowls in Pisces.

While his subjects got used to their new way of life, their King, their God, went on harmonizing the Earth with the heavens. Thousands of tons of earth were removed from the Pisces segment and added to the Aries segment by a fleet of fishing boats. Using pumps, the Pisces segment of the Zodiac was flooded with water until it became an archipelago of islands on which everyone had to wear flippers and snorkels. Interaction between the various signs was carefully controlled at the enormous central revolving door at the centre of Adocentyn above which God had my palace erected. God's palace, known as the Perfumed Palace of God's Delectation, was shaped like a erect penis bending a little to the left. Its marble walls were covered in frescos depicting my life; from Kyoto through World War Two, to America and finally Adocentyn. The frescos were created by Pisceans, the only signs on the island allowed to use paint brushes.

The Lieutenant-Governor lived for the most part in Aquarius and left all matters of state to his King and God. He was allowed to visit his wife, who was in Virgo, once a week.

Everything was good, everything was as it should have been. Adocentyn was heaven on earth, even if God does say so myself.

And then it all came to a sudden, jarring, stupid, tragic, halt.

THE 23RD

Britain breaks off diplomatic relations with Libya	☿ ☌ ♇
Origin of Species first published	☽ ✳ ♄
Dishwasher invented	☽ ⊼ ♆
Coup in Guinea	☽ ⊼ ♇
	☽ ⊼ ☿
	☽ ⊼ ♅

God and my second wife were in the celestial bedchamber when the latest bunch of paraspermologists from America came in to examine me.

'How would you like me, boys?' God asked.

'Mr Fontanelle,' said one of the men, 'we are not here to examine you.'

It was only then that God noticed that every one of the 'paraspermologists' was wearing a bright-orange life jacket.

THE 24TH

The Dreyfus affair ends	☽ v/c 6:35 pm
	☽ → ♈ 7:32 pm
Civil disturbances in Hong Kong	☽ △ ⚷
Announcement of plan to build Nissan cars	☽ ☌ ♃
in Britain	☿ ⊻ ⚷
	☽ ⊼ ♂
Launching of Apollo 14	☽ ⚹ ♆
Swaziland becomes independent	☽ ⊻ ♄
Troops fire rubber bullets in Belfast	

'There is no absolute truth. And those who claim it open the door to tragedy,' said the spokesman for the Committee for the Scientific Investigation into Claims of the Paranormal.

'Blow it out your ass!' God retorted masterfully.

'We are here to tell you, Mr Fontanelle, that your ship is sinking, and that it is taking thousands of dumb souls with it. Come in, number 9, your time is up!' said the spokesman.

'What in God's name are you talking about? And why the hell do you people always wear those stupid orange life jackets all the time?' God demanded.

'I had no idea,' God's second wife said, looking at God, her wonderful lower lip quivering. 'I thought they were research students from Duke.'

God reached for the phone to call my guards but one of the Committee members got to it first and pushed me back on to the bed.

'Mr Fontanelle,' said the spokesman for the Committee for the Scientific Investigation into Claims of the Paranormal, 'why weren't Uranus, Neptune and Pluto discovered by astrologers due to their influences on people's personalities long before they were found by astronomers?'

'What?'

'Mr Fontanelle, are you familiar with the work of Dr Gervey?'

'Who?'

'It is true, is it not, that people born under certain signs are more likely to become politicians or scientists?'

'Of course.'

'Dr Gervey compared the birth dates of 16,634 scientists and 6,475 politicians and found a random distribution of star signs.'

A Committee member opened a briefcase he was carrying and handed God a copy of Dr Gervey's paper.

The spokesman went on: 'Professor Silverman at Michigan State University found that married couples with compatible signs are no more likely to remain happily married than those with incompatible signs.'

'You're lying.'

God was given a copy of Professor Silverman's paper.

'Dr Bath and Dr Bennett examined the star signs of men who enlisted in the Marine Corps. There were just as many men ruled by Venus, associated I believe with love and beauty, as those ruled by Mars, a planet astrology associates with courage and aggression.'

'We don't have to listen to this,' my wife said.

But God and my wife did listen. We listened to it for hours as scientific paper after scientific paper challenging the basic tenets of astrology were thrown into God's lap. The worst moment came towards the end when the spokesman claimed that the great *Emerald Tablet* was a fake, written by some first-century European pretending to be an ancient Egyptian. The spokesman for the Committee for the Scientific Investigation into Claims of the Paranormal said the evidence for this was overwhelming and had been known by historians for hundreds of years.

'There was no Hermes Trismegistus, the Thrice Great One, the Maker of the Holy Pyramids of Egypt. The real author of *The Emerald Tablet* was as Egyptian as you are.'

God was speechless.

'What about my research, what about my paper *Seminal Ejaculations and Galactic Formations*?' demanded my wife.

The Committee for the Scientific Investigation into Claims of the Paranormal burst into hysterics, they slapped their sides, they fought back tears.

'Right, that's it, this has gone on long enough,' God said. 'You come to my Holy Island, insult my second wife, have the nerve to show me silly bits of paper challenging the ancient art of astrology, say that Hermes was a fake and that I can't prove that I make galaxies.'

'But you can't prove it, can you?' said the spokesman.

'Yes I can,' said God.

'You can't.'

'I can.'

'Can't.'

'Can.'

'Can't.'

'Can.'

'Can't.'

'Well . . . all right then, what if I can't,' said God, 'what if God doesn't stand up to scientific testing? What if astrology can't be proven? What about music? Do you want to put music into a double-blind test?'

'Mr Fontanelle, does music create this?' The spokesman of the Scientific Investigation into Claims of the Paranormal gestured at the room.

'What?'

'The mess that your stupid, half-baked childish ideas have made of this island.'

Then the spokesman for the Committee for the Scientific Investigation into Claims of the Paranormal said that your midwife exerts more of a gravitational influence on you at your birth than all the stars and the planets put together and God hit him.

A scuffle broke out.

In the struggle God's astrolabe was knocked to the floor. God was being hit from all directions by rolled-up scientific papers refuting the validity of astrology. God got down on my hands and knees and tried to get to the phone. The spokesman was shouting that we have a duty to ourselves and others to be rational, a duty not to demean our minds, a duty not to be taken for rides on silly ideas that lead who-knew-where.

God made another frantic attempt to get to the phone and caught my balls in the astrolabe just as Mars and Jupiter entered alignment.

There was remarkably little pain.

For a few moments neither God nor anyone else knew quite what had happened.

Then God put two and two together.

So did my second wife who started to scream and scream.

The creator of the Universe lost my manhood under this grim gaze of heaven:

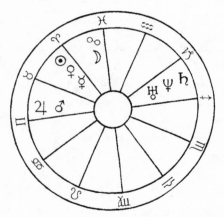

God should, of course, have seen it coming.

The last thing God did before passing out was crawl to the phone and call room service telling them that God wanted some ice cream on the double.

God had read somewhere or heard on television that it was possible to sew balls back on if they are kept as cold as possible.

God looked down at the astrolabe between my legs covered in holy blood and then God fainted. The last thing I heard was the kitchen porter nervously asking down the phone, 'Chocolate or vanilla? Oh, Thrice Great One?'

After dinner God and Miss Hughes watched *Star Trek*.

THE 25TH

Astronauts orbit moon	☽ ⊼ ☉
Divorce becomes legal in Italy	☽ ⊼ ♀
	☽ □ ♂
Deathday of Abbas I, Viceroy of Egypt	☽ □ ♃
	☽ ⊼ ♅
	♂ ☍ ♃

In the end it was Rocky Road. My Cosmic Balls were indeed saved thanks to God's quick thinking but the damage was so bad that it was deemed impossible to reattach them to my body; instead they were connected to life-support machines and given constant medical attention. Each had two doctors and a dozen nurses looking after it. God has to say that I was a little jealous of all the attention my balls were getting.

The Committee for the Scientific Investigation into Claims of the Paranormal left Adocentyn on the next available ferry.

In many ways the Committee for the Scientific Investigation into Claims of the Paranormal, who certainly never came to Adocentyn to castrate God, had done God a great service. They had ensured that my religion would last a thousand years. Resting in my bedchamber, my balls never very far away, God came to see that my castration had been my crucifixion. It was the best piece of marketing my religion had ever seen. It gave astrology a whole new lease of life. People all over the world talked about it for months afterwards. It gave God, well, depth.

Utter pandemonium broke out among my adoring followers when they heard the news. Many refused to believe it just as many in Japan had refused to believe WWII had been lost. There was concern that as a result of my injuries, the Universe might shrivel up or something. A similar thought had crossed God's mind, but when night came it was clear that the planets remained in their orbits, and that the Universe was taking it well.

A week after the accident God made an appearance on the top of my palace, and assured everyone that the Universe and I were fine.

A few days later, due to public demand, God's balls and their medical entourage toured the island, the right ball, so we thought, going clockwise, the left ball, fingers crossed, anti-clockwise. Everyone turned out to see the balls go by.

THE 26TH

✳

Birthday of Fred Astaire (dancer)	☽ v/c 6:26 pm
Channel Islands occupied by Germany	☽ → ♉ 6:58 pm
Invention of the roller coaster	☽ ⊼ ♅
Mohammed Ali Shah of Persia deposed in	☿ ⊼ ♃
favour of Sultan Ahmad Shah aged 12	☽ ⋎ ♃
	☽ ☍ ♀ ♂ ⊼ ♆
	☽ □ ♆ ☽ △ ♂
	☽ ♂ ♄

God cannot paint an entirely bright picture of my castration. For one thing was painfully clear even to those with no head for theology (such as Virgos): the Universe had got as big as it was going to get. The show was over. There were to be no new galaxies, God had finished my handiwork, had done my thing for the last time. God had been forced into early retirement and the Universe as it was would just have to do.

THE 27TH

✳

John Lennon fined £150 for possession of cannabis	☽ ✳ ♃
General de Gaulle announces devaluation of the franc	
Britain starts night-bombing of Germany	
Massacre of Mamelukes at Cairo	
Frozen meat shipped from Argentina to France	

This morning God received more fan and hate mail. One of the fan letters God particularly liked went:

> *Dear Japs Eye Fontanelle,*
> *You saved my life and restored my sanity.*
> *A Virgo.*

When God had finished sorting out my mail I and the Chaplain of the 82nd Airborne Division discussed a subject on which I am a world-renowned expert: masturbation.

'Did you Christians ever get the wrong end of the stick when it came to masturbation,' God said. 'Take your St Thomas Aquinas. He said the dumbest, saddest thing any mortal has ever said on the subject of masturbation. That crazy, sick bastard, said that masturbation was worse than raping your mother.'

'He didn't say that!' the Chaplain protested. 'He couldn't have said that!

'He did!' insisted God. 'Go and look it up if you like.'

'I will.'

'You do that,' God said. 'It's in his tome *Summa Theologiae*.'

The Chaplain stormed out of the mobile home saying he would be back in five minutes.

He came back an hour later and said God had been right. St Thomas Aquinas really had said that masturbation was worse than raping your mother.

To cheer the Chaplain up God told him who it was who had said the wisest thing any mortal had ever said on the subject of masturbation. This person was Woody Allen.

'And what did he say about masturbation?'

'Don't knock it. It's sex with someone you love,' God quoted and then asked the Chaplain if he wanted to hear God's pet theory that explained why Christians are so darn fucked-up about sex.

The Chaplain said that he wasn't feeling in the mood.

It was after his castration, during a check-up in the Things Will be Good For You Hospital in what had once been St Helier, but was then Happy Happy Days Town, that the Lieutenant-Governor told God of his idea to have painted on the Les Mielles golf course in Scorpio my birth chart in all its glory.

'God is touched,' God had said and gave the project my blessing.

When God was well enough I visited the finished work in one of those golf carts, into which I could only just fit. It brought tears to God's eyes. It was magnificent. After God had pondered it long and hard God spent a few minutes talking to some of the artists in their flippers and snorkels who had worked on the project and who were slowly dying of scorpion bites.

'You shouldn't have, really,' God said or something to that effect.

God ate a great deal following my castration. You tend to put on a lot of weight after a thing like that anyway, but I really swelled like, well, like some tremendous fat old guy with no balls. It was then, to add to everything else, that God lost the ability to lower my arms and they came to remain in the pose which, so many people tell God, looks as if I am in the act of surrendering to some unseen assailant, or to life itself. It was in the stars:

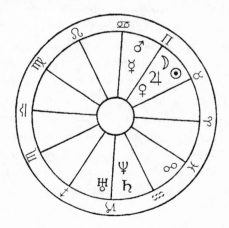

God had lost my balls along with my ability to move my arms. In addition the Universe had stopped growing. Depressing stuff, but an even greater tragedy was only around the corner bouncing up and down on the infernal pogo stick of the completely insane.

THE 28TH

✳

First commercial flight of Concorde	♂ → ♍ 7:28 am
Birthday of Jesse James (outlaw)	☽ ☓ ♇
Very first neon signs go on display	☽ ☓ ♀
	☽ □ ♅
Rising in Bosnia and Herzegovina against	☽ ☓ ☉
Turkish rule	♀ △ ♅

Four days after God's castration, Commissioner Pizarro called another press conference. Journalists went to it with considerable expectation. After all, the only other press conference the Commissioner had held, just before the Korean War, had caused a sensation around the world. The second of Commissioner Pizarro's press conferences turned out to be no less spectacular.

It took place on the thirty-eighth floor of the UN building in New York, Mars in conjunction with Jupiter, in Pizarro's old office that had, since no one had been found insane enough to take over his old job, been turned into a broom cupboard.

In this spacious broom cupboard with a fantastic view of the Manhattan skyline, Commissioner Pizarro outlined his case against God. He came bouncing in when the room was full and informed his audience that for the last twenty-five years God had been under close UN observation. The Commissioner said that he had decided that he now had enough evidence to prosecute. The Commissioner went on to explain what exactly God was being accused of.

No one was more surprised than God. I was watching the whole thing in bed in the Perfumed Palace of God's Delectation.

Commissioner Pizarro explained how my matter creation would, in the opinion of a great number of cosmologists he had spoken to, have profound effects on the future of Time, of everything, on what Pizarro called the Omega point, the ratio of density of the Universe to the critical density needed to eventually halt and reverse its expansion. To say Commissioner Pizarro blasphemed after that would be to understate things. It was a diatribe. To create a populated universe that would eventually die, Commissioner Pizarro said, was the cruellest, dumbest fucking thing he had ever heard of. It took the complete biscuit, he said. 'Why create conscious beings in a temporary universe?' It wasn't funny, it was mass murder and it was sick, sick, sick according to the Commissioner.

'I thought the volcanoes and earthquakes and typhoons had been bad enough, but,' said the Commissioner at his second press conference, 'it now looks, ladies and gentlemen, as if all that was just the tip of God's sadism iceberg. The Universe is a Goddamn bomb. We are all living inside a great big enormous fucking time bomb! This means, of course, that God is a terrorist. This fact will, I know, be hard for some people, especially religious people, to accept but the evidence speaks for itself.

'I, Commissioner Pizzaro, ladies and gentlemen, want you to know, that I will not rest until God is apprehended and stands trial for his almost incomprehensible crimes. A warrant for God's arrest has been issued and sent to all police departments on Earth. Thank you for your time.'

The Lieutenant-Governor and God's second wife were concerned, but God told them not to panic. When we had finished harmonizing the Microcosm with the Macrocosm the world would see the glorious benefits of astrology and all charges against God would be dropped.

In the meantime, God cast a series of horoscopes and Adocentyn officially declared war on the United Nations.

THE 29TH

London's main drainage system completed	Ψ D 7:10 am
	♉ → ♏ 9:44 pm
End of Thirty Years War	☽ ✳ ♂
Marattas outmanoeuvred and then heavily	☽ ⊼ ♇
defeated by Afghans	☽ ⊼ ♅
	☿ □ Ψ
Invention of the contact lens	☽ □ ♀

To this day God does not know how Commissioner Pizarro managed to convince the UN Secretary-General, who convinced the Security Council, who in their turn convinced the General Assembly of the UN to pass resolution 231337. But pass it they did.

Resolution 231337 called for the immediate detention for crimes against everything of Japs Eye Fontanelle. What was remarkable about resolution 231337 was the second paragraph, which stated that the UN was authorized to use 'Whatever force is deemed necessary to bring God to justice.'

God was public enemy number one.

Posters showing God creating a galaxy appeared everywhere. Underneath the picture was the following:

WANTED BY THE UN

FOR THE ALLEGED KILLING OF TIME
ZIZO YASUZAWA

DESCRIPTION
Date of birth: 17 November 1925;
Place of birth: Japan (also claims ancient Egypt)
Height: 5'; Weight: 600 pounds; Build: fat; Hair: black
Sex: male; Distinguishing features: hole in head,
no balls; Social Security Number Used: 136-94-3472
(invalid SSAN)

Aliases: Zodiac Man, God, Japs Eye Fontanelle, The
One Who Hath Made All Things The Spirit Of Spirits,
The Old One, Cosmic Being, Perfectus, The Light,
Benign Creator of Everything, The Infinite, Awo-Bam-
Do-Bop-Awo-Bambo! The Creator of the Universe,
King of the Holy Channel Island of Adocentyn
(Jersey), Maitreya Buddha, Avatara of Vishnu, Iman
Mahdi, Hermes Trismegistus The Thrice Great One,
and He-Whose-Figure-Of-Beauty-Is-Tinged-With-The-
Hue-Of-Cerulean-Blue-Clouds-And-Whose-Unique-
Loveliness-Charms-Millions-Of-Little-Cupids

CAUTION

YASUZAWA ALLEGEDLY CREATED THE UNIVERSE
WITH TOO MUCH MATTER IN IT, WHICH MAY LEAD
TO A BIG CRUNCH AND THE DESTRUCTION OF ALL
PROPERTY, HUMAN LIFE AND EVERYTHING ELSE
INCLUDING TIME ITSELF. YASUZAWA SHOULD BE
CONSIDERED DIVINE AND DANGEROUS.

THE 30TH

Maine-Canada boundary settled	4th – 6:11 pm
Silly Putty invented	☽ ☐ ☉
Wittgenstein starts work on *Tractatus*	☽ △ ⚷
Logico-Philosophicus	☽ △ ♃
	☉ ⊻ ⚷
	☿ ☍ ♄

A few days after resolution 231337 had been issued and the wanted posters put up, CNN reported that the 3rd US Marine Expeditionary Force, which called itself 'The Tip of the Spear', was leaving the island of Okinawa. The 3rd US Marine Expeditionary Force was composed of 18,000 blue-helmet-wearing Marines and was headed towards a little island in the English Channel with more than its fair share of concrete and the wonderful, soul-stirring, if hard-to-pronounce name of Adocentyn.

God and my nurse watched *Star Trek* tonight after dinner.

THE 31ST

London Zoo opened to the public	4th Libra
Pope Pius X elected	♅ D 1:46 pm
Italian fleet destroyed by Austrians	☽ ⊼ ♄
T. Yong establishes the wave theory of light	☽ ✳ ♇
	☽ ⊻ ♂
	☽ △ ♅
	☽ ⊻ ☿

Uncle Sam was coming to kick God's holy ass.

'It was in the stars,' God assured the citizens of his astrological utopia, trying to calm them, adding that the entire Universe was on our side and that consequently we could not lose.

When God had finished telling them this, God twiddled my fingers defiantly.

The people of Adocentyn burned the US and UN flags. God gave speeches cursing the International Community to high heaven. I made jokes about the UN Secretary-General's birth chart and asserted again and again that Commissioner Pizarro was completely insane. Which he is.

The Marines steamed east, crossing the Pacific Ocean and passing through the Panama Canal. Knowing that they would be off our shores in a week or so, we prepared our defences. Each of the twelve signs of the Zodiac formed defence forces. These were called things like the Libra Brigade, the Virgo Volunteers, and so on, and had snappy uniforms designed by God myself.

God spent every waking hour consulting the stars searching for a winning strategy. Given that the invasion was bound to take place in the sign of Taurus, God realized it would be reckless folly to use guns to defend our astrological paradise. Instead everyone on the island was issued with a bamboo spear. The tips of the spears were made from a different metal for each of the signs. For Libra it was copper, for Aries it was steel, Sagittarians had spear tips made from tin and so on.

God told my followers that when the Americans saw our bamboo spears and our determination they would realize that they could not possibly win.

♌

LEO

Fort Knox, the 1st

Birthday of Sir Oswald Mosley (politician)

Invention of the paperback book

Battle of the Pyramids

☽ v/c 1:17 am
☽ → ♌ 2:25 am

☽ ☌ ♆
☉ ⚹ ♃
☽ □ ♄
☽ □ ☿
☽ ⚺ ♂
☽ △ ♇
☽ ☌ ♅

God hardly slept last night on account of the cold.

High-flying planes, well out of spear range, dropped thousands of leaflets urging my followers to leave the island before the Marines hit the beaches.

To God's great surprise something like ten thousand people did just that.

God watched TV pictures of the Adocentyn boat people, as they were called, being helped ashore in England and France.

An ultimatum was issued by Commissioner Pizarro: God was to hand myself over immediately to the UN or Adocentyn would be taken by force.

Two days later, despite attempts by the Committee for the Scientific Investigation into Claims of the Paranormal to get the whole thing called off, the 3rd Expeditionary Force, supported by an unknown number of warships and the nuclear-powered aircraft carrier the USS *OJ Simpson*, dropped anchor thirty miles from God's holy island. The President the United States of America was shown on TV that night on the White House lawn with the UN Secretary-General and Commissioner Pizarro. All three men looked sombre and deep in thought, even Pizarro on his pogo stick.

The next morning Adocentyn was rocked by a series of cruise missile attacks. Three slammed into God's palace, turning it into a beautiful pile of rubble. Another two took out the control tower and the runway at Humphry Barnard Airport. Another took out the main TV mast on the island in Aries. Government House was also hit. As was my recently completed birth chart on the Les Mielles golf course.

God and my wife were unscathed in these attacks, having moved to God's command bunker in Scorpio, about a mile inland from St Aubin Bay. During WWII, God's command bunker had been a German underground hospital. Since then it had served as an art gallery.

The day the first cruise missiles slammed into the island God, the former Lieutenant-Governor and our wives were looking at modern art two hundred feet below sea level.

'What's this one called?' the former Lieutenant-Governor asked God, standing next to an object that looked rather like a gramophone.

'That,' God told him, 'is by a dear old friend of mine, Professor Asda.'

'What does it say to you?' asked Dr Hultcravitz.

'Victory,' God said.

'Bravo!' said the former Lieutenant-Governor's wife, clapping like mad.

THE 2ND

Marco Polo sets off for China	☽ → ♑ 12:05 pm
Hottest day in London since records began	♄ → ♈ 1:42 pm
46 countries sign convention outlawing	☽ ⌄ ♆
biological weapons	☽ △ ♄
Discovery of chemiluminescence (how things	☽ ✳ ♀
glow in the dark)	☽ ✳ ☉
	☿ ♂ ♎

An hour after the cruise missiles had hit their targets the pay phone in the front of the art gallery began to ring. Field Marshal Wells of the Sagittarian Corps reported that St Quen's Bay was being bombarded by naval gunfire, F-18s and Harrier jump jets. With two members of the Zodiac guard carrying the Death Ray and eight carrying forty-foot ladders, God and the Lieutenant-Governor made our way to the wall that divided Scorpio from Sagittarius.

By the time we had erected the ladders and managed to set the Death Ray on top of the wall the first wave of Marines had already hit the beach in their LVTP 7s amphibious assault vehicles.

The first battalion of the Sagittarian army hidden in the bunkers of the Les Mielles golf course charged the Marines as they came ashore.

It was quite a sight.

The purple-clad astrologers were cut down in their hundreds.

'Fire the Death Ray! Fire the Death Ray!' God ordered.

The Marines on the beach had, by this stage, spotted us (we were, thanks to God, a considerable target with absolutely no cover). Bullets started to whizz around us. Three Zodiac guardsmen standing in front of God were shot.

'Fire!' God shouted, wobbling with excitement. 'Fire! Fire! Fire!'

And then for the first time ever the Death Ray of Professor Asda, the most deadly weapon of mass destruction ever invented, was fired.

THE 3RD

Birthday of Ludwig van Beethoven (composer)	3rd – 3:12 pm
Invention of the tin can	☽ ☍ ♀
Russia forms governor-generalship over Turkestan	☽ △ ♇
	☽ ✳ ♅
	♀ ✳ ♇
	☽ ☍ ☉

At breakfast, God told Colonel Fleming that GIs returning from occupied Japan brought back for their wives and sweethearts something American women had never seen before: dildos.

The Colonel does not believe me but it is perfectly true. God saw GIs buying them with his own eyes. 'Think,' God said to Colonel Fleming, 'of all the American orgasms that would never have happened if God and other young Japanese males had not shot up Pearl Harbor.'

'I'm thinking,' said Colonel Fleming, chewing on a piece of toast.

God then asked when the Cobras/Samba/Fontanelle satellite will be launched.

'Very soon,' Colonel Fleming said.

I don't know quite what I had expected, perhaps a green ray or lightning, at least a sound of some kind, but nothing happened.

Except that the former Lieutenant-Governor of Jersey got shot in the arm and God ran up and down the wall, my arms upright, as bullets popped and whizzed all around me. 'Retreat!' God shouted, kicking the useless Death Ray over the side of the wall into Sagittarius, and descending with great difficulty back into Scorpio.

Somehow, alone, God made it back to my command bunker. The phone was ringing. God picked it up. 'Hello?' God shouted.

God could hear the distant sound of machine-gun fire and explosions.

A Captain Wilbothest of the 1st Sagittarian Division was at the other end.

'God, come in, God, over,' he said. It was hard for God to hear him, the phone being so far from God's ear, on account of God's dumb arms.

'This is God, son. How's it going down there?'

'All my commanding officers have been killed or taken prisoner. My unit's been wiped out. The Marines have walked right through us. Every time we try to charge them with our spears my men get cut down.'

'Hold on, I'll cast a horoscope.'

The phone went dead before God had finished.

God hung up. The phone rang again. It was a Major of the 2nd Sagittarian Battalion stationed at Humphry Barnard Airport.

'Hello, hello?'

'Speak up, soldier,' God shouted.

'God, we're being bombed to smithereens! Marine helicopters are landing on the runway, Your Majesty.'

'Hold at all costs. Defend till the last man,' God said, then added, 'Things will be good for you.'

Then God hung up.

The phone rang again. Marine combat engineers had blown a hole in the wall dividing Sagittarius from Capricorn.

'Counter-attack!' God told the Commanding Officer of the Capricorn Corps.

God's command bunker was then rocked by a tremendous explosion. A hole had been blasted in the wall dividing Sagittarius from Scorpio.

God used a small fortune in coins ringing round all the other signs telling them to get to Scorpio on the double.

'Each man will make it his duty to kill ten of the enemy before dying,' God shouted down the phone. These were not God's own words. Lieutenant-General Tadamichi Kuribayashi (Taurus) had used them in the battle of Iwo Jima in WWII. Kuribayashi had been a cavalry officer, a poet and a songwriter. His two most famous songs had been about his love for his horse and his love for his country. God has always admired the man.

THE 4TH

✳

War ends in Portugal	☽ v/c 5:44 pm
Invention of the electric guitar	☽ → ♊ 6:44 pm
Japan excludes all foreigners	☽ ☍ ♅
	☽ ⚹ ♃
	☽ ⊼ ☿
	☽ △ ♆
	☽ □ ♂
	☽ ⊻ ♄

Two hours after the initial assault had begun just about the whole of Sagittarius, including the airport, was in United Nations hands, mortar and artillery batteries were in place, Cobra gunships and F-18s were bombing the hell out of us. In short, God's beautiful zodiacal utopia had been shot to shit.

Our counter-attack was a disaster from start to finish. With the central revolving door having been taken out by the cruise missile attacks before the invasion, God's reinforcements had to scale wall after wall to get at the Marines. They were completely exhausted as a result and came over in dribs and drabs and were annihilated by the Marines' assault rifles, grenades, rockets and machine-guns. By the time the Geminis were ready to launch their attack it was nearly nightfall. They too were cut to pieces.

When the stars came out, effective resistance was over and Marine units were less than half a mile from God's command bunker and getting closer all the time.

There was no one left for God to phone, and anyway I had run out of coins.

God went down to the lowest level of the German underground hospital where with enough supplies to last them three years were the two teams of doctors and nurses looking after my balls, and my second wife. After a tearful farewell God went back upstairs. God had decided to crash-dive Captain Fuchida's Zero fighter on to the deck of the aircraft carrier the USS *OJ Simpson*. God's Zero fighter, fully fuelled and repaired, was hidden under trees nearby.

God left a note on the front desk of the art gallery. It read:

From Japs Eye Fontanelle to all surviving citizens of
Adocentyn. Battle situation come to last moment. I want
everyone to go out and attack enemy until the last. You have
devoted yourself to God. Do not think of yourself. I am
always at the head of you all.
God.

There was still some sporadic fighting going on in the wood outside the command bunker, multicoloured bodies were everywhere.

God made it over to my plane undetected.

Dusting the cockpit as quickly as God could I heaved myself in. It was only then that it dawned on God that in his physical condition there was no way I could fly, my hands being a million miles away from the controls.

God started to swear like mad.

It was then that Private Rafferly of the 3rd Marine Expeditionary Force appeared and told God to keep my hands right where they were.

'Fuck it,' said God.

THE 5TH

America discovered	1st – 5:10 am
	☽ v/c 10:25 am
QE2 arrives in New York on maiden voyage	☽ → ♏ 11:37 am
First automatic telephone switchboard goes	☽ ☌ ☉
into operation	☽ ☐ ♆
	☽ ☍ ♄
Volcanic eruptions in Iceland kill one third of	
the population	

Private Rafferly became something of a hero after he took God, the Supreme Being, prisoner. On his return to the US he entered politics and became Senator for Tennessee and among other things passed a law banning all sharp objects in the state.

It took the Marine Corps several hours to get God out of my Zero fighter. They had to use circular saws and a crane.

When God was removed from the plane I was taken to St Quen's Bay which had been turned by this stage into one huge depot by the Marine Combat Service Support Element. Showers were already set up and breakfast was being served in eight mess tents. God hadn't eaten for hours and felt absolutely famished.

God was marched into a huge green tent. Inside were a dozen Marine colonels, two generals and Commissioner Pizarro bouncing up and down on a camouflaged pogo stick.

God was then slung unceremoniously underneath a Ch-45 Sea Knight Helicopter and flown around the entire island shouting the following words through a microphone dangled in front of me:

'The war situation has developed not necessarily to Adocentyn's advantage. Should we continue to fight it would mean the possible destruction of astrology and thus the only hope for human civilization. God asks you therefore to lay down your spears and cooperate with the occupying forces. Do as they say. Do not answer back, I repeat do not answer back. This is only a minor setback. Things will be good for you. Thank you and good night.'

After that God was given some breakfast and allowed to collect two carrier bags of personal belongings from my utterly ruined palace. Then Commissioner Pizarro and God were flown to the aircraft carrier the USS *OJ Simpson* which promptly set sail for New York.

So long, Adocentyn; so long, wife; so long, Happy Ladies of the House of Fun; so long, extensive video library; so long, freedom; so long, balls.

During the three days it took us to travel across the Atlantic Ocean, all God seemed to hear was the tapping noise Commissioner Pizarro made as he moved around the huge ship.

After dinner tonight God and my nurse watched *Star Trek*.

THE 6TH

✳

Birthday of Nancy Reagan

General Strike in Barcelona

Siege of Leningrad lifted

Corn Flakes go on sale for the first time

☽ ✳ ☿
☽ ☌ ♇
☽ ✳ ♅

The Chaplain came by today. He wanted to hear God's pet theory that explains why Christians are so screwed up about sex. God had nothing better to do and so told him my theory. The problem stems from the Christian notion of the soul. God told the Chaplain that Christianity would one day be remembered as the great institutional schizophrenia, for with its notion of the soul, man is cut in two, his body becomes 'other' and with the body goes the world and everything in it. The soul, the crowning glory of Christian thinking, that shrivelled, atrophied idea is why Christians hate their bodies and sex so much. But why did the insane, preposterous, schizophrenic idea of a soul take hold so easily in the Western mind?

'Why?' asked the Chaplain.

'Because Western civilization originates from the Greeks who were —'

'Great philosophers?'

'Slave owners,' said God. 'A slave owner comes to associate all things physical with his slaves, and thus considers such things to be beneath him. Rather than get his own hands dirty, rather than *doing* anything, the slave owner prefers to sit around eating grapes thinking about abstract, non-physical things, like God and Truth.

'In time this leads to insanity; the slave owner ends up despising all things physical, including his own body and thus sex.

'The stupid Christian notion of the soul, the apartheid of the body and mind, fits in perfectly with western civilization's deranged, world-hating, sex-hating, slave-owner mind set.'

'And explains why the idea of the soul, of a hatred of sex and the body, took hold so easily in the West,' said the Chaplain.

'Precisely,' said God.

God's arrival in New York was supposed to have been kept secret, but news of it leaked out and two thousand astrologers were waiting on the dockside for me. From there I was flown to the South Street Heliport in lower Manhattan where God was greeted by members of the New York Police Department's Anti-Terrorism Task Force, agents from the FBI's New York office and dozens of UN officials. God was taken to the UN building and then driven several blocks to the Manhattan Correction Center where God stayed for two days before being put aboard an armoured supersonic train, normally used for transporting plutonium, and taken to Fort Knox.

And here God has now lingered for nearly six months in the company of my nurse, my attorney and Colonel Fleming.

Soon after God was taken off the island my second wife managed to get to the Hero of Pearl Harbor Harbor with one of my balls (possibly my right) and its life-support machine, which she cunningly concealed in a pram. Together they hid on a supply ship that left the island the next day and ended up in Hiroshima where Dr Hultcravitz built the temple known as the House of the Right Ball.

THE 7TH

✳

Crew of HMS *Bounty* mutiny

Bayeux cathedral finished

Birthday of Michael Caine (actor)

☽ v/c 1:28 pm
☽ → ♓ 6:24 pm
☉ △ ♅
☽ ⊻ ♃
♀ ⊼ ♄
☽ ☍ ♂
☽ ⊻ ♅
☽ ⚹ ♄
☽ ⊼ ♀

Commissioner Pizarro, the man God holds responsible for this whole, stupid mess, came bouncing into the gold vault after lunch.

'Are you here about the heating arrangements?' God enquired.

'I'm here because I want to know why you made the world the way it is. I want to know why we must endure all Mother Nature can hurl at us. I want to know why you made the Universe so hostile to life, full of earthquakes and volcanoes and tornadoes, and avalanches, and droughts, and floods, and hurricanes, and cyclones and terrible storms, and the million and one other things that fuck us up. Why?' asked Commissioner Pizarro.

'You can't make an omelette without breaking some eggs,' God told him.

Commissioner Pizarro said nothing and then left.

An hour later a press conference was held here inside the gold vault.

'What,' asked one reporter, 'do you think are the odds of you being found guilty, Mr Fontanelle?'

'About fifty-fifty I guess,' God said.

'Are you scared, Mr Fontanelle?' asked another reporter.

'Am I sacred? Of course I am.'

'No, are you scared? Are you afraid?'

'Oh, scared, I was a kamikaze pilot during WWII, I have

laughed at death so many times it isn't funny. Of course I'm not scared.'

'So you're not going to renounce your divinity at the last moment as the Committee for the Scientific Investigation into Claims of the Paranormal suggests?'

'No. Absolutely not. Never.'

'What would you like to say to the Committee for the Scientific Investigation into Claims of the Paranormal, Mr Fontanelle?'

God thought for a bit and then said, 'I'd ask them why it is they insist on always wearing dumb orange life jackets.'

THE 8TH

Tidal wave kills 150,000 in Pakistan	☽ → ♍ 11:32 am
Buddhists arrested in South Vietnam	☽ ⊼ ♆
Austria-Hungary declares war on Serbia	☽ △ ♄
	☽ ☌ ♂
	☿ ⊻ ♇
	☽ □ ♇

Cobras/Samba/Fontanelle was launched today at 3.34 a.m. Western time. It was astrologically a very bad time to launch a spacecraft as is borne out by its chart:

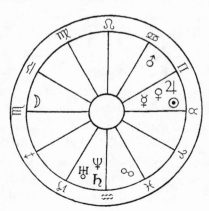

When America was planning to send men to the moon God wrote to NASA advising them to send Capricorns. They sent a Virgo, a Libra and a Gemini. God frankly doesn't know how they managed to get there and back.

At the launch of the Cobras/Samba/Fontanelle satellite was the entire General Assembly of the United Nations. They all wore safety helmets with their country's flag painted on. They also all wore dark glasses.

The launch took place at the French-owned Guiana Space Centre, two degrees north of the Equator.

When the rocket carrying the satellite had disappeared into the sky the UN Secretary-General made a speech which was broadcast live on TV.

'Ladies and gentlemen,' he started, 'I have just been told that the launch of the Cobras/Samba/Fontanelle satellite, probably the longest named satellite in the history of space exploration, has been completely successful. The satellite is now in orbit and performing Power Spectrum Analysis. All we can do now is wait for the results to come through which I have been told on the very best authority will be soon.

'Mankind's predicament at this moment reminds me of a science-fiction story I read once as a boy. I'll tell you about it.

'It was a story about a race of aliens who made contact with Earth. They made contact to ask permission if we would mind them dismantling a moon of Jupiter so they could use it to fuel their spaceship. I don't know what the aliens called their spaceship but its name was probably shorter than the name of that satellite we just launched. If we agreed to give the aliens a moon they promised they would tell us something of great importance. The leaders of the world discussed the matter and asked the very polite and well-mannered aliens which moon they wanted. The aliens said that they didn't really mind. So the leaders of Earth decided they could spare Io, which had a radius of 1,815 kilometres and a hell of a lot of volcanoes.

'The Aliens said, "thanks".'

'In return for one of the fifteen moons of Jupiter the aliens told the leaders of Earth something of great importance. They told the world leaders that they, the aliens, were heading out of the Milky Way because it was going to explode in little under one million years.

'Here is what the world leaders did when they were told this: They did nothing at all. Except demand Io back which led eventually to a war between the aliens and humans, but I'm getting off the point.

'The point is mankind's inability to think more then a few thousand years into the future. The truth is that we ought to have thanked the aliens and started packing up the moment we heard the Milky Way was a goner. We ought to have figured out a way to take the whole damn solar system with us. But instead we did nothing. The world leaders in that story were silly, were short-sighted and we can see why. But what if the aliens had told the world leaders that the whole Universe was going to collapse into itself and cease to be? What ought mankind do on hearing this news? There's no point us putting the masterpieces of our culture — our paintings, our books, our ideas, — into crates because where the hell are we going to put them? This is mankind's predicament today.

'What if Cobras/Samba/Fontanelle tells us the Universe is a goner, that it is indeed a dead duck, what the hell are we going to do? What the hell can we do? Somebody, and it wasn't God, once said about mankind that "*the most incomprehensible thing about us is our cheerfulness*". If Time does have an end this is what I suggest we all do: we will accept that life is ultimately meaningless and just get on with it. That's my suggestion.

'Thanks for listening.'

THE 9TH

General election held in Japan	☽ □ ♇
Mr Kyprianou becomes President of Cyprus	☽ ⊻ ♅
OPEC countries freeze oil prices	☽ ⊼ ☉
First International Skateboarding Championship held	☽ ⊼ ☿

No word from Cobras / Samba / Fontanelle.

After breakfast, Colonel Fleming handed God more fan mail and hate mail. One of the letters was from God's second wife still hiding out somewhere in Japan. In her letter she told God to be strong and that she loved me very much and that my ball is just dandy.

Another letter God received today came from the spokesman for the Committee for the Scientific Investigation into Claims of the Paranormal.

It went:

> *Dear Mr Fontanelle,*
> *I am writing to tell you why all of the members of the Committee for the Scientific Investigation into Claims of the Paranormal wear orange life jackets. You asked about this at your press conference a few days ago.*
>
> *We all wear orange life jackets because of something that William K. Clifford wrote a long time ago. William K. Clifford wrote that ideas were a lot like ships.*
>
> *No idea, just as no ship, William K. Clifford felt, was unsinkable and many ideas are a lot less seaworthy than people realize.*
>
> *Your ship, Astrology, for example, is a ship that sucked the moment man started to think straight.*
>
> *That's why we wear orange life jackets, it is also why we*

shout at you all the time, 'Come in, number 9, your time is up!'

> *I just thought you ought to know.*
> *Yours,*
> *The Spokesman for the Committee for the Scientific Investigation into Claims of the Paranormal.*

God showed the letter to my nurse.

Still no word from Cobras/Samba/Fontanelle.

THE 10TH

USSR walks out of Geneva disarmament talks	☽ ⋁ ♃
Germany declares war on Russia	☽ □ ♄
790 couples of the Unification Church marry	☽ □ ☿
at the same time	☿ ♂ ☉
Martial law imposed in Poland	

Several years ago, while on Adocentyn, I wrote to the great Humphry Barnard. I have a copy of the letter in one of my carrier bags here in the gold vault. It went:

> *Dear Humphry Barnard,*
> *I am writing to let you know what a pivotal role you have played in shaping the modern world. Yes.*
> *Many years ago I read your work* Star Sign Secrets *and well it changed my life, as it has changed the lives of many in Japan and Jersey. It made God realize how influential the stars and the planets are in all manner of things.*
> *God thanks you.*

*I had of course known before reading your work that I
was God but it was your ideas that led me to the conclusion
that I made galaxies with my genitals. It was you, Mr
Barnard, who allowed me to make that quantum leap, to
unify the small with the large. I and the Universe are deeply
indebted to you.*

> *Yours sincerely,*
> *Zodiac Man.*

For some reason he never wrote back to God.

On the TV tonight, experts are saying that there must be something wrong with Cobras/Samba/Fontanelle because its Power
Spectrum Analysis ought to have been completed by now.

THE 11TH

Birthday of Diana Ross (singer)	☽ v/c 2:47 am
Deathday of Ho Chi Minh (politician)	☽ → ♋ 2:20 pm
Colorado becomes a US state	☽ □ ♃
Napoleon Bonaparte becomes 1st Consul for	☿ ⊼ ♅
life with the right to appoint his successor	☽ ⊼ ♆
	☽ ✳ ♄

Colonel Fleming told God that some of his men are uneasy
about the idea of shooting a man who's got his arms in the air.

Later, God and his nurse watched what may very well be
God's last episode of *Star Trek*.

In tonight's episode the crew of the Enterprise are sent to
find the meaning to life but something goes wrong with the
ship's computer-tailor and none of the crew have any trousers to

wear. So the crew of the Enterprise have to go in search of the meaning of life without any trousers.

Later, God's nurse asked God what he thought the meaning of life was. God said that it was to live in accordance with the stars.

After a little while, God asked my nurse what she thought it was.

'I think the meaning of life is to give life meaning,' she said.

God told my nurse this was totally silly and she agreed and said that it probably was.

Later still, Miss Hughes asked God what I thought the secret to life was.

'The secret of life,' God said, 'is to live in accordance with the stars. What do you think it is?'

And Miss Hughes whispered, 'There is no secret to life, but don't tell anyone.'

Still no word from that stupid stupid satellite whizzing around beeping in space.

THE 12TH

Germany declares war on France and invades Belgium	3rd – 6:22 am ♀ → ♍ 2:24 pm
The De Lorean Motor Company announces plans to build a factory in Belfast	☽ ⊼ ♂ ☽ ☍ ☉ ♀ ⊼ ♆ ☽ △ ⚷
US air-traffic controllers go on strike	☽ ♂ ♃

According to Miss Hughes, God talked in my sleep last night. God talked in my sleep last night about a book I was planning to write. Apparently, God was going to call it *Bad Poetry* and in it I was going to assert that astrology was a confused mess of half-baked anachronistic ideas and childish nonsense, mumbo-jumbo of the highest order, a demented attempt to reduce the wonderful diversity and complexity of human personality. God was also going to say in this book that in reality there is only one star sign shared by everyone.

God told my nurse that this is almost as funny as the Committee for the Scientific Investigation into Claims of the Paranormal's idea about me renouncing my divinity in order to go free.

Commissioner Pizarro then came bouncing into the mobile home with an omelette which, he told God, proudly, he had made without breaking any eggs and left again.

It is still absolutely freezing in here.

It says on the TV that the results of Cobras/Samba/Fontanelle's Power Spectrum Analysis have been beamed to Ground Control at the Guiana Space Centre in the last few minutes.

Miss Hughes, bless her, keeps bursting into tears uncontrollably while making everyone lunch.

Mr Spillsbury, the greatest defence attorney the world has ever seen, is just outside the mobile home on his knees shouting:

> *It is true, without falsehood, certain and very real*
> *That that which is on high is as that which is below*
> *And that which is below is as that which is on high.*

God can hear the phone next to the door of the gold vault ringing.

It sounds like this: Berrr Berrr Berrr Berrr.

AUTHOR'S NOTE

✳

Annual reunions of retired kamikaze pilots really do take place in Hiroshima.

✳

Captain Fuchida really did exist. He really did lead the raid on Pearl Harbor, really did witness the aftermath of the dropping of the bomb on Hiroshima, really did write a book called *No More Pearl Harbors* and really did fly his old Zero all over America preaching about Jesus Christ.

What a life. (What he really thought of astrology I have no idea.)

✳

Professor Asda also really did exist and did indeed spend the war working on a Death Ray device which didn't really work.

✳

Hermes Trismegistus, the Thrice Great One, really was the founder of Modern Astrology. (See *The Encyclopedia of Occultism and Parapsychology*, third edition.) He was also, as the fictional spokesman for the Committee for the Scientific Investigation into Claims of the Paranormal claimed, a complete fake. (See *Giordano Bruno and the Hermetic Tradition* by F.A. Yates, University of Chicago Press.)

The Cobras/Samba satellite really does exist and really will perform Power Spectrum Analysis and thereby discover if the Universe will come to an end or not. What it will find and why it has two names I, like everyone else, have no idea. It will be launched by the European Space Agency soon.

The picture of God's genitals in this book is really a picture of my genitals.

And finally, the Earth really does go around the Sun, whatever astrologers say to the contrary, and your midwife really does exert more of a gravitational influence on you at your birth than all the stars and planets put together.

I just thought you ought to know.